good deed rain

5 NOVELS

Jackson Ferocious

2000

Harmonica

2001/2002

Velocipede

2002

Rose Petal Lantern

2003/2004

Copper Kettle

2005

INTRODUCTION:

I wrote my first novel in college and since then I've been writing at least one or two a year. GOOD DEED RAIN was created to bring these books to life, rather than have manuscripts sit in cardboard boxes until who knows when. I've been wanting to share them with you for a long time. 5 NOVELS, originally written 2000-2005, is my first collection of multiple novels, since *Ohio Trio*.

My friend Rob used to live along I-5 where it passes through Seattle and I still live a hundred miles north, with the highway in our backyard. We imagined it would be possible to send messages to each other; he could tie a note to a radio antenna and I could catch it as it drove by my house an hour and a half later. Then I saw JACKSON FEROCIOUS, up there on the overpass, with a fishing pole, casting at cars like a stream full of metal fish going past.

HARMONICA also started as an adventure with Rob. Back when I lived in a large Eastern metropolis, I had a little trouble with the law. To pass the time waiting for a subway, I drew a moustache on Cybill Shepherd. A movie poster of her, that is. Next thing I knew, I was getting a ticket from a portly officer. An art lover. Of course I didn't pay and the threatening letters that came for me, escalating by the week to horrific levels, contributed to my decision to flee that big city. I still can't remember if that officer's name was Callahan or Clanahan, but I think I've paid my debt to society with this book written in his honor.

When we moved to Bellingham, I had a factory job for a while. It was loud, hard work and I was definitely the oddball there. I made muffler guards for semi trucks. This became the setting for VELOCIPEDE. Interestingly, eight years later, I got a phone call from a woman at The History Channel. She was doing research on velocipedes for a television show. She was interested in my hand-sewn book which, alas, I had to tell her was a strange Western set in the future of Aztlan.

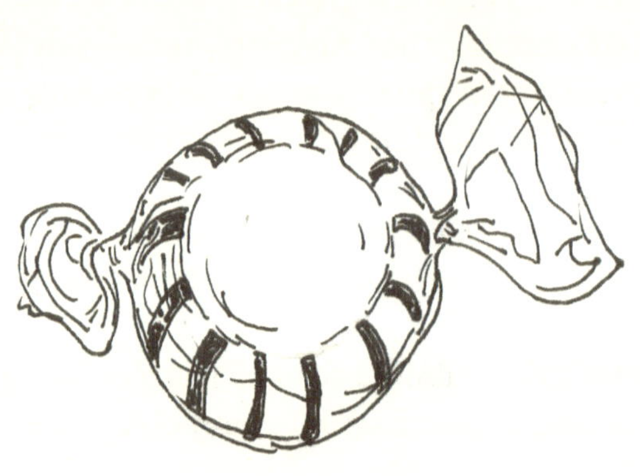

candy wrapper camouflage

In 2010, I published *The Mermaid Translation.* What wasn't included in that volume was its prequel, ROSE PETAL LANTERN. I've always been a fan of Charlie Chan and I wrote this with Sydney Toler and Warner Oland playing in the back of my mind. Incidentally, in 1935, Clark Gable filmed *The Call of the Wild* on Mount Baker, an inspiration for Sylvan Moore.

COPPER KETTLE came fittingly right on the heels of my ode to Chan. I wanted it to read like one of those old 1940s Republic serials. In fact, it began when my friend Miguel suggested we write a novel together online. He would write a chapter then I would, back and forth. So that's how this first appeared ten years ago. Oh, by the way, that candy store really existed. In one of the boroughs, there was a white painted storefront, like a wooden clubhouse, with candy wrapper camouflage papering it, and a narrow slit you could order your choice of drugs through. Standing there, you could only see the arms and hands of the person inside there. You also couldn't miss what leaned below, a baseball bat just in case.

I hope you enjoy this book. I do consider these novels to all flow together. You can't help but see the connections, and most of all I hope this leaves you excited to see what GOOD DEED RAIN has in store for you next.

Allen Frost
Bellingham, Washington
February 16, 2015

JACKSON FEROCIOUS

Part One:

In the Breeze

The giant Jackson Ferocious lived in a sort of onion on the bridge above the freeway. His house had been shingled with so many skins because of the fierce wind from the trucks and cars.

There he stood inside, big as a lifeboat, watching the road, swiveling a golden telescope, eye blinking through it, waiting. His breathing was an elm tree's leaves in the breeze. Calmly, while the river of traffic went by, he surveyed for the perfect one. And it wasn't too long.

Spying one, he bolted away from the magnifying lens, lumbered to the plywood door, bashed it open, and carried on outside.

At the edge, he stopped by a metal pole propped with line and a hook attached. Jackson hauled it into his hands, drew it over his shoulders like a rainbow waiting, waiting, waiting, then he let it go.

There was no mystery to this casting anymore; he had done it so many times. The thick line went out into the slipstream and guided by his perfect aim, the lure hit the shape flooding past. In the click of that, he bent back the pole, catching prey, arced it into the air and then he reeled it back. Against the blur of motion underneath, watery as any creek, he pulled in and hauled up what he was fishing for.

An awkwardly balanced piano set legs gently onto the cement beside him. Jackson smiled at the gleam of polished black wood. He let the line unhook itself, and linger almost feline, wagging its rope curves side to side.

He was surprised at his catch. It was a beauty and would bring him some wealth at the market. It should be enough to keep him in grapefruit for another month or two. This was how he made his living.

People went by so fast nobody noticed, or if they did, it was only a flash like a forgotten thought, awareness of something that was lost with all their wheels.

Up on the bridge next to his little house, Jackson had a truck contraption. The whole thing sagged on its suspension. With an engine full of rust, it didn't look like it could ever work. The piano was tied in back and wrapped with raincoat scraps.

Jackson unrolled a hawser tied to the front bumper chrome, coiled it over his arms and pulled. The truck followed him like an old dog. Away from the middle of the bridge, Jackson's motion was slow in the air. A squall of cars charged under both ways, some with lights on now for the deepening gray.

The world remembers. Every lively thing that ever was, will always be real. Bringing back the history of dinosaurs onto some green lawn, dirigibles in the clouds, even people of old can reappear here momentarily, shimmering, as they were, in a replayed movie to infinity.

The Saturn Circus reappeared that way. One sunny blue day in the middle of winter, birds were reviving the sky. The veil of a month of cold had lifted, maybe only for that minute, but it had the world feeling charged. Living memory ran through the spindles and another joy was brought forward.

There they were: the caravan, the animals and performers sending up tents. Like a flower, the conjuring didn't last long before the fade. It disappeared and was replaced by the modern cape of apartment buildings and parking lots, but a giant had stepped off the ride and fallen out of his time.

That was some months ago. Shipwrecked in this new world, Jackson Ferocious adapted to it as best as he could. Picture his vision from that other century when circuses crossed the country, when he made a living by magical means. Now he survived, stranded, by collecting worth from the roads that passed by under his feet.

The rain was falling in curtains as Jackson turned in to the parking lot. While he kept his head down pulling the rope leashed truck, he saw himself reflected in the splashing puddles.

He stopped the truck at a two story pale wooden wall. A sign surrounded by colored lights popped above the door:

AUCTION
Every Thursday 7 PM

Creaking the truck into its spot between two white drawn lines, Jackson stopped. His breath caught up with him. It was the beginning of night. The freeway sound toured as usual beyond.

Jackson left his prize tied up and went to the door. He was covered in rain.

The door swung open light as cloth.

He found the tiers of sale objects numbered with little yellow tags for tonight. The wind he let in turned them into rattling leaf sounds.

Around a corner of violins, an-almost-puppet man appeared. "Jackson!" He lifted an arm to point out the door. "You bring me a piano in the rain?" Clicking past Jackson nearly weightlessly, he touched him and pulled him along. "Come on. Let's bring it in."

Jackson wasn't interested in the details of the sale. He left that game alone. He moved among the aisles like a cloud blown down an alley. He walked past the shelves looking deeply into each old thing. They spoke their age…They were taking him back. His big swimming eyes searched.

A spider waved to him from the dark wooden edge of a box. A fine spin of web crisscrossed the black grains.

He took the box out of its dusty place and held it on one flat hand to open it and look at the postcards inside. Every moment

14

spun, some were written on, from ages ago to now…Taken away like him, he thought, and hanging in the waiting…Flipping one into another, pictures blinked all over the world in beautiful scenes. Then he stopped the movie at the photograph of a merry-go-round. That was how he would like to return…spinning through the air back where he came from.

His dream broke when some kid suddenly appeared from a trap door.

"Mister! You want your money?"

He knew where he was. He closed the box and put it back.

The truck was light on the return. The bumpy path chucked the wheels up. A few stars were strong enough to show through the milky clouds overhead. Casting a stronger orbit in the sky was the neon red of the Food Giant sign. Like one of those space station predictions from the 1950s, it sat amidst the blackness, flashing beacons around and around to guide you in.

Jackson pulled the truck up over the asphalt bump into the parking lot. Shiny new cars rested in rows. When he found an empty space, he took it over and braced his truck into place. He tucked the curb under its front wheels, tossed the rope over the hood and plunged his way on.

Before the doors, he stopped to grab a wicker-looking shopping cart.

He wondered for a moment if he might need two.

No, he pictured he could pile enough in one like a pyramid. Lifting the metal cart off the ground, he pointed it to the doors and went in.

The people of this time had it poured all around them, Jackson thought. Food Giant was one more wonder—rows of linoleum, music around corners, waving colored flags, stages set for a march of food that never seemed to stop anywhere. The circus had outgrown the tent, Jackson thought.

Like a galleon with its gold, the grocery cart pushed across the waxy floors, sailing through the aisles, then after waiting five minutes through the narrow check-out, left into the night with a heavy yellow load.

Jackson tipped the hundred grapefruits into the open truck bed so they rolled and poured and filled it up. The way people watched and froze for him, he was a star again.

In the back of the truck, the fruit rubbed, bumped and glowed like moons. Jackson towed the rope between the dark and light of the streetlamps. Above him, the air hovered with moths.

At the top of the hill he stopped. Below him was a slanted roll by the houses, black trees, to the gold yarn of highway burning through the distance like a line of bees.

Jackson got up on the hood. It had already been worn into a seat from the many times he sat there thinking, remembering, meditating, eating grapefruit. The truck creaked. His feet dangled in front of the headlights and cast wild shadows far ahead upon the road.

A gentle breeze took the smoke out of the chimney, over the current of traffic swerve where the lights plowed tracks back and forth.

Inside of his forgotten house, Jackson was quiet. Some candles lit the dark room. He was content to wonder in his way. There were halved grapefruits on the table top and around him the tacked, battered wooden lean of his walls kept out the weather.

Late night is a deeper ocean when the road belongs to the long whale shapes of trucks. As they glided by, dripping little orange and red lights on their sides, Jackson watched from above.

He fished patiently. Like a one-eyed mariner, he saw the breaching prey ride into view. It looked promising. He hoped the approaching truck with a heavily tilted stack might be carrying something precious from a carnival. He had seen them before. Sometimes in the dark of night they rolled deconstructed roller coasters, Ferris wheels, funhouse mirrors, to the towns waiting next in line. Maybe with circus parts he could make a time machine.

Busting out into the cool air to the cement edge of his bridge, he swung the fish hook lightly by its tether and gauged the approach by the tinder of the headlights fanning brighter. Even from his sky view, he could feel the rumble of wheels, weight and engine.

In a sudden motion, he threw the silver hook. It caught exactly, rope whirred out in a spool and Jackson held on tight for the pull.

But what happened next had never happened before—what Jackson caught was stronger than him. The cracking force of the line caught on the truck, yanked him off his feet and tore him through the wood and concrete, ripping the world apart from him, riddling a thousand playing card pieces of his bridge and home in a scattered explosion.

Jackson held on to the rope as he flew at cannonball speed high above the road. The force carried him along in the air like a kite. Hand over hand he drew himself forward toward the truck. He felt like a meteor in that fast pour of wind. His eyes were so filled with tears he couldn't see what had captured him. He wagged back and forth in the air and continued down, pulling himself into the coal tasting exhaust.

At the end of the line, he collapsed next to the thing that had taken his hook. It looked at him with big shiny eyes and gaping sharp mouth and when the truck hit a bump on the pavement, Jackson toppled into its darkness.

Part Two:

A Thousand Years War

The sound of chains pulled him back from wherever void he had been. Hearing their scratch, hollowed in thumps all around him, Jackson opened his eyes. From where he lay, he could see the sunrise out the big animal's mouth...yellow light and blue beyond, the sight framed by the creature's teeth.

He moved his leg and his heavy boot dragged a metal peal across a row of bumping rivets underneath him. Apparently, the monstrous creature that swallowed him was made of steel. With the strength he used to have slowly returning, Jackson crouched. His footsteps took him over the iron shocks to the teeth peering out.

"A stowaway!" a little figure in a white coat called up to him.

Jackson was half out of the mouth and bathed in the bright yellow from a phosphorescent ceiling.

"Come down!" the man continued in a surprised voice.

Jackson dropped out onto the wooden bed of the truck trailer. He twisted his head to clear the sore bend in his shoulders and saw the black and white whale he fell out of.

His mind clicked slowly around the place the whale carried him into. The space in between the walls was filled with tables and crowded with ocean animals...seals, otters, a walrus, and more fish than an aquarium. They couldn't be alive, not out of water, and some of them were only half formed. It was like being behind the scenes of a dream.

"I don't know how you managed to get into my orca whale," said the man. "Are you from the marine park?" He paused and regarded Jackson's patched clothes. "Maybe not..." he decided. He offered his hand to the giant. "My name is Le Grand. I live here." His hand disappeared in Jackson's grip.

Then Jackson touched his lips and shook his head.

"Can't talk?" Le Grand nodded. "That's good," he quickly smiled, "because I wouldn't want you to tell what you've seen. You've managed to make your way to somewhere you shouldn't be." Le Grand got silent, thinking.

Jackson was staring at a shark. Curiosity walked him over to the bench it was laying on. He picked it up between his hands and held it like an Italian sandwich. From head to tail, it was bigger than Le Grand.

"You're interested in animals?" Le Grand rushed over to it, touching its arrow shaped nose, "Maybe you should stay here? Yes, I could use you here. There is so much to do."

Why not? His house on the bridge was gone. Jackson nodded. He agreed to another new world dropped on him. He set the shark down flat again, but as his hand left it, a pocket-sized panel clicked open on its side. A gleam of circuits and wires were revealed.

"There," said Le Grand. "The secret of what we do." He pressed it shut and took a screwdriver from his coat to tighten it. "Not long ago," he explained, "the fish and animals used to be real, that is, they were all alive. But they have been dying. People are killing them off faster and faster as time goes on. Most of them can no longer survive in our world. See this fish over here?" Le Grand led Jackson to another workbench.

Frozen in a kind of amber block was a tropical fish. "This is a ghost." Le Grand picked up the brick and held it to the light, putting rainbows on it. "It's extinct. This living species will never be seen in the seas again. But look at this!"

He pulled open a drawer and took out a cloth covered object. It was wrapped like a flag around something holy. Le Grand held his breath then opened the cloth with a silver, delicate tool. The fish was duplicated. He held it by the fin's tip to let it glow like a candle. When he touched its tail, it miraculously fluttered. It blurred with life. Le Grand beamed, "It has come back!" He brought it to a blue tank of waiting water.

The surface rippled while it dug in. Freed, the fish swooped back and forth, finding shelter in some weeds. "Look how the spirit of the real animal inhabits ours." It regarded them with its little eyes—or the black stems of batteries.

"We are doing our planet a great favor," Le Grand said proudly. "We are creators and guardians. Any creature that is gone, or nearly gone, we will restore. Over the years we've been restocking Earth with animal replicas." His voice cracked up a notch, "And not only things from the poisoned seas. We will create animals and birds, rare insects, they're all disappearing too! Think of it! Elephants, and rhinos, wolves, bears, just like our fish, programmed and powered by circuits to roam the world again!"

Jackson had a cot set up in the aisle between fish tanks. The water bubbled and a faint buttery green color played over his eyes. He couldn't sleep. He turned over on his side and the wooden bed legs creaked on the rubber mat.

A year ago he had tried to find that exact place where he had fallen out of his circus-time into this mirage age. He thought that if he discovered that spot again, maybe he could return to his world, open a waiting door. But he went around and around streets and blocks looking and he didn't recognize a thing. They changed too quickly. Modern America had taken over with all its walls and signs and five story flights. This America had hidden everything familiar from sight. To be missed forever. That's how it went.

He turned over again.

In this haunted space, a hundred pages could float by in a sentence.

Fish made shadows like lullaby notes. An aquarium at night was a slow, dreamy thing.

Le Grand woke him every morning at sunrise. His job waited for him in the other room. Dawn turned into long day, into night, and another dawn and on and on. As long as he felt he was doing good, useful work, Jackson could get up every day.

There was a soldering iron on the table, a box of metal parts, magnifying lens, the split halves of fish waiting to be filled with works. While Jackson melted the silver fins to their springs within, Le Grand held up a picture of some new dream he had schemed.

"Your reward," he said. "Your faithful service here has not gone unnoticed. This will be your retirement." He pointed to the picture. Somehow the old man knew exactly what it took to keep Jackson there. It was a merry-go-round, a pinwheel of painted colors and animals. "This will be yours," he promised.

"You will have your circus reward," Le Grand repeated every so often, as the years turned into more animals. By this time it had become such a clear dream that Jackson could have hung it on the wall of his room, next to the one narrow window that looked out of the thick skinned wall at the rooftops stacked like tiles. The sun made them clatter by day and then moon after moon washed them calmly in the night.

The mechanics of the intricate pull of Earth and Sun begin and end with the chirping stir of a robin. Every morning, every evening, it's always that hopeful bird on a branch or fencepost that sings the yellow light up and down. Like a prisoner at his window, Jackson listened and relied on that song.

Each night Jackson climbed back to his quarters carrying with him another little piece from the mill—something that wouldn't be missed. Warped into shape from bits of soldered metal tubing, electric gears and swiveling parts, those somethings came slowly together. Over time it became a bird, and then with the colors of feathers added, it was clear, it was a robin.

Finally it could fan its wings with the power of flight. When he let it go, it could spin a small circle around the room and land on Jackson's hand where it began. That was only the simple beginning, the Kitty Hawk for what he planned next. Holding a magnifying glass, looking into the bird's silver heart, Jackson turned a wheel tighter than ever to adjust it and let its travel take it in a further loop than the confines of the room. It was ready to fly.

With the small window open, the morning came singing in. Some real robin somewhere had already begun as Jackson set his machine on the ledge. Giving it more winding energy than ever, Jackson held his arm as far out the window as he could reach and he let go of the whir.

He breathed painfully, pressed as he was against the concrete. His fingertips way out there trembled slightly like the tipped swag of a branch. He waited for the feel of the bird's return. Unless it ran into trouble, it would be coming back. After a minute, when the feet wrapped around his fingers again, he gasped and caught it.

Jackson pulled the bird into his room. For a moment he couldn't move, the bird contraption held with eyes closed.

Then he slowly lifted it close. Close enough to touch his face, Jackson looked into those eyes, while he rubbed the feathers like a magic lamp.

What was it like outside? he wondered. How much time had gone by? What of all the animals they had made and let go? Were there giraffes wild on the street?

Deep in the black of its bird eyes, a little movie played. Everything the robin had seen had been recorded for Jackson to watch.

Jackson saw the beginning, the brick wall with his arm imprisoned, held out. Vision rested on it. Then the flickering sight swept away. Jackson stared as the bird flew its boomerang journey. It was free, on the air outside the tall building instead of the corridors and workroom and quarters that Jackson had known for so long. Jackson read the passing letters painted on the red factory wall.

Le Grand Animal Sales. Exotic Animals for Your House Or Garden.

It was all just for sale! They were buying and selling the wonders he made, shipping them off to who knows where.

The vision cranked around the corners and sides of the industrial building, revealing the small locked windows, bricks, and a leaning smokestack until the robin eyes reeled back to him.

He set the bird projector down. What kind of movie was that? Le Grand Animal Sales…Jackson fumed. Not that he hadn't seen his share of schemes in the circus…Maybe all these years spent with animals, caring for them, repairing them, had made him soft, a rube, an easy touch…It wasn't something Jackson Ferocious liked to think about.

He was sick with sorry worry for the fate of his animals. Did they all end up tucked away, to be locked up in rooms or caged in yards? He had felt the freedom of the bird's flight, gazing through its eyes, and he made a decision. Animals need to be free, even if they aren't really real.

Jackson was hidden behind an elephant's ear, working on cir-

cuitry. He touched a white-coated wire and the trunk turned with snaking grace. This was going to work, Jackson thought. With Le Grand nowhere in sight, it was time to act.

Ten feet off the cement floor, Jackson stretched off the last ladder rung and seated himself over the gray elephant shoulders. Another animal was up there with him. The orange and black stripes of a tiger were tied behind him.

It had come to this; it was all he could do. So much time had gone by in this big green Noah's ark room. He had brought them to life, one by one, but now, like him, they deserved to survive in the world.

All it took was a little kick to send the elephant forward, toppling through the wall, into the rush of May sunlight.

After the crash, Jackson knew he had to be fast. He slid down quickly, untied the rope, pulled the tiger down and set it on its paws.

Jackson was dazed by his escape. For a moment he staggered. The world had changed during all that time he spent in the factory. He didn't see any people. It looked like the city had shut down. Had it been abandoned? There were ruins of it around him.

He shook his head and took a breath. The wind had a sound he had forgotten about, the air, the rush of the world, the feeling of being free could almost knock him down. The smell of lilacs and spring almost hurt.

With a wave, Jackson thanked the elephant who had already turned to go make more holes then he got onto the tiger's motorcycle back. A growl started it into life and they tore away from the rubble walls in one leap.

Part Three:

Jackson Ferocious Disappears

Running into weeds and trees lay a forgotten road. The remains could be followed to the clues of a bridge that had tumbled down long ago into a stream. Wild flowers and a willow bowed over where the granite stone blocks pressed shadows and a jagged arc made a deep cave.

Deep in there, past the green and flowering bend of the covering branches, a pair of yellow eyes sparked brightly. They watched the daylight birds tag in and out of the leaves and ferns, dipping their song in the creek. A growl sent them on their way.

The tiger brushed smoothly from the dark like a forest fire and padded out into the silver shallow water. It dazzled there and waited quietly…a garden of calm stained glass colors…the tiger, the stream, the flowers and the trees.

In an overgrown lot, Jackson used a maple tree limb to pry the edges and flip over a stone. He dug into the sandy dirt until he felt the soft ripples of a cloth bag. Taking it out of the ground, he brushed the soil back into the hole and replaced the stone. Jackson stuffed the bag in his pocket and stood.

An arrow made from purple flowers pointed to the spot. The clover had waited out cold ground for the spring bloom to remind him of the dollars he had buried there long ago. Back when he lived on the bridge and fished, he did this a lot. Whatever money he saved, he put in spots underground. He used the world as a bank. Money was hiding all over the city. This bag was enough for more grapefruit or a bale of spinach and it made him almost laugh to think life could be as free as this.

Finding a store that was still open though…that might be difficult.

Rhododendrons on the hill swayed thickly aside to let Jackson appear. He waved at his orange friend waiting for him. Digging his heels into the decline, Jackson half slid down. The tiger purred up against his side and followed him inside the hollow cathedral of stones.

Jackson set his backpack down on the blankets. He took out food. It was still light enough to gather firewood. The cave would stay warm through the night, letting the smoke drift up, out the rock seams, to crawl onto the mossy broken old road, blanketing it like ghosts too tired to go.

The tiger was aware of it first, when it was silent but near. Then, when it became a rustle in black leaves, both Jackson and the cat tensed. There was nothing planted in the tiger's way of thinking to make it attack, but in the dim pale of this place the sight of a tiger could play on fears.

They were both relieved when a deer walked out of the brush. It stirred through the water with antlers turned towards them like gentle TV aerials.

By dawn, there were more. A wolf and a panda arrived and the water shook with five Chinook salmon swimming upstream. They are finding the way, Jackson smiled. He drew them to him like a beacon.

While they showed up steadily by air, water and through the woods, Jackson left for another errand in the town. He followed in the gravel beside the passage of the stream. Every so often the flow glittered with the appearance of another passing animal gem.

Jackson emerged from a storm drain channel and climbed the cement slope to a sidewalk bordered by teetering warehouse relics. They were stuck in the ground like the husks of crows. Most of the city seemed deserted. The weeds and wild flowers strained from cracks and up buckled rusted fences.

Jackson snapped a jagged tear across the chain link big enough to step through. He walked across the yard straggle and crumbles towards the shadowy depths of the nearest warehouse, to an open door.

There were unwanted things in there he needed. He took a tarp off his shoulder and unrolled it on the floor. He could carry what he found wrapped in that. Off in the rust colored dark, he was watched by the mice, bats, and a barn owl baking in a broken wall clock.

Night had dropped over him as he sloped along with the heavy pack. The search for a few more junked things had taken him to the old edges of town where the alleys ran under wires spread like a web. Jackson was spidery, with a big round shape heaped on top of him, rocking and guided by the low drip of electric lines and shadows.

He found a space between warped boards where there were some oily black fossils of once-working machines. This was his last stop. He smiled at the round cog someone had left here. Perfect. He had all the parts he needed. He was ready to go home to his cave. He tucked the rusty cog into his finds and turned back towards the river.

Something flickered in the gray lane, moved low with animal motion to the overhang of an ivy fence. Jackson whistled, thinking it might be a timber wolf or arctic fox, something that he made on the line. It seemed to be waiting for him, the eyes were watching him.

When he was close, in the same long shadow, Jackson stopped. He held out his hand peacefully. He still wasn't sure about its animal life. It was hard to tell the difference between real animals and machines. He didn't think it mattered anymore anyway. Real was a strange word in this world. They regarded each other in the dim light.

Remembering a scrap of bread he had in his pocket, Jackson took it out and offered it. He tossed it forward. One of his machines wouldn't need to eat, but something alive would be thankful for it. The bread sat like an alarm clock on the paved sidewalk between them.

Jackson leaned against the handrail above the shallow river. He looked in the window of a closed shop, at the cloudy blue wool of the TV way back inside.

The Count Misfit Show creaked on the late, late air at a quarter past two like a silvery dream, with its visions of rubbery monsters and heroes on the run. In the jungle, the black and white creatures tangled with the fate of their lonely creator.

The Count stopped the movie at a suspenseful point and glowed like a candle before the camera. He reached out in that moment, beyond the piled up things in the repairs store—vacuum cleaners, a shelf of radios, a cactus, lamps and toys—before the screen blinked him away.

Affected and wondering, Jackson turned from that.

How could he have missed this little machine, after all the time he was captured here? America's favorite invention, the magical box that dreamed for you…It had even known about a life like his, seen feelings inside of him and shown him that something cares—like so many lonely Americans, he had a friend made of circuits, wires and picture tubes.

Jackson turned around to see the tiger standing in the water below the railing, growling hello. Jackson was also happy at the familiar sight of the burro that had come along too. He remembered the care he put into creating it.

The curve of a half-moon melon rilled in the stream.

With a hop, Jackson swung over the rail to join them. The tiger blinked softly, watching him near. The burro moved forward to offer help carrying things. Jackson, who was very tired, was glad for that. There was power in animals.

They used dark's cover to slip out of the city. The tiger, the burro and the giant flowed upstream like a nursery rhyme.

By the time the sun rayed on the tiger's back, they were among the tall tree chimneys of the forest again. Alive with birds and animals and sparking rapids, the tiger led the way to their bridge. When he saw it, Jackson stopped. The freed zoo was all around him, they had shown up like a mechanical painting.

The sound could be heard a hundred yards away. It purred around the cedars. Closer, louder, a curtain of ferns, berries, leaves, and then, where the tall summer flowers parted, the music came from a field, in the open late afternoon sunlight.

This was a memory the world could hold onto. It would carry this moment back and forth in time—Jackson Ferocious on his homemade merry-go-round—a big round wooden shape bolted and nailed together with lights on its roof, tilted animals on poles, curved and spinning like a record. Rising and falling, around and around to a carnival song, Jackson followed the fade, back where he belonged.

9:45 PM   6/14/2000

HARMONICA

• DREAMS OF BEING

While the water came to a boil, he rested. The murmur from behind the door was a lull from another world. Spring worked at the window with a picture of blue. On the wooden chair behind the door, the hotplate began to breathe and form the first bubbles in the tin pan.

Callahan reached into his deep coat pocket and pulled out a crackly packet of Instant Noodles. "It's going to be good," he smiled. Chicken Flavor. He tore the seam and tipped out the square silver packet of spices into his palm, before he tapped the dried noodles into the popping hot water splash.

There are rituals to all things—building steeples, crossing streams on stones, just moving from bed into the day. Callahan spun the cooking noodles with a fork he always kept in his pocket. He had dreams of being a cook, in the middle of a steaming big kitchen, with pots and pans hanging overhead, chefs all around the stove line…Instead of the wooden office of his chief.

He didn't need to taste a noodle to tell if it was ready—he was beyond that—he was so accomplished at this, he just knew. As he unplugged the hot plate, the water felt the temperature drop and the noodles settled in their white foam.

Callahan lifted the pan over to the sink. It was a little sink, tapped into the pipes that ran chipped paint up the wall to the next floor. Hot water poured off around the dish he held over the pan. The sink was littered with cigarettes, plastic chopsticks and their emptied paper take-out boxes stamped with red and black pictures of dragons.

Callahan tossed the noodles into the yellow bowl. Next was the packet of chicken seasoning. Contemplating as he let the powder out, he jumped when the door broke open into the room.

"Callahan!" Chief of Police Clanahan flung himself in and roared, "What's going on in here?!" Out there behind the opened door, the station sounded like a barnyard, the voices of a hundred cows, roosters, goats and donkeys, horses and ducks. It seemed unreal.

Callahan put the bowl gently down on the table, to slowly pass by his boss and look into the cartoon other room. "What's going on in *here*?" Callahan repeated, stopped at the doorway, pointing at some people he knew who were clucking like hens.

"Can't you see? They've been hypnotized."

He recognized all the signs. "The Hypnotist…" Callahan whispered. "He was *here,* right?" They weren't coming out of his spell. "How do we wake them up?"

But Clanahan was busy eating the noodles. "Where's the salt?" He started tossing papers about.

Callahan walked into the midst of the next room. It was like being in Noah's ark. He shook his head as he passed everyone he knew, back when they acted like police officers, talking on the phone eating sandwiches and coffee, or passing through on their way to their cars. Callahan snapped his fingers at them. That used to work for those television magicians, but that didn't cause a change. He clapped his hands. Nothing…Callahan didn't have any effect on them.

"You'll have to do better than that. You'll have to think of something unusual, Callahan!" Clanahan had to shout at him through all the animal echoes. There were phones ringing without answer now. Shadows and light bent in the darkened room from the half-pulled window slats.

"I have no idea!" Callahan yelled back. Wouldn't a loud shock do it, he thought? He didn't carry a gun to shoot in the air. He had a harmonica, but he hadn't played it in years.

In the half-darkened room, he reached for the light switch and snapped it on. The great row of florescent light bulbs planted in the ceiling poured on, "What a zoo…" and he turned the switch back off. Light had no effect on their spell. Did they need a special word?

"I'm sending you out to track The Hypnotist down," Clanahan came up behind him. He gestured with a fork of noodles towards another door and moved, "Come on," and out into a hall.

Its steep path led to the underground garage. "I don't know who brought him in here, but he did what he did and got away," Clanahan explained between bites. "Fortunately, we still have some officers who were unaffected—you, me, and a few others who weren't here when it happened."

Down a cement stairwell, they came to the level that screeched with tires pitching corners back up to daylight patrol. The sharp smoke in the air from the gasoline engines burned their eyes as they crossed the painted lines and numbers, past the parked steel interceptors. Some of them even had rockets and folded wings attached. Callahan had always wanted one of those, but Clanahan took him right past them.

Clanahan was still talking, chewing up the air like a propeller, talking about how only Callahan could stop The Hypnotist. "He's got to be hiding somewhere in this city, Callahan. I want you to find him fast before he strikes again." When they stopped, he slapped him on the back. "Go get him!"

Clanahan pointed at the forty year old van parked in the corner of the garage on patches of oil spill. Parked well alone, some gray from the day colored its blunt edges. In a couple of footsteps they scared some pigeons up off of it.

"What a picture!" Clanahan stabbed at the white and rusted van with his noodles. "Fully equipped for surveillance..." He passed Callahan a key attached to a big metal loop.

Callahan slipped his hand into the loop and took the key.

They walked up to van's door.

"There was a raccoon in it the other night." Clanahan looked in the black window. "I think it's gone now."

"This..." Callahan began. He cracked the door open and waited for a moment before he said, "I'll try my best, boss."

Callahan slowed in the web of all the city streets, got caught in traffic and stopped. The giant van relic steamed and coughed amid the bicycles and electric things. He had to watch the dropping fuel dial; it kept running on the blood of the earth. Rushing again when the green light flowered, Callahan steered in a fever, trying to keep from crashing.

He turned onto the older cement road that led to the highway. There was less traffic, only the occasional other gas car with police markings. Every once in a while he passed a wooden carriage at sixty miles per hour. He looked in the mirror to see how they shook in his contrail. He felt like the futuristic creation of Jules Verne.

He let the car drive him, unsure where it was taking him. The highway was a good place to think though, to watch the city shift and turn like an animal as he drove beside it.

Some people were walking on the narrow edge of railing ahead.

He was required to stop anyone walking on the highway. It wasn't allowed. He touched the brake and the van shuddered. He could have let them go; he could have gone on by like a cloud. But he had to reach out the window and put the detachable siren-light on the roof.

The van cramped into the cement curb and stopped. He dropped out the door and walked towards them. A feeble blue light and electronic bleating noise sat above him in the air.

Callahan took note of all the things they carried. Bicycle wheels. They both carried maybe twenty tires on their backs. They stood there staring at him. There was nobody else on the road. He could hear his footsteps scratch. Further off were some crows, and the tinkering sound of the city.

Callahan walked to within a couple feet of them, stopped and announced, "It's illegal for pedestrians to use the Interstate." In a tired motion—he forced himself to do this—he reached for the ticket-book in his coat pocket.

The quiet between them lurked while he tore them a ticket.

He thought about it as he left them in his wake. What he thought was, from their point of view he had dropped on them like bad weather. He imagined the trouble that had been caused because of their hitting that law. He didn't like it, he didn't feel good about what he had done, it was getting more and more clear: this job was for someone who could turn off their mind, feelings and otherwise, and just carry out the law.

The shapes of old billboards flew by, there from the days when everyone had cars up here, planted to catch the attention of rushing hours. He watched them fallow as he numbly drove, until out of a curve, like a hello, a billboard spoke to him from the past.

It said:

See THE HYPNOTIST. Appearing

There was a tear where the sign had torn off in wind a long time ago. It may have been a fifty year old message, but it was all he had to go on, so Callahan took the next exit ramp back into the city, braking to muddle with the rickshaws and horses.

• THE PAPER

It was a relief to fall among all the people out on the sidewalk, leave the van, to drop in anonymously for a while and get a cup of coffee and something to eat while he read the paper.

On the corner, he put twelve quarters into the newspaper vending machine. Before it popped open with the paper, the lock dial spun numbers randomly.

He never won the lottery. As usual, he looked away until they were done tempting his fate. Another losing combination, but the latch was allowed to open.

He pulled out the offered paper and tucked it under his arm. He would wait to read it until he got to sit down.

• TIRED OF WAITING

A dream waited for him. It sat in the hawthorn tree for a still moment. It wished the sun would hurry and be done with this waste of time. As soon as night took over, it would float in to show him a vision. Keeping track of him, it passed from the tree branches reach, onto an old telephone line, sagging along shadowing Callahan. It was getting tired of waiting, wondering when Callahan would stop wandering and wake up.

Callahan took a second cup of coffee while he reread the advertisement in the middle of the newspaper. He crackled the crisp rice paper closer to stare at it. It mentioned The Hypnotist. He would be appearing at The Albion tonight, in one of those movie shows, with magicians, trained animals and who knows what else.

Callahan had to go. He tore the announcement out and stuffed it into his coat. He cupped his hands around the hot coffee and smiled. There was an hour before the show.

• THE ALBION

The Albion was a few streets away from the Main Aqueduct. Callahan hadn't been in that theater for over twenty years.

Here is why: When he was in school, he used to come here to see movies, when that word had a different meaning. Movies were films. It didn't mean people were moving on the stage, they were other creatures projected magically. Movies were a part of his world, as much as dreams.

Then there was a time when all the wonders were attacked. They stopped making movies. The place was boarded up for a while. He was scared to see what the war had done, and afterwards, during the Reconstruction—that was worse—probably its balcony was gone, and the green-eyed statues on the walls, and of course all the gold trim and those heavy red curtains over the screen, scrapped.

Though it had the lights on again and people went into The Albion, Callahan could only remember what this place used to be…Archaeology…Rome, or whatever…No, that wasn't right. Under the layers here, before the invaders and wars, it was only a few hundred years ago when the coast trees were still green forest and the sea had been clean. Weren't things always changing?

Just as long as they left the ceiling, he thought, so he could look up…like he had seen children do, during the lull when the curtains were closed, to see the stars painted there, where the wishes made a long time ago were glued.

• SOMETHING FAR MORE

Callahan was past happy. The world hadn't changed terribly in here. It was the same well-worn feel of a lullaby. Film was gone, but like in the old days, he was waiting, eating a bag of popcorn, watching the curtain when it shucked across out of the way.

A table was in the middle of the stage. It was draped with a banner, plain letters that read *Marconi the Magician*.

Some one person in the audience clapped frantically.

Marconi was a stagger on the stage as if reeds, rocks, feet were digging into mudflats. He tossed aside his dropping cape. "Thank you, ladies and gentlemen. I'd like to thrill you with a magic trick. Enjoy!"

He reached into his sleeve and pulled out nothing.

He tried to cover, as he bowed and grabbed the cards off the table cloth.

"I wonder if you can guess what card I'm holding?" he asked the audience. He showed them the card back and forth. "I thought so…" he nodded as he looked at it too.

The curtains fell back together. The orchestra played loudly.

Callahan folded another crease into the program. The Hypnotist should be next. This was it, simple. Callahan rehearsed in his mind. He would get through the show, follow The Hypnotist backstage and arrest him. Callahan would have him reveal the secret word and the city could go back to what it was.

The curtains pulled away onto a spotlight on the darkened stage.

The drummer was going wild on the rolls. Everyone waited nervously before a disturbance from the height of the aisle turned everyone around.

"Excuse me!" A voice came from behind all the chairs, up the aisle, over in the Exit sign's green. "Excuse me please…"

The Hypnotist traveled down the aisle with a huge bodyguard, shaking hands, starting murmurs and applause and delight. He went by Callahan in a blur and tossed himself up onto the stage, hitting the spotlight that was waiting for him there.

"Thank you!" he held up his hands for calm. "Thank you…" The orchestra wound down like a wooden watch.

"You've probably all heard the news by now," he started, "The demonstration of my powers…The police station has been hypnotized!" The applause started again. "No please, it was not that difficult. A mere spell…Something far more amazing is in the works, just wait. It will change your lives forever."

Callahan stopped eating popcorn, he brushed his hands off while everyone applauded and yelled, reaching into his pocket to get his notebook and write it all down.

He wrote *Something far more* and then his pen stopped as he was seized, held frozen by an invisible force pinning him down.

The Hypnotist quieted the crowd so he could continue, "Tonight…As I walked up to the stage tonight, I read minds… There's someone among you…" he paused as the lights went down and the orchestra buzzed like a bug trapped helpless under a plastic lid.

Another spotlight had joined him. Its beam reflected off him and made him look like a lighthouse shining out over rocks and ocean.

Callahan was dizzy enough to fall, like some others in the audience, but he was locked in place.

"If you will allow me a moment…" The Hypnotist pressed his forehead with a finger, "There is someone out there I must warn…You are following the wrong path. You will only meet confusion and danger!" There were some screams in the rows of watchers. The drum rolls had begun to drown his voice, cover him with a water as he shouted at the crowd, "You must not go any further, turn back before it's too late! Take my advice, save yourself!" but the curtains fell and he was gone into a song.

Callahan gasped for breath.

The weight left him. Up he rocked from his seat like a bell buoy. On the stage all the yellow lights returned for a dancing act.

The sound of shoes were hitting wood while Callahan bolted, forced the curtained doorway, through the lobby to the glass exit out.

51

• FIGURE IT OUT

To find a peaceful place to think, figure it out, or at least conceal himself safely from that mind, Callahan looked for a park.

Of course the city needed more places to rest from walls. Sidewalk trees were anxious and bent between avenue and building, holding up the world alone. He put his hand on that bark and got nothing but exhaustion from it.

Away at the end of five minutes walking, he found himself below the leaves of trees unfolding soft as owl feathers underwing. The park was the hush of an ocean calmly breathing, the pearly inside of the shell, where after all the swirling he could rest. Past the gated metal scrollwork and wisteria, Callahan took a seat on a bench in the blue grass.

"Ohh," he held his temples, elbows resting on knees, sighing, no rest. "Ohh…What now? The Hypnotist can read my mind. I can't catch him if he knows I'm near. I don't know how to do this. Why can't he just tell me what to say to wake up the department? Then we can end it and both go." Worry, worry, another worrier at night…

A dog started barking in front of him and his thoughts were scratched. Before Callahan knew what he was doing, he had snapped, leaped to his feet. "It's illegal to bark in the park in the dark!" Carried away, he had his ticket book in hand.

The man with the dog was a painted shadow staring back. "What?"

Callahan's pen was already writing; it couldn't be stopped. He watched it go, a creature with its own life. The moon was all it needed to see and write. By the time it got to the end of the paper, he was starting to wish it had never started. But another feeling he knew better took over. "It's the law," he explained palely. He tore the ticket from the book, held it out, let it grow away from him, trembling in the wind, no more power on its own than a new born Luna Moth, or bat. "Look, I'm sorry I have to do this…"

"Are you?" said the man with the dog. "Then who are you doing this for? Not yourself? Who?"

"I'm just doing my job. I have to do this..."

"It's a stupid law."

After the man took the papery flicker ticket and left with his dog, Callahan sat back down on the bench. No…It was worse than before…He had ruined the peaceful hopes he had here. He had to go back into the city, at least until this was all done, then he could be himself again. But as he slushed through the grass, he happened upon someone taping signs on trees.

The slippery figure hurried away from the yew, onto the stonework path, "I'm just a pedestrian!" she said, getting away.

Callahan looked at her sign left behind. It was an invitation to Jerk Theater, tomorrow. He was sure there was a law against that too, but he let it slide. She was gone. He wasn't going to go on and on in the dark all night long, one little thing leading to the next til he cornered half the city, yet couldn't sweep The Hypnotist from his mind.

• WISH IN TIN

Callahan called the station from a phone stuck on the wall at the back of Prairie Market. He rested his elbow on the piled bags of rice, listened to the ring on the other end of the line.

"This is Clanahan." A voice in a soup can.

"I found him."

"Did you get him?"

"Well, no, I—"

"Callahan, listen to this place…"

Inside the heavy metal receiver clamored the animal show he dialed into.

"I'm not a zookeeper, Callahan! I want that hypnotist! He's the only one who can change them. I've had magicians and veterinarians in here all day and nobody can do anything! Arrest that nut and bring him back here now!"

A donkey brayed loudly in his ear and the connection broke.

Around him, a hand truck stacked with cans of tomatoes pushed against Callahan. He stepped out of the way. No small amount of miracle would be needed. He wished they sold one in tin.

Callahan sat in The Albion alley. Pigeons huddled warm together above the worn rain-wet stage-door exit, watching him from their iron rest.

At last, he stood up from the garbage can. The way in stared at him, but he couldn't get himself to go. Not that helpless terror again! The next time they met, he had to be prepared somehow to defend himself from that mind-control.

All at once, the door shook open to orange light.

Callahan blinked at the silhouette holding a head.

The shadowy creature stood there breathing the night, letting out the orchestra air and then Callahan could tell who it was.

"What a night," The Rocket Man said, noticing Callahan. He sighed, "Still got another show to go though…After that last one, I don't know. It's murder inside this can."

Callahan studied him. It took three seconds. He had an idea that would get him in there to safely arrest The Hypnotist. "That helmet—is it made of lead?"

"Something like that…Awful heavy thing." He turned it in his gloved hands.

"Let me ask you…" Callahan made a move like a cricket into the lighted doorway. "You're tired…Nobody knows if it's you under that costume or not, right?" He flashed the coppery star of his police badge, "I'm supposed to go around doing good deeds. Want me to take over for you? I could do your last show, you could take it easy."

The Rocket Man paused for a moment, not long. "Aww…I must be crazy doing this," he said. "But I'm really beat." He started to pass Callahan the helmet, "You know my act though? You've seen it before?"

"Sure," Callahan nodded, tapped his head. "Memorized."

"All you gotta do is chase the monster off the stage," he told Callahan. "Except make it look real. Give him a sporting chance. Let the people wonder if you'll be able to survive. Even lose a little before you win. And—"

"Don't worry," Callahan clapped him on the arm. "I've been chasing monsters for a long time. I'll be fine."

• AFTER THE MARTIAN

Callahan ran into the wall again. It was okay though. Backstage, everyone rubbed in a beehive. Callahan couldn't see much through the helmet eyes, just the rush of colors in their inches. Finally, he asked a flower in the lapel of a tuxedo, "Have you seen The Hypnotist? Is he around here somewhere?"

"He went home half an hour ago," said the wilted flower.

Callahan was going to wonder out loud where that home coul be, but the heavy pad on his shoulder got hit as someone barked at him.

"Get out there, you're on!"

Slowly, Callahan stepped onto the red, dreamy surface of Mars. His breath came heavily, steaming the insides of his helmet. Trapped by a purple sky and rocky hills, he heard a violin sort of sound climbing up as he walked…Waiting for a life-form to appear in this desolate world…He didn't have long to wait.

Waving wings and popping open eyes like painted umbrellas, it came out of a cave slashing long tentacles at him.

Callahan fell backwards. The weight of the helmet and costume carried him over onto the hard wood floor.

A cymbal caught the crash. He could hear the audience roar.

The orchestra banged, sawed and blared like a Chinese opera as the monster parried around him.

Suddenly Callahan realized, he remembered he was in the show. The music and the people in the crowd reminded him.

He laughed inside the helmet at what he was afraid of—the painted backdrop and the stitched-together monster before him. The way it moved looked like someone riding a unicycle.

Callahan got to his feet, rocking back and forth with all his Rocket Man weight. The bolted seams on his arms waved at the monster. Faster and faster, with the band going wild in the orchestra pit, Callahan stomped after the Martian, each heroic step to more cheers, on to end where they couldn't be seen.

Callahan was caught by the tuxedo who yelled, "That was

great!" and pushed along out of the way of the next act going on. There wasn't much Callahan could see through the steamy helmet eyes.

He felt his way along the wall, past the sets and ropes and pulleys, performers and colors, to the hallway that led to the dressing rooms and the backstage door.

Callahan pawed out of the same orange lit doorway as an hour before, only this time he was The Rocket Man and in the alley of long cast shadows where he was before, that tired actor was waiting for him.

"How did it go?" he asked Callahan. The same garbage can rattled.

Callahan took the helmet off so he could talk, flooding himself with the cool spring atmosphere, distant rain, delighted by where he had been.

• SLEEP

What a day…Callahan sighed to himself. Before he tossed onto the top of his cot, he had called the station. When a cow answered him, he knew that nothing had changed over there. Too bad for them…Until The Hypnotist was captured, they would stay that way.

No surprise though, he got in my mind too, Callahan thought. It was close, I could have become an animal too if he desired, but he just wanted to warn me, make me wonder to myself what I'm already wondering, Do I need to go on with this, the way things are?

Callahan stared at the newspaper clipping he had tacked over the wallpaper stripes. He had been a star on the stage of The Albion tonight. Smiling, he yawned, reached over to the lamp and pressed it off.

Dark…Time to slip away…Through the thin wall of his room, he could hear the owl in the elevator shaft.

Sleep wasn't far away.

Here.

• HOW TO MAKE MOVIES

Callahan stared at the night sky. It was always this way in his dreams. He saw thousands of stars, then among them moved gold spinning wheels. He didn't know what they were, but they were always there.

The trees were other lives like his, moving each black winter branch held out, only slower. On the path and looking around, he came across someone in the woods.

The person who answered him was only a child. The field was a watercolor, washed with moonlight and fog. "The Hypnotist lives on Forest Hill Road. You can't miss the house. Go…" Just like when they knew how to make movies, the night twirled around him, inside and out. "Go!"

• FOR ANYONE AWAKE

Callahan woke up. It was still dark. He heard a train down in the yard, a mile away hauling with its horn calling for anyone awake to listen, beware.

This was the fourth time the child had been in his dreams, but this was the first time he had ever heard him speak. "Forest Hill Road," Callahan repeated out loud so he wouldn't forget. The sound of his voice was still heavy with the dream.

He reached from his bed and wrote the site in his notebook because visions can disappear like ghosts come the dawn. The next dream can wipe it out, be careful.

It was a midday that glowed through the green new leaves of May held above the boulevard. On top of the apartment roofs, the windmills turned slowly. A white van drove below, shaded by trees and spin, and surrounded by pushcarts and people.

Callahan followed a girl riding a bicycle built with a tray full of tulips for sale. Soon, he left her and turned the vehicle onto the ramp that climbed towards the freeway.

Some crows scared off the cement, spread black patches before him away in the air.

He pressed gasoline into the engine, arteries, poured on speed, hurried over the cracked surface with smoke and a rattling roar that filled his ears. The van shook as it pushed through space so fast.

Callahan wasn't thinking about them—he surely didn't want to go through that again—but there were the same two tire peddlers ahead of him on the shoulder step of the road, breaking the law again to save some time to their next destination.

Callahan shut his eyes on what he didn't dare to see. When he opened them again, after more than a blink, he saw the peddlers seeing him and then he couldn't believe it…They jumped over the railing to get away.

Wheels smoked and slid, then Callahan scared the van into reverse to the spot where they disappeared.

Callahan tore from the metal door. Loud engine, his heart charging, he ran to the drop and grabbed the gray rail to look down.

Tin covered roofs, dog deep pools of rain, shoots of rice and other gardens strung apart with white kite rope. He saw there were some people gathered down there too. "Oh no…" was all he could say to what never should have happened. It didn't make sense. He wouldn't have stopped them again, he was tired of tickets. He didn't mind them anymore, really.

Callahan ran back in front of the grill of the police van and jumped inside the cab. The gears chopped the road into moving again.

When these bad things happen, he knew, it was part of the job he had to see it through. He flew over the potholes of the next exit, steering and slowing.

The van bumped off the last remains of cement and landed on dirt and grassy weeds sprouting where the road used to be. He drove on the cloud he made alongside the tall pylons that held the freeway so high in the air.

Little farms grew beside him, plotted between raked up piles from the junked last century, shaped with the pushed memory things only the old-timers remembered anyway.

As Callahan saw a crowd, he slowed. He turned off the engine and let glide. Turned into dandelions, he stopped. The ones he ran over sent scatters of their seeds across the field.

The drop from above—he stared—it must be fifty, seventy feet.

How could they survive? He hurried for the backs of people he saw ahead of him, everyone looking at something. He knew it was those two he had scared into falling.

"Excuse me!" he pushed their backs and arms until he reached the edge of the mud. It sunk over his shoes.

All around him, in a circle, everyone looked with him at the sight of the thick bubbles forming, dropped rubber tires looped and half sinking around the spot on the bog where shapes fell in and never came out.

Callahan pointed, "Did they fall in there?!" then he noticed the faces staring at him.

The city was divided into different neighborhoods, puzzled around the castle towers of downtown: He was in Blue 22. This was a Code M-13 zone. Nobody answered him. Of course not, he thought, then abruptly, "The van!"

The picture ran through his mind.

He escaped as fast as he could. When he broke from them, he could see his van parked not far ahead.

"Hey!" he yelled. "You're breaking the law!"

The bunch of them stealing parts from the van saw him coming and scattered away.

The silver chrome trim had been lifted off, mirrors, the antenna, hubcaps, and some handles. He stopped running and looked at the tossing bushes.

Well... He unlocked the door and got inside.

The engine started with more of a roar. No muffler anymore. It sounded like a wounded dragon tearing from Blue 22, smoking and chunking over the slabs of cement that drifted into becoming the more solid road and then the jolt of the ramp up to the freeway.

The missing strips of chrome left long scars in the color of the hood he looked down. "We're both lucky," he tapped his hands on the steering wheel, "We could have been left with nothing."

The van seemed to be glad to be tilting the speedometer fast. That was lucky, he smiled. There were all kinds of hundreds of stories about those lost in Blue 22.

• IN THE VINES AND EVERYTHING

Forest Hill Road had a faithful sweep from its trees—tall, kingly chestnuts and oaks, maples, firs, cedars, and alders. As Callahan drove he looked from right to left at the mansions formed in them. How would he know which one The Hypnotist lived in?

Then it was right before him. The familiar scene from a dream that was shown to him a night before…If he could only believe it.

He found a place alongside an ivy-colored wall to park. Nosing into the juniper, there were enough shadows and overhang to let him nearly disappear.

"That could be where he lives…" Callahan whispered. But what if it is? How can I arrest someone who can control my thoughts, knows where I am, what I'm doing here hiding in the vines and everything? It's mind against mind, he decided. I have to think in ways he can't comprehend.

The start of rain dropped small prints on the glass.

• PRETZEL

"He's still out there," growled the thick words at the picture window.

"Yes, I know," The Hypnotist replied.

"You want I should go bend him like a pretzel?"

"No, no, no, I don't think so. What's he doing, just sitting in the car still?"

"Yeah. I think he's reading a book."

"A cookbook," The Hypnotist muttered.

The big thug at the window put down the telescope he was looking in and asked The Hypnotist again, a squeak of a whine in his heavy door voice, "I don't see why I can't go out there and bend him like a pretzel. Just a little bit…"

"Leave him alone, Ambrose. He needs to discover something. In due time…" He turned to go into the kitchen, "Besides, it's raining. He won't go anywhere, will he?"

• ROUTINE WATER TRACKING

Callahan listened to the rain rustle over the metal roof.

The sound had given him an idea, an inspiration that would allow him to look less suspicious if anyone happened to pass and notice the rusting van in the dripping foliage beside a stone garden wall. It had to blend in to the air like a cloud.

In the glove compartment, he found a marker pen he could use. Making sure it was waterproof, reading the little print on it, Callahan opened the door and stepped into the soft wet loam outside.

Along the side of the van, he stopped by its blank hull to write:

Routine Water Tracking.

The lettering came out a bit crooked looking, bunched together in places and heights. It wasn't easy to write on that kind of space, it reminded him of having to write on the blackboard back in his schooldays, but it had to be left good enough. It was raining lightly, it was getting dark.

This was the swaying in the dark that he had been waiting for, the veil of shadows so he could look around for signs of The Hypnotist.

• PUDDLES IN HALF

He hoped it would be as easy as finding a painting of a radiating all-seeing eye on a mailbox, *The Hypnotist*, or the obvious whirring black and white pinwheeling light coming out of a Lugosi basement window. Instead, he broke puddles in half, raked in rain beads off ferns, climbed and tumbled over fences across yards, taking stumbles and waking up the neighborhood dogs. Why wouldn't the dream tell him exactly where to go? What if it *did* and he didn't know?

A spotlight shot across the next lawn and he crashed through hydrangeas to hide. When he pulled himself over a wooden fence, he fell off the top and landed in a chicken cage, through the wire mesh and splintered the thin wooden roof. The birds ran yelping out of the wreckage. Lights went on in the house.

Untangled and tearing himself from there, feathers and ripping, slipping on the mud when a door opened and slammed, Callahan dived under a hedge.

"Who's there?"

Callahan didn't answer, he held his breath. Being a spy wasn't easy. It was all he could do to keep the juniper, or whatever scratchy leaves they were, from shaking and giving him away. Closing his eyes, he tried to make himself invisible—to escape his body here—the same way dreams lift out of you when you sleep, the same way your soul escapes when you die.

After a frozen while, when Callahan was aware that the commotion had cleared back to a quiet night, he rustled out. He got to his feet, found the sidewalk, and ran, collecting and clutching shadows of each big umbrella passing tree.

Returning into the van, Callahan shut the door tightly on the weather. He sat there looking across Forest Hill Road, at the mansion. The thing felt so familiar it had to be something he had seen before, but the dream's message was slipping to the back of his mind.

"Aww!" he cried. He had to try it at least. The Hypnotist might even be asleep. He couldn't read minds if he was asleep, could he?

Callahan opened the van door. If he could just get a look inside that house, maybe he could sight a clue…As he neared, he went over how to do this right. He acted out something in his mumble that he remembered from the police exam. It worked on paper.

The big walnut door was before him. He took a deep breath and knocked. There was a *No Peddlers* sign patched into the brickwork around the white frame. He cleared his throat.

The door roared open to reveal the scale of Ambrose. "Yeah?"

"Is this the Fitzgerald residence?"

"Who wants to know?" His big hands bent invisible shapes.

Callahan set the bait, "You may have won a million dollars," edging his foot nearer.

"Hah!" Ambrose laughed. "We already got millions!" and he slammed the door.

• A FEELING

Callahan pulled off his coat, threw it over the passenger seat and pressed himself between the chairs to the back of the van. Behind the driver's seat was a big latched box labeled: *Survival.* Whatever was in there was probably too late to help.

A wooden table ledge above that had a wind-up telephone. First, he had to push the antenna through the guides in the ceiling. It went up like a periscope, out. Then, with the receiver cradled against his ear, he cranked the antique wheel.

A crackle formed a picture in his mind. His call was racing through the ether on its way invisibly to a destination, a far off window in a cement building downtown.

"This is Clanahan." His voice chewed across the miles.

"I think I found him."

"What do you mean, you *think* you did?"

"I'm parked in front of his house. I think." Callahan listened hard to the ocean sound cupped to his ear. In the background he thought he might still hear hens and things.

"Have you seen him in there?" Clanahan asked in a voice straining patience. Suddenly it boiled, "Have you, Callahan?!"

"No, not yet. It's a feeling I have, I just know that—"

"A feeling?! I won't even tell you what things are like here at the station, how few officers of the law can actually function in this city, because if anyone besides me actually knew, it would be bedlam, Callahan! Bedlam! I'm depending on you to find this hypnotist so don't tell me how you have a feeling! Go to the usual sources, Callahan. The docks, the flea-bitten hotels, the underground. Dig him up!"

"Yeah, alright."

"Take it apart, Callahan. Then put it all back together again."

"Sure, Chief."

"Leave no stone unturned!"

"Alright, I won't sir." Callahan finally hung up. He crawled back to the front of the van. From the driver's seat, he looked at the dark and the rain's return. The trees and the square yellow lit windows of the mansion wore the night exactly like his dream. Oh well, he started the motor to lose it again…On to the next.

• ALL THE SCRAP OF THEM

Callahan parked the police van in the lot of the Prairie Market at the farthest end of the roll of tar where the chain link fence hit the brace of willow leaves. He turned down the window.

It was quiet and dark and the air still smelled of rain though it had stopped some while ago. Who knew what time it was?

The van door shut behind him and echoed across the parking lot. There were rickshaws left closer to the store and a sway-back horse scraped its hoof to eat the weeds growing through the cracking tar. A puddle reflected the stars.

So whatever happened to cars? Oh, they left their breath forever in the atmosphere, otherwise they were all but disappeared. Only the police used them anymore. The parking lot memory of them faded, leaving yellow spaced lines scratched wide enough for three horses or five bikes, and oil stains, the bruises where they once sat. All the scrap of them had been melted down into what could be used again.

Callahan walked a block. The little tinker shops were closed. He walked down their street, observing their smelting chimneys stuck out slanted roofs and black window buttons hung on walls. During day this section crawled with pushcarts. It seemed to go with visions of another time, moving letters and pictures pulled by the propellers of windmills.

Callahan passed the bins of the alchemist and looked in.

More failed experiments left to pools of rain water. The smoothed shape of one of them on the pile caught his eye. No bigger than the knot in a pine, he took it out, put it in his pocket, where it fit bending with the spiral-bound notebook he carried.

Tall rigged masts pointed above the rooftops. Callahan leaned into their direction, the docks and the brine. It didn't seem likely that The Hypnotist, a performer wearing a tuxedo, would hole up here, where wooden, creaking warehouses had washed ashore. The hulks of the buildings staggered about, some throwing long, tipping, slatted docks off to sea. A greenish light shone for a freighter taking on a load due somewhere weeks across the curve of ocean.

Callahan observed from a shadow. He could hear the men carrying on like a pirate crew as they heaved crates and craned the weight above in hemp nets. He even watched silently as some men were dragged in slumps and thrown on deck. Shanghaied, Callahan guessed, and he was glad to be hidden. If he showed himself to them, he too could fall into a blackness, only to awaken in the soaking breeze, far at sea, to slave reefing lines and shrouds for a living.

No, Callahan decided, no sign of The Hypnotist here…Just the same old centuries working ways of the seafarers and the on and on sound of the water below the boards.

A yawn turned him from the docks. The first place on Clanahan's list of the usual criminal haunts was checked off…Now on to the next.

Not far away he came to the rows of hotels and pool halls. There was a movie theater with neon bulbs lighting up the street. Clanahan wants me to find the most flea-bitten place, Callahan paused…A rattling bicycle load of tin parts splashed beside him.

"I don't know," he groaned, then settled on The Hong Kong Hotel. He crossed the gravel street to its cracked teak-plastic entry. It had a door made of painted green aluminum plates, nailed together, overlapping like the scales on a dragon.

He opened the door and walked onto the worn red carpet trail.

There was a tired counter with a silver bell. He noticed the cigarettes for sale, but he didn't want to be a cop and arrest anyone, he only wanted to drift in for some information, then leave.

He didn't have to ring the bell. By the time he reached there, he had been observed by a man who walked out like driftwood in plaid. The man stared at Callahan the way most people glance at a cloud.

Callahan spoke. His sentence croaked, it had been a while since he talked, "I'm looking for a friend of mine. He might have registered here. He's a fancy dresser, I guess. Wears a tuxedo suit…"

"Yeah," the clerk pointed a branch at the door, "He goes to the movies."

Callahan nodded. He tried to show he wasn't amazed how easy it was. He quickly hid his face by looking over to the hammer dented door, then left for it with a parting, "Thanks."

"Wait a second," called the clerk. "I got something for you to bring to him. Let me get it."

While he was gone, Callahan stared at the red and gold wallpaper, the seams of it running up the stairway to the rooms. Maybe The Hypnotist bided his time up there. It was possible. Yet Callahan felt so sure that his dreams had taken him to The Hypnotist's lair before. Why had he doubted himself?

The clerk reappeared holding a cardboard shoebox. He held it out over the counter for Callahan to take. "Here, let him have this."

Callahan took it and started to tuck it under his arm.

The clerk shrieked, "No! Be careful with it! Hold it gently..." His hands cupped around an invisible egg. "Just get it to him in one piece."

"Alright, alright..." Callahan carried it in front of him like the crown jewels in a rotten sort of peeling paper box.

The rain outside the door drummed on the cardboard lid as Callahan walked across the street to the neon covered awning. A yellow painted taxi rang bells near him across the cobblestones and gravel. Some sailors veered close to him and he clutched the box tightly, getting into the light off the street.

Someone bouncing drops of rain reached out for him.

Callahan laughed, "What do you do, walk around Chinatown in the rain in all that lead and tin?"

"I've been looking for you." The Rocket Man grabbed Callahan by the sleeve.

The box almost fell out of Callahan's hold. "Watch it!" he bleated.

"What did you do to my act?!" He shook Callahan. "They want me to do what you did! What did you do?"

Callahan grabbed the box out of the air. He warned, "Calm down! You're rattling yourself to an early grave." The Rocket Man sounded like a bicycle going down stairs. "I don't know what I did. I don't think I could do it again, whatever it was. I have no idea. It just happened."

The Rocket Man fumed and gave up, swerved on his heels to look at the brick alley. Everything looked patched together the same way—bricks, moonlight, garbage cans and cardboard, and a string of dull colored bulbs running up the rainspout along the gutter with the stars and some clouds in the air. "Ohhh..." When he shambled into that alley, his silver costume reflected leaf-sized bursts of light, dwindling until he became a silhouette.

"How am I supposed to remember what happened?" Callahan mumbled, then forgot about it anyway when he looked at the movie posters on the wall.

There were trained animals, trapeze acts, musicians, magicians…and The Hypnotist, with a picture of him, gaunt and shadowy.

Callahan paid the queen bee beauty in the ticket booth. She was all bright with wax candles cornered in glass and she let him go on in to see the show.

Past a curtain, he saw the rows of seats all staring at the stage. Up there, a girl dressed like a bird walked on a tightrope, step by step, as sure as she could.

A band played music for her on antique sounding horns and guitars.

Callahan searched the backs of the people sitting in the audience. There were only a few. The tuxedo really stood out. Compared to the rest of the audience, his black silk shoulders leered in there. It could be him…

Callahan made his way into the narrow fit of chairs to where the tuxedo was alone. But Callahan stopped, almost there, when he realized it wasn't The Hypnotist. A strange face tore from the girl swerving above the stage to blare at him.

"Ummm…" Callahan stalled, then finished his task to sit next to the lad. "This is for you," he passed him the rain-dotted box, "from the clerk at the Hong Kong Hotel."

The boy sat twisted in his chair. He held the cardboard in his hands and stared at Callahan.

"That's all," said Callahan and he got up to leave.

He walked away from Clanahan's flea-bitten part of town, gathering steam as he hurried in the rain, imagining himself going to sleep soon inside the wide metal shell of the van.

• COAL BOMB

As he crossed the street, there was a thump sound, like a thick beehive falling out of a tall tree and from the doors of the theater poured a heavy black cloud of soot. It stung into the lamp lights.

Forsaking the stalled jitneys and nervous horses in the street, Callahan plunged into the cloud.

The exploded bomb left everything soaked in black. He could feel it prick into his skin and painting the folds of his clothes. If he didn't already know the way in the door, back to the stage and chairs, he would have been lost in the ink.

The hotel, that paper box, that kid…Callahan lurked through blindly, realizing, *I gave him a coal bomb.*

He bumped into someone falling and coughed, hurried on, feeling the back rows of seats.

A woman's voice was yelling. "Help!"

The dust was beginning to clear, he could see shapes in the gray.

"Help!" called again from above the stage.

He could see her, the bird-girl holding onto the trapeze, twenty feet in the air.

Callahan racked through the orchestra pit and climbed off a tuba onto the stage.

Looking into the gloom of the ceiling where she chandeliered dimly visible, he called, "I'm here! I'll catch you if you let go!"

She yelled, dropped like a piano falling out of an airplane in the fog, and when she hit into his arms, he collapsed with her onto the wooden floor.

He held her smooth crow feathered body dough and helped her to stand.

"Oh," she clucked, "Are you okay? You saved my life, I'm sure."

"Yeah," he wheezed. "No broken bones? What happened anyway?"

"I don't know. Some guy in the middle row had a coal bomb. It just went off during my show."

Callahan looked out into the chalky murk. "I'll...I'll go take a look."

"Thanks, mister," she said as he clambered into the orchestra pit.

His back gave him a terrible shriek, a pinched nerve or something, and he gritted his teeth over to the row of seats where the poor tuxedoed kid had been.

There was enough sift in the gloom for Callahan to see between the chairs, padding towards where he had brought the coal bomb not long ago.

The coal was thickest here. Callahan sunk into it and it clouded so he couldn't see below his knees.

When he arrived in the center, he stopped. He reached and plucked at the remains of burst balloon clothing strips. Some burnt cardboard...Pulling the tuxedo rags up, coal poured off onto the floor in a stream.

Callahan shook his head sadly. He let all that was left drop sand from his hand. He started coughing, coughing, he needed air.

• PENNY SORROWS

Wandering found his way into the hall of a place he hadn't been in years, a time before the police. The smell reminded him of days working here. The colors were the same. Callahan was reliving it all, where he felt some of his shadow had stayed ever since, waiting, watching for him, catching up with him at last, and almost knocking him down.

He strayed in the corridor that led off from the crowds and noise. There was a sofa to sit on while he observed. Its cushions had been deflated over years and filled with penny sorrows. He was going to sit down, when someone nearly ran into him with their guitar.

"Kelly Jo Philberts!" Callahan startled.

"Yeah…" she stared at him, knew him, didn't know, knew, wasn't sure, "Callahan?" Her hands switched the guitar so she could touch his hand.

"You playing here tonight?"

"Yeah."

"I remember," Callahan said, "It was a long time ago when I was washing dishes at this café. When I was always stuck knee deep in soap and hot water and half-eaten food, I would listen to you while you played in the dining room. That was the best shift. The dishes came at a peaceful rate. I could hear your music and keep up with the pace. Thursday night. I don't know if you remember. It was a long time ago."

"Five years ago," she said, smiled.

"That's true." Though it feels like many more before, he thought. "So, you're still here, out there playing your guitar?"

"All the time almost. How about you? Do you still play that harmonica?"

"No, I don't really have time. I've been swept away in other things. But you know, things are always looking up. The last time I knew you, I was living in a van."

"So how are you now?"

"Oh, well…I'm still living in a van, I guess," he stopped.

Kelly Jo nodded, understanding, "It's a sign of the times."

Callahan didn't want to tell her he was a cop and all that.

It seemed to drive a cloud into wherever he went. "I better let you go play."

"You going to stick around?" she asked.

"No, I wasn't really going to. I'd like to. I'm just happy to see you again. I'm sort of passing through. I miss listening to you though. I know it will be a good show."

"Alright, Callahan," she said, "I'll be seeing you."

"Yes."

He watched her go past the low sofa, open a door and take her guitar in. He thought she might look back at him.

Oh! He forgot about his color! No wonder she wondered if it was him. He rubbed his black hands. It wasn't coming off. The coal bomb had gone into him deep. He laughed, he had to. Well…

He flowed through the crowd, not thinking he would see someone else from the past. It just happened that he did.

On the other side of the half wall that separated him from the kitchen, the cook stirred filled pans over flaring heat.

"George!" Callahan called to him and waved. Back in his washing dishes days, Callahan had been friends with the cook. He used to flip the records for him while they worked. Those were days that now he wished had never ended. "It's me!"

George looked up from the grill.

Callahan came closer, close enough to put his arms over the ledge, accidentally knocking a complete row of spices into the pot of cooking chili below.

"Callahan!" George bleated. He jumped over to the spot to dig all the tumbled spice shakers out.

"I'm sorry," Callahan dipped his hand over and knocked another salt shaker in.

"Callahan!"

"I'm sorry," he goofed. "This night has been this way since the sun went down." He remembered working with George always ended up like this, before he left dishwashing and joined the police force. But after this last fiasco in the underworld, he had to retreat, back into the crowd, to the door, and let the noise out.

• ROOSTERS

Dawn woke on the roofs of the city, a blue gentle light, soon followed by the sound of roosters off the peaks of the police station downtown. They flopped their arms, folded in like wings, and screamed at the orange rising sun.

Two carts full of hay and feed creaked a big shadow across the street's cobblestones and stopped underneath the eaves. The front door of the station cropped open and a weary Clanahan came down the steps to pay them off. He was wearing denim overalls.

• BICYCLE

Faraway, in prison, all a boy's concentration was projected on a bicycle…Drawing it from the side of a blue and white house, catch-wobble-balance…Moving its wheels, turning the pedals, pushing it across the dew and garden roll. The boy watched it move like a dream, felt it glide on the sidewalk, hop off the curb and pour on speed past every sleeping house.

• THE EVERYDAY MAN

A usual man stepped out of the morning pace and sort of sleepwalked into a bank that just opened for business. His eyes webbed in everyone in the bank, as he walked in and caught each mind. The doors locked automatically. There was a lull. From the man's eyes a sort of radio-wave directed everyone.

The entranced tellers left their beginning work and went into the safe to collect stacks of money. They brought bindles to a door that led out to the staff parking lot.

The parking lot ground was filled with a dense flock of pigeons. More waited on the sloping telephone wires. Each pigeon wore a pocket harness tied on.

One by one, the money was slipped to the pigeons who poured into the air like a faucet, until the money was all gone and the birds were turned off.

The staff returned to the bank. Everyone in the room blinked into where they were before the interruption, counting, talking, whatever they were doing at 8:01.

The everyday man who had been used to carry the trance into the bank wondered why he came in. He felt embarrassed. He left the bank quickly and silently. A cup of coffee was all that he had gone out for… The café was further down the street. He smiled at his mistake.

• IN THE LEANING

Callahan tried to keep sleeping. He pulled himself tighter in the flannel, brought an arm over his ear, but it was no good. Whatever was going on outside around him was just too loud.

He got out of the sleeping bag.

He stared at his hand, his skin was still painted over coal, both hands, turning them over—guessing probably all of him was coal that wasn't covered by black clothes.

A yellow and green light from the new day in the leaning willow filled the windshield screen. He let that light hit him as he crawled to the door.

The windows showed him people setting up tents on either side of him. "Oh…" he remembered, "It's Market Day today, that's why." So much for staying unnoticed in the morning on the far edge of the old parking lot…Far from forgotten, this was the one day a week it turned into a circus.

He creaked open the door and stepped among them, next to someone tying a colored streamer onto the van's bent radio antenna.

"It's okay," Callahan waved at him. "Don't worry, I was only sleeping, I'm leaving now."

He felt like he had slept in a spinach can. Living in a van was getting old. He sort of creaked when he walked, like the Tin Man's trouble in the rain.

He got away, jumping in between the bent gap seam of running chain link fence in front of the van. A few lilac blossoms still lingered purple on the branches. A junco flew from him. There was plenty of laurel growing and the postcard of rhododendrons and soon tall cedars for a little bit, a city block at the most, before he stopped under a tulip tree flapping above the next fence.

He could see the ocean over the tops of houses. The water was blooming with the rays and the unshrouded islands further across there. The seamill churned in the bay, all silver and gray, making the power to start the people in town, the workers and drones beginning with their alarm clocks, to hot showers, while the burner on the stove made breakfast for them automatically.

He broke through the yarrow into the waking hours of the neighborhood. He brushed the pollen off of his arms and legs as he passed across someone's back yard.

The trouble was, he could barely keep his eyes open. He wondered what was happening to him. Slowing down in between houses, shuttered windows, dropped rainspouts, down, chipped paint, oar-colored siding. He felt like he was changing into cement as he went. The adventure was so tiring.

He turned for the sea avenue, even slower. A few more minutes he made his way before he dropped to the ground, too sapped to move anymore, putting his back against the nearest lamppost where he was fast asleep.

• MONEY FROM THE BIRDS

The big suit on Ambrose laughed hard as he collected money from the birds. He and The Hypnotist stood on the terraced roof of the mansion with a hundred pigeons cooing at their feet. The Hypnotist tossed out another handful of seeds and the birds shifted, weaved blue and dense as a blanket fluttering.

Ambrose was in them, gamed in some sort of heavenly dream he played, laughing and romping like a boy, pulling dollar prizes off their wings. "This is great!" he called out. He shook his head in disbelief, "Look at all this cash!"

The Hypnotist maintained a cool profile against a curved cherry trunk. All the blossoms had blown off last month and the leaves had turned rust on the branches casting over him.

• ALL THE INFORMATION IN DREAMS

Callahan was fast asleep against the lamppost. A city worker reached up to the lamp and doused the candle light. Callahan didn't stir as he started to dream. First, it was a picture, then it started to move.

He was inside a prison, staring at a wall and another wall and then he recognized the boy who had been giving him all the information in dreams.

"See, I can bring you to sleep anytime I want to tell you things," the boy echoed.

Callahan was locked and silent in his dream, listening.

"Why did you leave Forest Hill road? That was his house! Why didn't you go in and get him? You don't have to worry about The Hypnotist. I kept him from hurting you."

Callahan stirred, "Why are you helping me?"

"I'm in jail. But I can send my thoughts out. I pretend I'm in a movie. I saw you when you were in a dream. You need help. We can be partners and catch The Hypnotist together."

"Why are you in jail?" Callahan asked.

"I was born here. My parents were Rs. You're the police, you know about the law that keeps me in here too."

"Yes, I know…I don't like that law…I'm sorry."

Then Callahan had a funny vision of catching The Hypnotist. Newspaper reporters from *The Herald* crowded around Callahan, taking photos, writing things in ink on paper, headlines, 'America's Sherlock Holmes Smashes Hypnotist Racket!' while children on the street corners hawked his latest adventures like a super hero.

The boy was looking at something happening on the other side of Callahan. "It looks like you're going to go away for a while," he said, "but remember where The Hypnotist lives. You were there before. You can—" but the dream turned off with a shock.

Callahan wasn't the only one waking up in the dark and creaking. Sunlight came in knives through the slats from outside and all the black and poor men in rows were waking up like him, holding onto oars that ran to portholes out to the sea.

He scrambled himself back to the living. He reached for his forehead and pulled on the chains that kept him locked to the ship's beam.

"Shanghaied..." Callahan sighed deeply. It did happen to him after all. There were other curses and moans around him as the others discovered what was happening, realized the way it goes, how they should have all known to beware.

He slumped against the oar drawn against his body. He listened to the clashed gong sound ahead of him somewhere.

They all blinked at the silhouette breaking in from the sun. The daylight sparked on the bullet belts looped over his shoulders and the pistol handles out of holsters. They could hear gulls crying outside, while he walked on the boards in the aisle between the chained rowers.

"Look at this..." he yelled back at the door he had come in. "Is this the best crew we could get?!" He stomped across the hard wood, "Have you ever been to sea before?" he grave-dug his voice at them. "Put your hands on the oars, let me see you lift them and drop them in a wave." He kicked the heel of his boot down to the keel and they all jumped to follow his command.

The ship moved as they dug at the ocean. Their chop began to grow together and when it went steady, he told them, "Just keep going this way, keep an eye on each other to make sure we drive the same speed. We'll get there...Then you'll be free to go."

Sure, Callahan laughed, if only you knew who I am.

Laughter had never been onboard. Callahan's crashed in the air like breaking plates.

The rest of the ship continued to row while Callahan smiled. "I'm a cop," he explained. "There's been a mistake. I was on a case when I lost track of time. I'll just get up now and leave. Thanks all the same." He tried and couldn't get anywhere.

"Oh, allow me…" the sailor unlocked Callahan and helped him to his feet. "Follow me, this way."

Everyone else rowed together, sweeping their arms back and forth clockwork, raking the sea, avoiding the doomed look of him as Callahan was moved out into the sunlight wind.

The ship had already cut some way from land, only a thin dark line on the horizon remained.

Callahan rubbed one wrist, then the other. He was going to laugh and say how mistakes can happen when the man behind him suddenly gave him a push and Callahan crumpled over the rail, between the oars and into the icy freeze of the sea.

Callahan came back to the surface screaming and lashing. He gulped a wave. Coughing, trying to breathe and stay afloat. "Where's land, where's the boat?" his mind shocked frantically.

His thrashing was drowning him, yet all the terror in his thoughts somehow changed into the still picture of the boy radiating. Callahan didn't feel heavy anymore, he wasn't sinking.

When he opened his eyes, he was looking into a wet steady face. Big dark eyes and skin gray as a seastone. Then it ducked underwater.

Callahan felt himself lifted by seals. They were carrying him; he just sat on them like a throne.

He could see the land over the crest of swelling water. The seals were taking him there. It was a miracle. He was going to live…Be calm, sit in the churn of cold curling wake rolling along. What a dream this was, but it was happening.

The land was quickly getting closer, it wouldn't be long before he could sop ashore.

• DRAWN ON THE WATER

The seals took him up onto the polished white and black stones of the beach. Turned as drowned and cold and crooked-shaped as a shipwrecked anchor, Callahan crawled like a starfish dropped from a wet paper bag.

The heavy evolution from sea to land was taken in slow stagger steps and handfuls of sand to steady him as he went towards the trees.

Among the firs he saw a rough home, built with driftwood walls and roof patched with bits of plastic washed ashore. He fought gravity all the way there, bracken ferns grabbing him. He stopped when he felt heat by the stone circle gown of a blackened smoking fire pit. He called as loud as he could, "Hello?!" as he settled down to the ground.

Numb as he was, he fumbled some branches into the fire memory. He was starting to shake. Blowing on twigs and bark, he caught a fire off the embers, fed it dry pine tinder, crackling scratch branches until he could feed it more from a pile of good-sized wooden bones. The heat began to soak into him. He waited for whoever might be around to appear.

There was a rope line strung between two trunks. At least I can hang my coat up to dry, he thought. Going through his scallop suit pockets, he pulled out things—the notebook, harmonica, the alchemist object, tickets and scraps—lined them up on a fallen nurse log near the fire. He shimmied the string down lower, closer to the tide from the fire and hung the coat on. A loud jay went up steps in the bough. He took time to get warm, rubbing his uncoaled hands, arms and legs now and again.

Soon his clothes, the kelp he wore, steamed. After a long while of that, the sizzle and smoke of his clothes and shoes getting crisp, the shore breeze, his back against a tree, Callahan sighed and thought of making food. He got up and walked for the house.

There was a white sign nailed to the door. When he was close enough, he could read its message:

He paused, but he had to go in, he was damp and hungry. Pushing the door open—it was only made of wooden patches—he stood inside the autumn colored light of the room.

Someone had left in a hurry. The place was haunted by suddenness. There in the middle was a tipped over cable spool table. On a shelf touched into the corner, he noticed a familiar sight. A package of Instant Noodles…He had everything to be thankful for—he could have been sunk in two hundred feet of water right now…He could see the beveled sand, the crawl of gray creatures from over the weeds towards his final place of pale rest…But that dark coral might-have-been never happened, he was brought here instead.

It was with that in mind, he took the package from its shelf. He bowed before it like a holy relic. That was the thanks he felt as he left. Dark green bent over him as he passed outside with the pan in his hand, back towards the warm fire.

When he stopped over the surface to look, he saw what was drawn on the water. A ghostly reflection, that wasn't himself. Someone looked at him for a full couple seconds before the wind brushed the face away.

"Oh," Callahan said, seeming to realize, "I'm here at your camp. I'm just lucky to be alive. Thanks to you, I'm just going to have a little food while I get warm and human again. When I leave here, I'll leave it as it was."

The water became water and Callahan took that water to the waiting fire. He set the pan on the bent metal frame over the wood and coals. He held the package close to him, preparing for the next step. It never came.

The ferns and forest others shored over, crushed from a rush and attack. It was so fast it was in slow motion. Police, all in masks and black, surrounded him. Elephant guns were pointed at him. He heard the latch of hammer, strike and catch.

"Wait! I'm Callahan!" He dropped the twenty cent package of noodles as his arms went up. "I'm on the force downtown. I'm here on a case. Don't shoot!"

Someone knew him and the others did too. They laughed through their masks. "You were almost dead!" Those big guns went down to point at earth. "What are you doing here?"

"I've been following something, a lead," said Callahan. They piled around him. "What are you doing here?" he asked them.

"This place is ruled out, Callahan. You better come with us."

"Wait a minute," said Callahan, "I have to get this back on," and he took the kite-like flap of coat off the rope. He scooped up the pocket-things and stuffed them back in. "You never know when someone might wash up from the sea," he said to the noise of them scuffing out the fire with water and kicked dirt.

Callahan, sogging in his old wear, followed them, wading in their footprints where they had slashed a way out of the bracken shock and broken split branches, traveling back towards where a van that wasn't like his waited on the shaded channel. Dirt and broken ages of small rocks slated off the hills.

They all got in it and sat down in that clam and when gasoline charged it and moved it, they all started talking again.

Callahan's clothes fit him like tap water. "What's going on downtown?" he asked above the roar of the van drone.

"Another bank's been dropped," Gorcey said. "The Hypnotist again…Has to be. The tellers, the bankers, everyone in the place just conked out. When they came to, the vault's wide open, money's gone. Nobody knows how it was done. It has to be The Hypnotist, Callahan. I talked to them and they all woke up from the same dream, they all remembered feeding the birds."

"Hmm." Callahan nodded. "Birds…"

"So you find out anything about this Hypnotist character?"

Callahan tossed as the van hit a hole. He jostled a mumble aloud at the wall.

"What?" Gorcey said.

"Ideas," Callahan repeated louder. "He's like tracking something that can hide in another dimension."

"Hah!" Gorcey laughed and the others too.

"In other words," Pirch grinned, "You got nothing."

"Wait til Clanahan finds out!" the driver laughed. "What a pair! He's been farming and you've been out here swimming and camping!"

Everyone in the van was laughing, but Callahan grumbled, "It's where it all ends up that matters."

Gorcey patted his shoulder, "Don't fret, pal. We're just giving you a hard time."

"Sure," Pirch said, "You shoulda seen me today. I had to bust that Jerk Theater in the park. Wrote out sixty seven tickets. Got stung by a bee too."

"Clanahan's got us running ragged," Gorcey admitted. "We're outnumbered. We're counting on you to find The Hypnotist soon."

"I'll find him," Callahan said. He could see the towered city gates drawing them in.

• ANOTHER FEATHER

Clanahan pulled Callahan out of the barn-like atmosphere into his office. He slammed the door, tucked his thumbs under the straps of his blue overalls and walked around to the other side of his desk and sat down with a groan. He rubbed the sweat on his brow with a handkerchief.

"Ummm…" Callahan paused. The glass on the door buzzed from the vibration on the other side. He was going to say something about it.

"What's this look like to you?" shot Clanahan, as he dug into his desk. He set, "Exhibit A…" down lightly on the faded pine.

"A feather."

Clanahan continued the routine, "Exhibit B…"

"Another feather." Callahan looked at them both. They were curled slightly on the desk in front of him, color grayish-purple.

Clanahan pressed them into a white envelope. "Take them," he spoke. "Look at them. That's all we have to go on. Two bank robberies, two feathers."

"Pigeon feathers?" Callahan guessed.

Clanahan drummed his fingers on the table. "How can two banks in two days be bumped off by a bunch of pigeons? I don't know," he shook his head. "I already have enough troubles with animals," he pointed at the other room.

"They're not really animals though. They're people."

"They are what they think they are," Clanahan told him. "Now take those feathers out of here, Callahan. And oh, here's a list of names Gorcey made before I sent him on another case. He talked to those zombies at the bank. He wrote down the best witnesses, such as they are." He shook his head, "Aww, it's all just a dream to them anyway! They probably don't know, Callahan, but see what you can squeeze out of them. Then get him!"

"I'm trying," Callahan mumbled quietly.

Clanahan stood up, "I have to get back to work." He jabbed at the window, crunching clouds on the wall. "You find those pigeons, you find The Hypnotist."

• LERNA ZEMMER

The late Spring sun kept light lingering on. It was past 9 PM and still bright enough for Callahan to sit in the park, watching. Kites flickered about high above the grass, one by one drawing back down to the ground as families went home. Bits of gold electricity shone in the hills past them in the windows climbing up from the bay.

He was waiting for Lerna Zemmer, the best name on Gorcey's list. After leaving the station, he had called her at the bank where she worked and she agreed to meet him here.

For an hour he had been watching people pass, guessing for her, until time passed on and he started looking at the changing sky instead.

As the last of the kites tugged down, the air tracked with the jerky orbits of little bats striking back and forth. Night had begun.

Still, getting up to leave the park bench took longer than he realized. He had been watching the stars topple closer in the dark. They appeared with the lamplighter in his creep along the water path, turning the lamps on. Finally, Callahan gave up on waiting for Lerna to show, because maybe she never would.

He passed beside the sigh-breezed leaves. He could hear the lap of the windmill fans out on the point of land. There were ships out there too.

An older woman walked with a cane that made green luminescence on the ground when it tapped. He thought perhaps that was her arriving late. She must have had to hobble in a hurry from the downtown crowds by cable car to here.

At any second, as they neared each other, he expected her to say hello and stop him. He even slowed enough to match or mesh into her pace, but they passed without her becoming more than seconds in his life. She wasn't the one.

No other soul around either, so he guessed the whole hope was over, that was all, it was done. He thought of forgetting everything and going back to sleep in the van he hoped was still there.

Then he felt a tap on his back. Not much to know someone was there, but when he turned, it was obvious.

There was a lady dressed in black veils.

She said quickly, "You are Mister Callahan?"

"I'm Callahan," he said, "You can call me Callahan."

"Sorry I was so late," she apologized.

"No, don't worry. It's okay. I stayed busy. Shall we walk along and talk?"

"Yes." Her eyes glittered jewels of moment and darted, the only part of her revealed from the veil. Gorcey hadn't told him that she was an I. Oh, they were a mystery to him, more than Rs, something he read about in the reports that sent him a feeling he couldn't quite describe in the ordinary alphabet.

She said, "I work at the bank," and sensed his parched look. "I was there that morning we all forgot."

"What happened?"

"I remember someone came in. I don't know who. It could have been anyone. Then we must have all fallen into a trance. Like a sleep. I had the dream the others remembered having too. Something to do with the birds."

"Pigeons?"

She said, "Yes. They were pigeons in my dream."

"What were you doing?"

"Oh, dreams are strange, you know."

They walked from the park onto the dry cracked cement, becoming more of the same as it led them to the line of callow sills and repetition balconies under the towers built to resemble forever, no end in sight.

"You know what I was doing?" she asked him. "I was feeding the pigeons. Actually…Yes, it must have been money we were feeding them in our sleep. After they had their fill, they flew away." Her veiled eyes tipped to the sky. "And I don't know what next. I woke up in the bank. All of us did. We looked around and said, 'What happened?' It was like a spell had been cast, waking up from poison, or whatever."

They had to walk along in a silence while Callahan observed it in his mind.

"There's a hypnotist on the loose," he told her. "He's been using people and controlling them to follow his wishes. Apparently, he can even hypnotize the birds to carry out his plans…Poor birds," he shook his head sadly.

There was a crash that broke the window next to them. Callahan needed a second or two to crawl back into his skin. He saw a hole drilled into the glass, shatter marks cracked away.

"I think someone just took a shot at me," guessed Callahan.

That was it for Lerna. She saw that and she was gone, frightened away fast as any leaf blown down the street. The breeze took care of her, taking her around the nearest corner.

Callahan wasn't so sure. As he looked at what happened to the window, it might not be a bullet hole…Who used guns anymore anyway? The police…Maybe he had just dreamed it was gunfire. But now it was too late anyhow, she had disappeared.

He kicked at the little diamond dust. His clothes still felt carped and woven by ocean as he turned and walked them in the direction of the Prairie Market van.

• GREEN 12

To see him move, to watch him as he went in and out among the neighborhood gardens, it was plain he was oblivious. Instinct was walking Callahan. He was deep in other thinking until he crossed the street into Green 12.

Gardens cracked open long overripe cement where people grew the food they needed, repaired what needed new and jobs were just what was needed to keep their cycle going. Sometimes all it took was a few tending hours a day. That was all. The rest was family and play and being alive.

It made Callahan feel like a ghost. What was he doing? Where was he from?

Music played like junebugs on the balustrades. Canopies of washed clothes were floating on the lines above the streets, waiting to dry.

• FISHING

Callahan stared at the van. He had left it there for only one day, but like a cocoon it had changed so much it scarcely recalled its old shape of wheels, windows and walls. He only knew its form because that's where he had left it before, on this edge of parking lot.

Callahan approached it slowly. Someone had turned it into a little red and gold house, with a pipe chimney out the top. No, it wasn't a house—someone had repainted over where *Routine Water Tracking* was. Now it said, *Skillful Mending, Tailoring & Shoemaking.*

The back door was open, orange light swung out of a lantern and a man was sitting there, dangling his legs with the smaller legs of a child next to him. They could have been fishing.

Some distance away, Callahan stood there by the fence and leaned into the bough of a spindling tree.

He liked the way it had transformed into this new night moth beauty.

He didn't mind at all. He would have to come up with something for the station though; he would just have to tell them the van flew away.

The next day, Callahan was driving another car, a little electricar, a Ford Sinatra. The station had folded it up in the garage, ready to be accordioned open. It was bright red as a fire engine toy.

All the other vans and squad cars were taken by Clanahan to clear the station's hypnotized occupants. Clanahan was moving his flock to the country where he said they belonged. Space to roam, fresh air, stars at night, and for whatever other reasons he had left written on the door before they left.

Two old men on a cart stopped next to Callahan at the traffic light. "What station are you listening to?" one of them asked him, cranking a metal box stuck with antennas and wires, the size of a porcupine.

"This is all this car plays," Callahan admitted. "It's a Sinatra."

They watched his car leap at the green light and intersection, gone from them in a moment. Their donkey had its own motion, taking them along with footsteps, rickshaws and bicycles and other traveling animals.

Callahan swerved under the arched tiers of the aqueduct, parking the singing car in a curtain of some uncertain piled ivy.

Also, a family used this room underneath the water to hang and sew and patch rugged sail cloth. Callahan brushed past a bolt of canvas as he joined the cobbled sidewalk.

It took him along the thrilled out wurlizter of birds, in banks of heavy blackberry bushes, to a flattened clover-topped yard where giant, rusted machinery grew.

To look for pigeons, Callahan had come to ride a gondola. He opened the door of it and was alone inside. He stood next to the window. Round cogged blackened gears gripped the wires that sawed the suspended car uphill to the observation tower.

Ground dropped away, roofs, alleys, colors, angles making distance as the gondola rode over the trees. While it clunked, he scanned the low sky for a sign of blue wings tricking along the tiled eaves or leaves, but the ride was over before any birds showed up. The gondola tapped and cramped on the wire, pulling wheels, slowly as a mule groaning to its stop.

Callahan stepped out the doorway onto the tower's wide observation platform. The gondola swung around and went back down its deep loop.

There was only one other person up here, a man whose back was turned. Callahan ignored him, went over to the rail where there was a telescope. Like this tower, it seemed to be salvaged from a time of airships and clippers, built with a creaking-breathing metal that wasn't forged anymore.

His eye looked through and poured across the world turning round.

"You came all the way up here to look back there?" said the man who had stopped behind him.

Callahan turned around and recognized him. It was Derby Chagrin, The Watchman of the City, The Town Crier. "I forgot you were up here!" Callahan grinned as they shook hands. "It's been a while."

Derby had his rocking chair, his weatherproof timepiece, telescope and gong and all day long he would keep track of the city's clockwork runnings, halloing on every hour, down to below, through a brass tubewarbler. Most people couldn't hear him though; even Callahan forgot he was up here.

"You looking for something?" Derby asked him.

"Oh…" Callahan began, then realized, of course, who better to know, "Have you noticed anything about pigeons?"

Derby pointed his finger at two places in the town, "There and there. Strange…Hundreds of them gathered at those places in town on different mornings and then they flew off to the hills. It was low clouds those days so I couldn't see exactly where they went."

Callahan nodded.

"I haven't seen them do that again," Derby added.

Callahan drummed his fingers on the iron railing. "Well, if

you do see them in a flock in the early morning, keep an eye on them if you can. See if you can tell where they land."

He put his eye back to the telescope and spun the view to Forest Hill. "My feeling is they're going there…Maybe you could keep an eye on that place for me too." He was finished with gazing at those little far away things. They would come to him sooner or later. "Anyway, I have to go to a pet store now."

"You can't stay for a while? Can I get you something to eat?"

"Umm…" Callahan stalled, "Do you have any salad?"

Derby stared at him, "A cop who wants salad?"

"No, that's okay. I should really get going."

"I don't have salad, but I have—"

"Don't worry, I'll come up again. I'll see you later. Here comes my ride."

The gondola had docked against the tower's edge again. It swayed there like a big green acorn.

"Hey!" Derby called one last time to Callahan. "What about getting a cat or a canary or something from the store for me?"

"Sure," said Callahan, smiling. He buckled the door. "That might be good for you." The last thing he heard his friend say was a joke about salad, but he couldn't hear more than that word while the gondola began its slow descent with him, towards the picture of sky, sun, and wind mirrored on the bay.

• EVER

Far below, Callahan wouldn't have seen more than a peck upon the sea, a ship rested, tied to the docks. There, The Hypnotist left a journeyed gurney. He carried a heavy bag full of money. He shifted it to the other hand and walked towards the line formed before the gate.

He stepped in near the front; the rest of the people were blank eyes and let him cut in. Reaching into his pocket, he showed a white strip of newspaper that became a ticket to the eyes of the man in the blue uniform.

"We're only boarding women and children right now, sir. You'll have to wait."

The Hypnotist scowled. He might have struck more of his power into this, but he felt why bother, why play their minds too much on the job? They were stuck with this sort of thing for life. He could let them think he was just another face in the day after day.

So he went over to the dock edge and looked into the water. He could see into the green depths. The smallest fish tagged around the pier legs.

In a little while, he heard the electric microphone call out for the rest of the passenger boarding. He smiled as he approached the line but suddenly he couldn't move.

He felt pinned like a butterfly. Something was wrong...Someone with powers like his was checking and stopping his mind from working. There was no way around the frozen feeling. For the first time ever, he stood there unable to move and his mind raced with fear to find a way out.

He couldn't...Every turn of his thoughts hit another wall. He watched helplessly as the rest of the passengers boarded.

The hawsers were tossed off and the big ship was tugged into the harbor, on its way to Hawaii without him. When it was far enough away, the heavy dream weight peeled off of him and The Hypnotist staggered back to life. He laughed. "Okay..."

around the frozen feeling

• THE ANIMAL DISTRICT

The trolley rocked to a stop at the Animal District on Charlotte Street, giving Callahan only another block to walk. He took to the street and sidewalk, past some wind-moving pinwheels planted in the sod. With no idea about which store to go in first, he simply started with the nearest place, on the corner. He saw big discount signs at the end of the block that looked interesting, but it was too late, the conveyor on the sidewalk had already grabbed him by the feet and was drawing him in.

The doors opened automatically and he was inside.

The walls were tiers of honeycomb glass and each place enclosed a different bright pet. He stepped off the magic carpet towards the canaries.

They jumped around on a polished branch. The soundproof glass thicked out their songs until he pushed the red button next to the frame. Suddenly their radio station blasted into the room.

"Can I help you?" a man dressed in a butler's uniform bolted from an aisle to switch off the birds.

"I'm looking to buy a bird. And a cat. For my friend up in the city tower."

"Any specific breed of bird or cat in mind?" the butler threaded each word into the other. "No doubt you are aware of distinctions within the species."

Callahan pointed at a golden one, "How much for that canary?"

The butler wrote the figure on a tablet and showed it to him.

Callahan coughed. Those birds were jewels in a chandelier. "What about that black cat, the helpless one?"

The tablet had another numbers parade.

"Okay…" Callahan wheezed, "How much for a sand dollar?"

"I think perhaps you may want to try a *pet store*," the butler slated.

The carpet was turned off for Callahan, he had to find the door himself and walk out onto the sidewalk. He made for the distant discount signs tacked into the gingko leaves above the cement. "That will be more like it," he said.

The leisure of exploring took him beside more windows and signs. Some of them he thought twice about entering, then, almost to the end, he did stop when a shock of pigeons strayed low over him. They sailed above the wires and dropped on the other side of the roof holding the building next to him. Looking into the reflecting sight, he tried to see what was happening in the local bank.

Nothing out of the ordinary…He was almost disappointed to see the everyday scene of people waiting in lines, holding papers and faces let down.

He was still suspicious though. The Hypnotist could be at work nearby. He passed the bricks. The sky was tilled with cirrus, otherwise empty. Those pigeons must be somewhere…

He craned around the next window, the sill of the Peerless Pet Store. Inside of it was just as Lerna Zemmer had described. He could see straight up the row of sacks of food to the counter where it was just like watching her dream over again.

Callahan burst in the door to stop it from happening, knocking the bell above him clattering. He ran to where the zombies were already disappearing at a shuffle out the back door. "Wait!" he screamed.

He passed the counter and out after them to a patio yard in the middle of tall fences and tired turned backs of buildings. The two pet store workers were dumping bags of birdseed onto a spilling lake of pigeons.

Callahan jumped backwards to avoid crushing the birds under his feet.

The whole thing was happening the same way as the bank, so…

Callahan scrambled back inside. There should be someone serving The Hypnotist's signal. Sure enough, like a coat rack next to the sawdust, Callahan saw the poor hypnotized sap standing there.

There was nothing in the vacant eyes, but Callahan said, "Who are you? What are you doing here?"

The zombie was holding a piece of paper. Since nothing was moving inside the hand, Callahan took the paper from him and read it. It read, 2230 Charlotte St.

A loud flack blasted from outside as the patio cloud took off past the door. The pigeons were gone.

In a snap, the man before Callahan lurched forwards almost into a fall, stepping a foot out to stop himself. "No, this isn't right," he blinked. He quickly turned away from Callahan who was too unprepared to do anything else but watch him track out.

"What's going on in here?" the store echoed.

Callahan stared at the two women behind the counter. "What's the address?" he hurried.

"2232." She held the sides of her head like a deep sea diver with a goldfish bowl helmet. Her friend was the same muddled way.

"That's what I thought..." Callahan told her. "He had the wrong number."

He left them, went outside and looked at the numbers painted on the bank next door. "2230," he read. The bank missed being robbed by a door. "You could have picked a better zombie, Hypnotist!" he laughed. It was good, it meant The Hypnotist wasn't perfect.

He was so pleased with things that he let himself in the very next store, Double Discount Pets, dark as an attic inside.

There was a table with a green lidded light hanging down over a strange crew of card players. The first person Callahan noticed was the man with a gray parrot on his shoulder. The bird opened and shut its beak like a silent film star.

Callahan drifted close. He wasn't noticed so he took himself over to a bubbling mossy fish tank to observe.

It didn't surprise him too much when the game ended up with a movie sort of quarrel, chairs and arms flying.

The parrot shrawked out, "Cheater!" From that shoulder view

it grabbed a card with its beak, shifting it to its feet when the man grabbed for it. Turmoil.

Callahan harbored in. He slipped the parrot's claws to his own hand and saved it from being strangled.

"Gimme that bird!"

The place was an interruption. Callahan shoved his hand like a gun in his pocket, "Everyone stay calm…" as he leaned out of the action, "Let's nobody worry. I'm leaving. Everything is alright."

It worked. He was back onto Charlotte Street like he wanted, with a bird. "You want to go live with Derby in the sky?"

The big parrot pulled on his ear.

"Yowch!" Callahan let out a scream. He stopped against a pitched fence to pull. On the other side he could hear the deep shush of land diving off.

The city was built around the curves of the sea, the lap and purr of water was never far away. Waves made piers appear, a place for the come and go travel of here and now.

In that falling down rush of air to sea, he reached for a twig to let the bird step off out of his life.

"That's a fine bird you have there," chuckled a voyager, someone blown up from the tide. "I've been looking all day for such a fine animal."

The parrot finally let go and scratched its claws back onto Callahan's hand. "You want him?" Callahan held his weighty hand out. "He's yours."

The parrot stepped right off onto the pirate's shoulder and was instantly at home. The two were together, a picture was completed.

• THE ORIGINAL DISCOUNT PET STORE

Under the funny lime colored leaves of the gingko trees, The Original Discount Pet Store was billboard sized. The cartoons of animals and signs and arrows pointed him to open the door.

He smelled the place, the sawdust, seeds and caged lives in the wait. When he opened his eyes again, he expected to see himself standing in an ostrich pen.

Callahan walked up to a conversation going on at the counter. There were two men.

"It looked like a bamboon," the first man said.

"A what?"

"A bamboon."

"You mean a baboon?"

"Yeah, whatever it is, one of them monkeys."

"Actually, the baboon is a member of the ape family."

Then Callahan interrupted them, "Can I ask you a quick question?"

They both stared at him.

"I have a question about pigeons."

The man on the other side of the counter touched his glasses, "Yes?"

"Do you know anyone who keeps a bunch of them? Has them trained or whatever?"

"Oh, well you know pigeonry is a popular pastime for many folks. I can think of several people with flocks."

"Could you tell me? I mean people with a lot of them."

"Let's see…there's Jeff Toffs, he's an amateur but shows genuine interest. Up and coming. Oh, and there's that remarkable hypnotist fellow. He's been in here getting feed before."

"That's him," said Callahan. "Do you have his address?"

"Well no, I certainly don't! He's a celebrity, he cares for his privacy I should think."

Callahan grumbled a word. A silence fell down for a couple seconds.

"What about that monkey?" said the other man.

"I told you, it's an ape."

Callahan turned around. He found himself looking at the cage full of kittens. They were so small and soft. There was so much in the world waiting for them.

Callahan left the store with a cage holding a canary and he had a cat in his coat pocket, looking out. The Elevated Line with gondola service to the crown of the hill wasn't far away. He pet the kitten while he walked past vacant parking lots growing fields.

He had to pay a couple silver coins to ride. This time he got on the gondola with some young Japanese students. They were so excited about this, his day to day world. He smiled and looked with them at the sights out the window gliding by.

He listened to their thrilled words and laughing going so fast. It was funny to think of all the languages out there he would never know. When you're stuck in America there are things you might never understand.

He closed his eyes and listened, as if to the birds when they go so cheerfully in the dawn.

A sudden stop halted the gondola at the top and the Japanese feathers departed out the opened door. Callahan got out too, looking for Derby.

He saw the bad familiar sight of two officers by the metal rail.

"Callahan," one of them announced.

"What's going on?" he said. He could feel something ready to fall on him. He set the birdcage down carefully.

"The Town Crier is dead."

"What?"

"He fell off of here. Didn't you see the mess below?"

"Derby?"

"Yeah."

Callahan bit his teeth and looked away. He saw the bird hop along the perch in the cage. He kept waiting for it to sing or talk or do something. Meanwhile, there were the sounds of the city never stopping. He felt like he listened to them for a minute before he dropped, "What…Why?"

"He just fell. Or jumped. Something happened."

Callahan didn't want to be on the tower anymore, he picked

up the cage and turned away and around and found the Japanese in the way of the gondola. With a mumble, he bowed and offered them the birdcage, pulling the cat out of his pocket also. "Will you please take these?"

Leaving the scene empty-handed, he held the rusted window sill of the gondola, wishing his grip would hurry it faster. Behind him, he heard them laughing and saying loving words to their new animals.

• GHOST LAND

Whatever empty ghost land awaited him at the end of the gondola drop, he wasn't sure. He didn't want to notice the crowd and official metal cars. Photographs.

He walked from that newspaper in progress. He didn't want to be haunted with another something that would follow him forever so he tried to keep it away from his eyes.

• SO MUCH DAY

He tried to forget and be hardboiled. Like the detectives and cops you read about in fables. He walked along the city streets and thought that way: concrete. It wouldn't be to notice the green leaves and sparrows, but he couldn't help it…and he couldn't remember where he left the Sinatra.

So much day had passed, someone had probably taken it over. Oh well, the department made enough in fines every day to pay for another car, or more. Let it become a greenhouse or a tailor shop, or a shrine, or whatever.

Callahan kept walking until he came to the water.

He sat on a bench and listened to a beautiful sound coming to him.

It was not a floating phonograph. It was a bird. He could see its dazzled shape on the sun's reflection. Even though life was taking him in dangerous directions, people shooting at him or not, friends falling a hundred feet, mystery and tragedy, sorrowful and forgetful, he had been reminded now.

The new next sound was the harmonica he kept in his pocket, quiet all this time. No hurry, letting it roll, boxcars.

"My name is Will Patton," the words fell on him like a satellite. "I'm a scout. Where did you learn to play like that?"

Callahan stared at the man in the sofa-shaped suit. "I don't know," he said. "It's just a harmonica," and he put it away.

"Yeah, yeah…You're coming with me, pal. I need you to play that again. We need you, we're making a record. Look, follow me."

Callahan followed along over the crowds of daisies, buttercups, clover tended by bees who flew away.

There was a black solar-car parked by the curb. When they reached it, all the silver wings folded up on top to give them room to enter it.

"Have a seat," Will ushered him in. "We're making a record and you just appeared out of the blue for the last song. We'll take you to the top, you'll be one of the stars."

"What do you mean?" asked Callahan as the plexiglass began to motion. "I have things to do."

"Don't you get it? I discovered you! Just sit tight. I'm taking you to David Tinpan, the bigtime, you bet! Decca Records!"

"I can't believe it."

"You can believe it. I've got an ear for talent, that's my specialty. Hey driver, step on it." The scout took out a ledger to make some notes.

It dawned on Callahan where the street was leading. "Wait a minute…" he said. They had reached the clearcuts, starts of fences stitching and rubble pounded down into the grass, where the last past of a civilization nightmare had been. It had a dark violence to it that had never been changed. It was so terrible, it had to be kept here in its past. "This is the jail."

"That's right. Don't worry though," he laughed, "this won't take long, just a song. This job is destiny!"

"I'm not too fond of this place." He didn't want to say what he did for a living, sending people here. If this was all going to be a mystery then okay, but it was too late anyway, they were already entering the gate.

The solarcar pushed into a tunnel of riveted steel and ran through the dim on its batteries until the driver stopped them before a waiting murmur of people.

The scout jumped out right away and Callahan could hear their conversation as he got out too.

"You can play?" said the man in the middle of all of them.

"This is David Tinpan," cut in Will Patton, "He's the record producer."

"Why do we have to be here?" asked Callahan.

Tinpan boasted, "Decca Records is producing a new recording entitled *Prison Harmonica*. The sound of the imprisoned, you know. We just need one more track."

"That you're going to play!" Will Patton added.

"Come on," Tinpan got them all moving down the corridor.

They were underground, they could have been underneath Paris by the look of the dark chopped stones that made the walls, trapped their candlelight.

"In here…" Tinpan stood beside the iron gate of a cell.

Inside the cell was a steel folding chair and a microphone stand with wire cords out the bars.

"I don't know if I like being in here," Callahan paused outside it.

"Who does?" Tinpan gave him a shove. "That's where the sound you play comes from. There's nothing else like it." Tinpan put on a pair of enormous headphones. "Take a seat. When you're ready, I'll start rolling."

• OUTSIDE

Callahan was waking up with outside air. He coughed and opened his eyes and sat up. "Where are we?" A fence, a breeze.

"We're in the yard," Will Patton told him. "We had to bring you out here. After you played, you passed out. We had to get you fresh air. Mister, I thought you were going to die!" He held his arm and helped Callahan stand. "Makes for great liner notes, though."

Through the chain link fence, Callahan's eyes focused on a group of young children in stripes. They were kicking around and pecking at the cement. Above them floated a little blue paper kite. It was actually reaching out over the fence.

Callahan followed the string down to where it held a boy in the corner of the yard flying it.

The boy looked over his shoulder and bolted his eyes to Callahan.

With those buttons on him, Callahan began to sway again.

Will Patton grabbed him, "Hold on! I got you. Say, I have to get you out of this place!"

• CLOVER

The next time Callahan woke up in the breeze, he heard water. He was staring straight up at the sky. Dragonflies opened and closed drawers in the air. A pigeon chopped wings by him overhead.

He sat up on the bench to look at it go and a piece of paper fluttered towards him.

It was that blue diamond shaped kite he had seen earlier. It was made out of newspaper. He could see the words spiriting through the paint. The rein of its frayed thread had been broken, to somehow lead it here.

There was nobody else around. By the bright low stare of the sun he guessed it must be either seven in the morning or in the evening. He didn't carry a clock though. He crushed the kite into a coat pocket, realizing with a sudden clumsiness that it was only structured with twigs and tore of course.

Pigeons. They were always darting around somewhere—they found cities wherever they were grown—they were part of history—while the buildings rose and fell forever. More of them had flown than he would ever know.

Gravel took him into a birdhouse telephone booth and he put all the silver he had into it. He waited for the call to go through.

"This is Clanahan."

"This is Callahan."

"Hah! There you are! Are you done now?"

"No. Almost."

"Well, you might as well be. You can't beat it, Callahan. The people love The Hypnotist. He's even giving away all that money he took, passing it out to those in need. And guess what? It happened to me! This morning I found a hundred grand in the hedge."

"So you're not coming back to the city?"

"No!" Clanahan laughed, "No, why should I? The trance wore off. Everyone's okay. I don't need that job, that lousy salary working with hypnotized animals. Listen, I have to go Callahan. Figure it out, okay? See you around."

Callahan hung up and looked out the little pane of glass. People stood in the green and yellow lights of the Gull station across the street, beamed on while they stopped to fill up their lanterns.

Returning to the world, it was a strange haze. Callahan wished he knew what time it was, whether dawning or eve. Tangles of morning glory tried to hide everything. The sunlight nearly made a sound, pushed onto the roofs and dropped on all the second hand carts in a rickshaw lot.

Some minutes later in the hollow crater of a gone building Callahan saw people making a park. The people were doing it themselves, miraculously, taking care of it themselves. They were planting trees and flowers, turning over the broken slabs of gray cement.

He read the signs they had made.

Welcome Para Todos!…Imagine…Have More Fun…Make This Pit A Park…Stay Free…Community Garden…Welcome All…Participate In Your City…Do Something Deconstructive!…Resistance Is Fertile…Be Good Family… Never Forget Everything Is Possible…Begin

Past there, into neighborhood, he listened to the creak of windmills on the summits. There wasn't much wind, just a flutter, enough to turn them, making slow electricity going.

Mostly he watched his feet though, sometimes looking up at the sights becoming familiar.

A blue police kiosk stood glued to the corner by the lamppost. Callahan smiled when he stopped at the striped paint curbside. He didn't need a key, the door was unlocked. When he pushed it open, there was his next car hanging on a rack inside the narrow space.

He took it off the hanger and shook out its pleats like a pressed suit. It took shape, a Ford Astaire, the air filled it, an origami car.

There was a red warning label on the dashboard: *Do Not Drive In Foul Weather.* Alright, Callahan agreed, as he got into the little cabin and turned the key.

The engine hummed and it sprung across the tar on nimble spinning wheels. Not that it was all that fast, some children even ran alongside of him, laughing, outrunning him for a couple blocks.

He enjoyed its papery float, the pleasant way it drove like a kite around corners.

When he stopped not much further, he was near the station. He got out of the little car in the peppery sunlight and shade of wooden trellises.

Someone immediately clopped up to him, "Can I borrow that for five minutes?"

Callahan let go of the handle, "Sure."

"Okay, thanks. I'll be back tomorrow."

Callahan laughed. Two lovers walked on the other side of the street, she with some flowers he must have given her. There was calliope and fresh fruit being sold, clover coming up the sidewalk cracks.

A boy found Callahan when he was almost in front of the precinct and hovered, "I got stung by a bee the second time." He held out his small thumb.

"Yeah?" said Callahan.

The boy took time to explain it the right way, "The first time I saw the bee, then I pet the bee and I got stung."

"Oh…" said Callahan. "I used to pet bees too, when I was little. You have to be careful."

"I know."

Callahan opened the station door to enter.

His first surprised thought was that he had gone in the wrong place. The hall was filled with the sound of playing children. Had the station melted out of sight from this spot? His big shoes clopped like kettles on the hallway floor.

Pictures on the wall were paintings of animal creatures and

suns that were smiling, rainbows, bugs and cartoon flowers.

"Ha!" he laughed out loud at the door that used to go into the old sight. *Good Morning Day Preschool,* it said.

"This is good," he mumbled, "this is good, this is right." They were starting to learn here.

He was too. He had come far enough to know by now. He might as well get rid of the badge in his pocket, the tickets, and the feathers and alchemy thing and everything.

He saw a tray of dirt set in the window sun's living light, so he set all his pocket contents on it.

Maybe when they found them, they could play them into some lesson for the class, or just forget about them under the leaves that were sure to grow.

Without that work anymore, Callahan turned around. He listened to the sounds of the new school in between the chucks of his shoes taking him back outside.

Clover light.

Across the street in the little yellow window of steam, he could see the real work that he wanted all along: dove-white shirts of chefs paging back and forth like a cook book, the aroma wind and seas that fanned out vents into the breeze into him.

Early Summer 2001

GOMEZ

He woke up a few minutes before the alarm clock. It was 6:40 in the morning. The lace curtains held the start of the blue day. His wife was warm as a rolling hill along his side. He tried to send out a mental bolt to freeze the red digital numbers on the clock but it ticked seamlessly into 6:41. He had two minutes to go before the peace in the little room would snap.

With effort, he managed to get his elbows under him. The blankets washed as his wife brought her hot leg up over him. She was still in her sleep. Her black hair fell all over her face.

Near their bed was a smaller bed with little Mira, sleeping too.

6:42. Oh, it was too late to be feeling this way. His wife was so lovely though. Her shoulder was soft, brown and bared out of the sheets. That leg over him. The light in the room was calm as a candle and he brought his hand onto her.

6:43 caught everyone by surprise.

WHEELER

Wheeler Treen was sent from The Untied States of America in a government car with a briefcase full of papers in the back. There was a book about desert flowers and a map on the dashboard and he was following the line drawn on that folded paper towards the town beyond, in Aztlan.

ZOOT & CLOVER

The border was a serpent scene—stalled colors, crowd and noise bound low to the ground with little blue smoky coils of charcoaling taco stands.

It took Zoot and Clover most of the day to get through that from one country into another. Zoot put their stamped papers in his suit pocket and had to nearly drag Clover on the way. Clover, carrying all their heavy bags, had that dazed look Zoot had seen so often before. He had to find shade and somewhere peaceful, fast.

"This way," Zoot said, "We'll rest in here." He led Clover into the alley between two buildings. There was some breeze moving through, enough to brush the clothes on the ropes above them. Clover was staring up at their folds and shadows. Zoot stopped him and let him rest against the clay bricks and watch the sky. "Well, we're here anyway…" he sighed. He took out a handkerchief and wiped his forehead.

GOMEZ

The rust on its walls made the factory look like a tiger. It shined in the sandlot among all the weeds and parked old cars. The sun blinded on every bent part and warp of the building.

For those who didn't have a car or discount velocipede or bicycle, there was a path torn next to the road. Once his walk took him to this part of the morning, where the factory was in sight, he gave himself a deep breath. He would be gone in that factory for the next nine hours. From this spot he could start to hear the machinery pounding out the end of the graveyard shift. It kept going all hours until Saturday and Sunday when they stopped making velocipedes until Monday.

Anyway, he had to hurry. He was a little late today.

ZOOT & CLOVER

One thing about Clover, Zoot watched him and smiled, he could eat tamales like nobody he'd ever seen. "Maybe we're in the wrong business," he joked, "Maybe I should enter you in eating contests instead." Still, he already talked to the cook and found out where the wrestling places were. They could start tomorrow. There was no rush. Aztlan was a whole new big country.

GOMEZ

He had a funny way of letting his mind go while he worked assembling muffler guards for the velocipedes. There was so much noise on the floor as metal was stamped and cut and run across in pieces on the assembly line, you got lost in your thoughts after a while. After long hours there, rackety aplomb, each of the workers' faces could be read like a book.

Gomez always ended up thinking about his family, remembering what they had done last evening, wondering if they were at the park now or what things they would do when he got home if he wasn't too tired. He knew by the time he got home, he would be exhausted. He would just want to lie on the bed. Sleep was all he would want. He began to think of that too. That's how the time went by.

Each time he set up a full pallet of muffler guards, a forklift came by and took it away. Then it was start over. Oh, the shift went by, as they all made their movies in their heads, and then finally went to clock out at 5.

Gomez's replacement was an old tall American man with a long white beard. He didn't have an ordinary name, all he had was a letter to be known by. It was C.

"Hello C," Gomez said in English and held up his hand. He smiled at him.

C was a character. C would talk your ear off about why he left the States. In broken Spanish C would explain, "El Norte, mucho loco."

"Si," Gomez would say, smiling, also part of the routine.

Nobody was sure exactly what would happen to C now that Aztlan was back, or even if the factory would keep running. They were all waiting to see what the next week would bring.

"Adios," C said as he took his place at the big machine. C wore big black rimmed glasses the size of goggles. The fluorescent ceiling lights checkered on their lenses when he moved his stiff arms at work.

Outside, in the warm start of evening, it was quiet. Castle colors lay on the land. The day shift belonged to the outside again.

Gomez split from the rest of them when he took to the trail. There was a half moon, a pale half balloon in the sky. His feet kicked up a bit of dust. The bugs hammered on the tall golden weeds on either side of him.

ZOOT & CLOVER

Zoot had found them a hotel called Los Lost No More. It was an okay place. They got a big room painted sand yellow, two beds facing a TV and a couple doors that opened onto a porch where they both went and sat down, waiting for a breeze. Zoot had his legs stretched out against the rail and Clover just watched.

Zoot ran his hands over the newspaper listings. Clover watched the strange purple lantern hung off the trim of the roof. Every so often a moth or other winged bug looped out of the flitting crowd surrounding the light to get too close and touch. An electric shock sparked and it was no more. All of that purple trick and agony nonetheless sat in Clover's eyes.

WHEELER

Wheeler's road went on and on and he was getting tired. He still had a ways to go in the U.S. This time of night the stars were his friends. He had the window rolled down so he could sometimes lean into the wind and look up. Not only did it keep him awake, he liked to stare at the sky in the blast going past.

The headlights spread an orange yellow ghost ahead of him.

When it seemed nothing more could stop sleep, he started looking for a hotel or motel. The land around him was black with moonlight touches on hills and silver tops of trees.

What are you supposed to think about when you drive so late? He chose the radio and as he chased through the dial he was so happy to find an old show. It was Roy Rogers. There were rustlers on the prairie, hiding out somewhere with everyone's cows. Pretty soon the heroes were hiding in a cabin, with outlaws surrounding them everywhere, when suddenly Roy Rogers appeared in the window with a "Hello everyone!" and a rescue plan.

Wheeler laughed at the childish storyline until he remembered that adults would also listen in great belief, lost in a world that spun them away from long days of sorry work or whatever, needing escape. Just like people were still doing.

GOMEZ

Gomez got home where the flowers grew and he could hear Mira's voice piping through. He opened the door.

Mira was running around the middle of the room, trailing a balloon and a doll by the hair, singing away. She stopped when he walked in. She looked at him and knew what to say, "Bu-Bump!" It was the sound of Chicken Heart, a story he told her at bedtime last night.

That was enough. He ran by his wife, managed to kiss her as he was pulled along to the bedroom.

"You go first," his daughter told him.

"Ohh! So I have to see the monster first?"

"Just go!" she pushed him with her little hands.

He pretended that he was scared of something hiding in the shadows of their bedroom.

"Turn on the lights!" she shrieked. "All of them. Over there and there! The closet too!" Her eyes brightened on him.

"Okay…" Gomez ran into the room, made it yellow, then dived under the covers ahead of her.

She was right behind him. He held up room for her to jump in beside him, kicking legs and yelling.

Under the tent of blankets Gomez laughed at her excited small face. "Bu-Bump!"

"Chicken Heart is hungry for people!" she screamed.

"What about me?" he laughed. "I've been at work all day. I haven't had my supper."

"I have an idea," she told him. Her ball of weight climbed all of him so she could listen out the edge of the blue sheet. She whispered a distant sounding, "Bu-Bump…" and looked at her father. "He's leaving…Go get us some food. Get some Beetle Chips and Spider Juice."

"Oh no," he replied. "Not that again." He brushed pretend crumbs off of himself. "I was shaking crumbs out of this bed all night long. No more food in here."

She was laughing as he carried on.

"—and that Spider Juice! It always gets spilled! I end up sleeping in a lake!"

"Go! Go you lump of mumbles! Go while Chicken Heart is gone. It's safe now," she told him urgently, pushing him out of the covers.

He landed on his knees on the floor and hurried out to the kitchen.

His wife Mina looked up at him from where she sat. She had been with Mira all day. She needed some rest.

Gomez grabbed a crackling bag of tortilla chips and opened the icebox door for the bottle of juice.

Mira sing-songed for him to hurry.

"I'm coming!" he ran back in and flapped under the blankets. "I made it, we're safe!"

Mira stuffed her hand in the bag and laughed as she pulled out crumbs of, "Beetle Chips!"

ZOOT & CLOVER

Zoot couldn't sleep. He finally tossed his long body out of bed. The moon and mariachi in the drapes wouldn't let him rest. Besides, he had to see this city at night. A scrap of paper told him how to reach the wrestling arena. That's what he couldn't stop thinking about.

Clover was out, drifting in some dreamland miles away. Neon lay over him in a blissful sleeping blanket.

When Zoot reached the door, he let in some of the music and bright yellow light as he quickly slipped into it and was off like a carnival moth.

The first thing he saw was a Ferris wheel half over the tiled roofs. An old billboard reflected the rainbow of it.

Zoot smiled at the sight. Little velocipedes putted by him in the road, crowds illuminated by the strings of candle lanterns, everyone out enjoying the night.

He straightened his tie and walked with the rest of them towards the arena, where the barrio leaned.

WHEELER

The Untied States hung onto these places. Fences in the night. Gas stations were still to be found though the prices kept most people walking, riding bicycles, velocipedes or other forms of travel. $52.95 a gallon wasn't as bad as he'd seen it in the city he came from. He laughed whenever he remembered the old days. He could remember clearly how the roads used to teem with cars and trucks making the air shimmer like a thick river. The car steered onto the tar, rang over the hose bell and he parked next to a pump.

A door in the office swung open and a gray man in a wheelchair clacked out to fill the tank.

GOMEZ

That night he had a dream of Heaven. Even while it was happening, he knew it must be a vision. He was driving one of those family-sized velocipedes. Mina and Mira were with him. Along beside them glided a field that flowed across to a mountain. The scene seemed so familiar, then he heard a voice say where it was and he knew it but he was already aware that when he woke up he would forget.

They stopped and stepped from their velocipede and walked in the right direction. He actually stopped so he could breathe the dream air. It was like nothing he knew in life. It was a glorious delight. A beautiful light was on everything.

All of a sudden, the mountain became close and had windows. A pathway was open letting the three of them go in.

WHEELER

Finally he couldn't go any longer. He waited for the road sign to tell him which place to stop. When a sign said The Last American Hotel, he had to roll off at that exit and follow the arrows.

He steered over the popping gravel and stopped in the empty lot. When he got out he was amazed by the cold air and stillness of the night. Shutting the car door was so loud he startled himself.

There was scant pear-colored light from the office door. A red neon Vacancy sign buzzed and crackled in the ink.

Each one of his steps broke into the quiet, taking him towards the door, up onto the porch and scuffing to a stop in the wooden shade.

After 11, Ring Bell.

He couldn't believe the cracked wall, the exposed wires and circuits around the button. I'll probably get a shock if I press it, he thought, but what can I do? Who knows what it will do to me?

He was right. The last thing he knew was the jolt, a fierce white light, and he seemed to be picked up by the wind, carried away into the black starless night.

ZOOT & CLOVER

They were both there. While Zoot stood in the crowd, Clover watched from a dream, a window sewn with cigarette smoke high in the top of the tent.

Zoot had his notebook out and a black pen was writing down everything he could describe happening around himself. He couldn't hide his pleasure as he thought about how perfect it was. Costumed superheroes, good and evil, throwing each other back and forth between the ropes, everyone was going wild, screaming, treating the fantasy as if it was real.

Clover would fit right in.

Zoot was the last in the crowd to leave. The sweepers broomed down the aisle, pushing piles of paper and bones.

WHEELER

A dull diamond light tricked in the bare branches. Wheeler rubbed a hand across his face, his eyes. The pain of his crooked cradle sleep woke him. He kicked his feet, spun and grabbed around the trunk of the tree to keep from falling. His eyes were wide open while he held on.

He could see the ground down there, fifteen feet away. Tall weeds grew in gray crowns around the roots of his tree with the rows of grapes below. The tree snapped and shook as he positioned himself so he wouldn't fall, so he could figure out what to do. He was finding grasps for his hands, where the branches twined out of the brown trunk, when he heard little tin whistle cries reaching up in Spanish.

There were children dressed like spinning tops who grew between the aisles of the orchard. They were waving at him and calling more and more people over.

Wheeler waved at them. He felt like another Gulliver, watching them wobble a ladder over. But as soon as the top step hit the edge of his apple tree, Wheeler was on his way down to the ground. "Thanks folks! Gracias!" He edged away, followed the path between the trees to be gone before he became a bigger scene.

It had been a while since he had to run. He felt like an ancient iron thing. His breath left rusted clouds over him.

He couldn't stop wondering, "How did I get from the door of the hotel into a tree?"

It didn't make sense and neither did his blind escape. He couldn't tell if the vines were running towards a way out or not. They grew on wooden posts like tangled telephone lines running on either side of a road. Little bees and yellow jackets took off from their leaves. Luckily, he didn't see anyone anymore when he glanced at his past.

Over the green ahead of him sailed The Last American Hotel sign. The big plastic thing held onto its corner of sky.

Wheeler appeared at the edge of the parking lot. His car was waiting. It took all night and the dawn for that missing picture to develop.

"I flew all the way from that hotel door, back over there…" where he looked over his shoulder into the dipping roll of orchard. "The bell on the wall must have been attached to a powerful flow of electricity…" he reasoned aloud…Something invisible and strong enough to throw him, giving him the power of flight.

Then he wondered more. The papers were full of America falling apart. Bombs were going off all the time, like whatever had shot him across all that distance into the tree. Except it wasn't a bomb…the door was still there and he wasn't harmed. He only had a few scratches and this lasting bewilderment.

Wheeler looked at himself in his car window. A charge of strange light flickered in the glass. He reached into each pocket looking for his car keys. They weren't on him. They were locked inside, still in the ignition.

CLOVER

He could feel something hovering just out of his reach, watching over him. It slowly ebbed from him with the quiet knowing motion of a creature living in the foggy white of a cloud. When Clover squinted out of the dream, the vision dissolved into a pale yellow curtained window. It was morning.

Clover opened his eyes and the thing had slipped out the edges of the wallpapered room.

GOMEZ

What would happen if I didn't get up? Gomez pressed a button that mechanically curled a sheet of metal to where the staplers caught it in the corners. He had been thinking that before he got out of bed this morning and it was still with him. What if everyone decided not to get out of bed? The factory would stay quiet after the late shift left. There would be no replacements to come work the machines. And then what would happen if the next shift didn't show up? He could imagine this big loom of iron arching out from him turning into rust and wind when the roof broke in and weeds grew through it all.

Each time the steel velocipede shell was curled over and stapled, he grabbed it and stacked it on the pallet next to him. He looked at the other people he could see. Everyone was in their own thoughts. He imagined them as radio towers he wasn't tuned into. Except for old C—he was talking out loud as usual. C was competing with the factory sound. His beard unrolled with each loud every other word. As long as he kept up with the work, Gomez thought, they would keep him on—he was the token American and he did work like a maniac.

Gomez smiled. He took another sheet of metal and flopped it on the track. He caught the curls and put them into hinges.

That's what he was thinking at 9:37 in the morning while time passed on.

WHEELER

Wheeler had to wait there in the Rose Café. He already made a half hysterical call to the one locksmith in town after the call to the police station told him that they would charge him $500 to open his door. Wheeler watched out the window with his coffee wrapped in his hands. He couldn't even eat his pancakes. They lay there like life preservers before his wrecked morning. Wheeler looked out the window, waiting.

Finally an electric horse appeared. It was pulling a tool wagon and the man driving it stopped it beside Wheeler's trapped car. Wheeler left some lead coins and creased certificates on the table before he dashed outside.

The locksmith was standing there like the first out-of-tune strum of a guitar that's been leaning in a corner. "I haven't seen one of these for a long time," he began when Wheeler was near. "A gas guzzler…You must be on government business?"

"Can you get it open?" Wheeler snapped. He didn't have the time to be misunderstood. He had to be on his way.

"Sure." The locksmith stopped. He stared hard at Wheeler. "You can leave us here. We'll get by," he shoved a slim piece of snarled metal inside the door, "You can take your gasoline government car. You can go and get—you're as good as gone already."

ZOOT & CLOVER

Zoot had his best suit on. Clover was standing beside him, wearing his stage uniform. He was covered in red and blue, with white pointed stars. Tall as he was, his body was bent into corners. He looked like he had been sat on all his life.

"Here's the contract," said the promoter Gonzales, returning to the room with the paperwork, "We can match him tonight. All you have to do is sign and we'll set it up."

Zoot leaned right into his signature on the page. He laughed, "This is great. You'll love my boy. This'll be great entertainment. There it is!" He pushed the contract across the table.

"Welcome to Aztlan," Gonzales shook Zoot's hand. "Be at the arena at 9 PM." He was wearing a gold watch the size of a sundial.

GOMEZ

Every day at this time, there was the blat of a horn from outside the corrugated walls. The foreman dropped the lever on the conveyor and everyone had a ten minute break to go outside.

The Snack Truck was parked next to the loading bay door. Gomez would go out too, even though he knew better and by now he saw something so bad in that silver truck waiting for them in the stark sunlight.

The factory had a deal with the company that drove in snacks at 10:15 every day. Painted on the tin were the American names and logos representing salt and sugar in easy, tempting, slick plastic bags. The American driver hopped out, wearing sunglasses, t-shirt and khaki shorts and he broke open the hatches for the show. Everything was priced up to match their location far from stores.

It bothered Gomez to see these people he worked with throw away their pay for a quick couple handfuls of that filler. He wished he could change their minds, as he stood alone, finding shelter in the clear air.

WHEELER

Oh, he thought about how he left that town. It kept coming back to him—that last American town on the approach to Aztlan. That upset locksmith opened the door and didn't take any silver in return—he just left Wheeler to his opened car and clucked his electric horse away.

"These folks down here think they're losing the land they grew up in. They think it's all gone. They're wrong. They're just trading flags. Aztlan will take back what America took away to start with. They're missing the point. They can stay. They can adapt. It's all the same planet wherever you go. Take a step away and look. History is one empire after another. We're in a cycle, spinning, never ending as long as we're not knowing."

He sighed and talked out loud to himself like the radio, "But how can they understand that, when I leave them to their fate, while I drive away with gasoline at 65 miles per hour?"

There were plenty signs of ghost towns now where the people had run away.

ZOOT & CLOVER

"Gather round! Gather round! El Contest! Evento Especial!" Zoot crooned. There was a crowd forming about the wood paneled stand underneath the palms. "El Contest! Tamales! Who can win? El winner?! Is it you?"

Clover kept getting the attention of every sentence, feeling eyes on him. Like a superhero lost on another planet, he wore his costume for the world to see. He stretched his colored arms around his chest.

After one and then another challenged him and lost, it became sort of the way it was going to be. Clover could eat tamales endlessly. Nobody could match him.

"No mas! No more!" Zoot shouted to stop it all. The breeze took away the crumpled papers and challengers. Zoot explained with a microphone, he made it really seem like a dream they were all in with the unbeatable Clover in their midst. Words that still wouldn't stop echoing over the crowd and off the walls and flags, could be heard down the dust colored alleys...Clover couldn't lose. Why try to be against him? Throw your life into a propeller. Clover could prove to anyone who they were. And guess what? He was wrestling tonight at the arena! Don't miss it!

MIRA

On a sandbar ten feet from the shore, Mira crept on all fours, mooing like a cow. "The farm got flooded!" she told her mother who kneeled in the shallows beside her, "What did cow say?" She splashed along, knees and hands digging in the soft underwater sand. Then she turned to face her mother with another idea. Her mind was as quick as a dreamer. She stood up, "Pretend I'm a clumsy chicken," and she folded her arms into wings. "Pretend I can't swim."

Out further in the sea, the black line sketch of a ship was bound for America. It had to rake up a full row of gray sails to catch the warm wind. Papery and hovering in the distance like a ghost on its journey across one watery room to another, miles away.

WHEELER

Somehow Wheeler had strayed off the road. It was easy to do. The highway was crumbled, frail, and the color of it was mixed with the earth of this hot sunny land. He had the map, but it was thrown like a dropped cobweb on the floor long ago. The mirror showed a cloud of dust where he had been.

He had to hope sense would soon appear ahead. Didn't it all look the same though? From here to where the sky ducked underground was all the same dry wolf color.

He wasn't going to turn around, he decided. He was going to keep going. The world wasn't so big that he couldn't find somebody in the distance.

Zoot laughed at the handful of Aztlan money in his hand. They were in a new place doing the same game just as well. "You better take it easy now, Clover. Go rest, siesta. Digest all those tamales!" he roared. He stuffed his pocket. "Oh, here's the hotel key if you want to go back. I'll meet you. I have to take care of some business, place some bets and what not. We're doing good…So far so good…" Zoot patted him on the shoulder, "Be seeing you."

Clover watched him go. Clover couldn't move from the folding chair. The flags fluttered shadows on him. His eyes closed but opened when someone spoke to him.

"Excuse me. You're from America aren't you?"

Clover in all his flag colors from that foreign country couldn't believe someone couldn't tell where he was from by looking, but then he couldn't help noticing her too. Strings had already started tying them together.

She said, "My name is Vida. I was from America too."

GOMEZ

What a racket the machinery made, a mechanical musical rhythm, as the clock on the beam overhead slowly moved every time he looked at it. Sooner or later all this work was gone and he was home, then he was back here again. The spell was broken by a little bit of evening each day and a weekend, that's all. He wished he had the power to change the way it worked.

Are they thinking about this too? He looked across the factory. A forklift went by all the presses and stampers and people wrapping full pallets with plastic. He could see himself in each shining curl of metal. His eyes looked to him for some kind of help. What am I supposed to do? He worked until it was time for his break. He had been waiting for this.

He hurried off the line so he could be the first one to get to the telephone. It kept him going to hear their voices at home. Sometimes Mira would answer the phone. It was her new thing to do. Her voice sounded like borrowed cloth from a moth.

WHEELER

At first he was stopped by the dead sea. Then he got out of his car and stepped into the shallow water. He walked a couple minutes into it before he decided it wasn't getting any deeper. His car was left a hundred yards behind him and the water still barely licked over his boots.

In the not so far distance he thought he could see something shaped in the waves of heat. It could be a town…How far away could he be? Aztlan had to start somewhere. Why not at the end of a dead sea?

Wheeler turned and returned to his car. The splashing circles his footsteps made were the only sounds in any direction around him.

Back behind the wheel, he started the engine and steered into the ripples. He followed his footprints and kept going over the smudge where they stopped to turn and walk over themselves again. A spray jumped up from either side of the car. The faster he went, the faster he expected the tall beacon towers of some Aztlan town to appear. He waited for them to show. If they didn't he would run out of gas.

Gonzales smiled and nodded and took Zoot by the arm. He had to pull him from the pile in the middle of the betting table. "Before you get too carried away, I think you should know your contender."

Zoot had both hands full of money which he had to stuff back in his pockets quickly. "But I—" he tried.

"Just follow me. Otherwise, who knows, you could disappear after tonight." Gonzales led Zoot through a doorway into a hall. "This way…" The sound of mariachi became muffled.

They were under the arena. Zoot had been here for an hour before this happened. He had a list of bets going and wouldn't you know this had to happen when he was getting somewhere. "Where are you taking me?"

"Not far."

The hallway was sloping, going down. It was getting steeper and it was getting colder too. Zoot could see a door at the end of the hallway. They were getting closer. The door seemed to emanate cold. Under all these feet of ground, Aztlan seemed to be ice. They could see their breath.

"That's it," Gonzales puffed and pointed.

The door was a heavy looking thing. It had a silver latch that locked it into the end of the hall. There was a little window cut in its white surface. Bluish light glowed.

Gonzales led Zoot right up to the freezing space in front of the door. He pulled his shirt over his hand and wiped the window. "Look…" he said.

Zoot slowly got to where he could see into the blue porthole. An arctic white place was in there. It took him a few breaths to try and make sense of what he saw.

On what seemed a sloped and molded bed of ice, a strange sort of beast slept. It should have been a polar bear, but it was not. Zoot knew what it had to be, but he laughed and stepped away from the door window. His laugh still hung frozen in the air for another moment.

"The Abominable Snowman," Gonzales said. "What do you think of that?"

THE ABOMINABLE SNOWMAN

His eyes were closed. Dreams took him here and there, in any time, into anything, anyone, anywhere.

MIRA & MINA

She has so much imagination and seeing, she was so easy to send a picture to. Mira woke up crying from her nap on the back of Mina's bicycle seat.

Mina used a tree to stop and lean against. Her daughter was screaming for the neighborhood on the sidewalk.

Loud as it was, that's just the sound of a mother and her daughter still only a few years into this difficult world. Distant from the heaven where Mira came from, she had to learn she landed here (again) and it would take a whole lifetime to get back where she began. So Mina had to show every day to her, her daughter had to learn as surely she would, as these days turn wheels into months and years.

WHEELER

His car was sunk in the dead sea in a place the map on the floor didn't even know. Wheeler sat on the roof with his legs over the windshield.

It might be a riddle, but he was waiting for nightfall because he knew if there was someone with electricity anywhere around, they would show up in the darkness. Then he could wade his way to their lights.

The car battery still worked. He leaned over the unrolled window and turned the radio on. It was tuned into Aztlan frequency. Somewhere in the shallow water traveling, he lost America and found his way across.

CLOVER & VIDA

Of course Clover was curious about the swell in her middle, but he had spent time in carnivals and seen all kinds of people.

Vida said, "It's nice to be able to talk with someone from home…Even if they can't talk back to you…And even though we come from different worlds in America. I've never paid much attention to the wrestling wars. I don't even know the rules or all the different costumes." She was sewing while she talked. She had a small blanket nearly finished spread over her lap. "But I like the stars on yours," she continued. "See…" she held the blanket up. "I'm putting some on here. You've inspired me."

Clover sat there, on the wooden chair in the sun, with the courtyard around them, listening to her and the birds in the palms overhead, warmed from tamales and lemonade. The ice cubes in the two glasses popped and cracked as they melted. They couldn't just casually turn into water, they were too full of life for that.

warmed from tamales

GOMEZ & MIRA

The world out the window bounced up and down and sang a song. The orange sky held a jumping tree with a white cat holding on to it tight. Mira stopped leaping on the bed and pointed at that, "Dad, look!"

Gomez moaned, opened his eyes to be back where he had to be. He was shaken again as Mira bounded next to the window's lace curtains.

"Look, it's the spirit cat!"

"Ohhh…"

That white cat sat on the branch beside the glass.

"What's he saying?" mumbled Gomez.

"He's telling me about his eye he lost."

Gomez made a loose sound as his eyelids fell.

"Well, he doesn't remember much, it was a long time ago. Dad!"

He woke up suddenly, "Oh yeah. He lost his eye to a shadow."

"Dad!" she repeated.

"One day, a long time ago, he climbed a tree to catch a woodpecker." Gomez yawned. She was listening to him. "The woodpecker saw him getting closer and got so mad the bird threw his sharp shadow at the cat. That's how he lost his eye." Gomez closed his eyes even though he knew it wouldn't last.

"No, that's not true. Mom!" Mira shouted and jumped over him. "Mom!" Gomez listened as she ran to the next room. "Mom, Dad is making up stories." The little radio of her voice told on him as he smiled and opened his eyes. The one eye of the white spirit cat was still looking at him like a fur camera.

WHEELER

Dead gray birds spread out wings like library books and the floating silver frozen pages of dead fish made stepping stones across the dead sea oil spill. Wheeler walked on them to get to the reflected light of the town that night had brought to life. It was a carnival. Music floated from the sight. What beauty.

It made him hurry. He couldn't wait to get there, off of all this animal funeral. His feet dipped and missed bird and fish and he sunk a shoe into that deathly tar. "Aghh!" he shouted, sprang, leaped, swung his briefcase full of papers and in the next second, he was flying.

ZOOT & CLOVER

"This way," Zoot told him. He opened the heavy iron gate for Clover who came into view around the corner with one last wave to Vida. "Come on, Clover! Don't you remember why we're here? You have a match tonight! And believe me, it's no cakewalk. I don't even want to tell you about it til I get your mind in the proper attitude. Come on, in here." Zoot patted Clover's back and sent him ahead into the cemetery.

"This is what I'm talking about," Zoot caught up with him and led him along the swept path in between towering thick hedges. He stopped Clover beside a gray marker stone. A skull looked off of it. "This is dead serious, Clover. There's no time to think about her," he pointed over the wall. "All you're going to see from now on is terrible! I've brought you here to prepare you for it. This match tonight…I've seen your opponent and I don't even know if he's human. He's…" Zoot shook his head. He clawed at the worried furrows on his brow.

"Clover, as far as I can tell, he's some kind of Aztlan monster." He gave Clover a horrible stare. "You gotta be prepared for what you're going to see. If you can keep the terror of this place in your mind, what is there to be afraid of in the wrestling arena?" Zoot took Clover around the hedge to where he hoped a whole chilling view of cemetery awaited.

"What—?!" Zoot yelped. The field wasn't what he wanted it to be. There were stones and signs of death alright, but not the heavy-ended piano chords he was used to hearing. Every stone was a crayon, painted and planted. Dusk was coming and strings of colored lights were going on. There were families visiting, bringing food and music and flowers for the night.

WHEELER

Just like when he flew from the hotel, Wheeler landed in the sky again. This time he was seated at the top of a Ferris wheel. His sudden landing creaked and rocked him back and forth in a bucket chair and he gripped the metal bar in front of his knees. "Hah!" he let out, surprised as the faces looking up and down at him from the other parts of the steel circle ride.

He was where he wanted to be. He waved to them with one hand so they could look back at the colors, feel like flying over town and laugh with each other. The wheel went slowly around. His seat came near the ground then started to climb again.

"How did I do this?" he asked himself. "Can I fly?" He looked at his hands as if he could will feathers from his skin. "I don't even understand my power. Where did I get it? What exactly can I do?" He was afraid some part of him would make him leap again so he held on tight as the Ferris wheel rode to its height once more.

GOMEZ

Their family of three in the cab of the pickup truck was pulled by donkey into the line entering the Twin Drive-In movie field. A giant screen pushed against the purple sky. There was another screen at the other end of the field. The traffic split at the ticket booth for two different movie choices. The back of the screen facing them had the titles. Tonight's Features: *20,000 Eggs Under The Sea. Blue Anthem Wailing.*

Mira chattered and held her animal toys to the window to see. She wanted to hold the money to pay for the tickets. "Pretend I'm a green dog with manners," she told her parents.

"Okay, green dog," Gomez said as he eased them to the booth. "Three tickets," he said out the window to the woman in her narrow wooden box. "For the 20,000 Eggs cartoon. You have the money, Mira?"

She quickly put the money in her father's hand, then got shy and hugged into Mina. They all laughed. Gomez gave the string of red tickets to Mira as he steered them into the darkening car garden. They bucked a few deep holes, the weeds brushed under their fender like thick water. He found a place to park where the screen filled the windshield.

ZOOT & CLOVER

The room made a concrete bell, humming the walled-in air with the muffler roar coming from the arena above. Zoot paced past Clover who sat peacefully on top of a green table, legs hanging down, swinging a little.

Finally Zoot stopped. "I don't want to have to say this," he said, "but I have a lot riding on this match tonight. I can't afford to lose." He stood close to Clover and took a ring from his pocket. "This is how we're going to make sure we win. Watch…Here, give me your hand."

Clover stuck his arm out. He felt the ring and wriggled the rest of his fingers clumsily. It felt strange.

Zoot seized his hand, held the ring finger up to Clover's face and explained, "The middle of the ring here has a gas pellet. It'll put your opponent to sleep. All you have to do is get close to him, like this, see," and he grabbed Clover, one arm under his chin and the other shoved up to his face, pressed under his nose. "The ring will break easily, just get it as close as you can." He laughed, "Don't look so worried! You'll be fine."

WHEELER

La Saturna blinked in a hundred flashing shades of light bulbs ringing the tops of poles, making a halo overhead. Wheeler's dazed-like walking suddenly changed as a thought came to him underneath. "Of course!" he said it out loud. He was stopped, looking at the painted canvas pictures of superhuman wrestlers that flickered like movies in the multi-light. "That's me…"

The river of Aztlan people laughed and talked and ran all around him though he was perfectly still. His dappled brown suit checked with rainbow colors, his suitcase still hung off his hand. "I am a superhero," sawed the words out of him. "I have been brought here to accomplish a great task…" then he tried to see what was hidden, "I just don't know what it is…"

GOMEZ

The inside of their car had become a warm colored aquarium filled with the cartoon paintings from the screen. The donkey's head was low and tired and Gomez's wife and daughter too leaned into each other, half in dream.

Gomez watched in the rear view mirror to follow the film that played behind them on the opposite end of the Drive-In. It was a different thing entirely. He had heard about it from C at work. It was filmed with a hand-held camera in black and white like an absurd throwback to the days of the monster movies and invaders from Mars. He yawned, trying to follow it, backwards, with the sound of the children's movie coming in the open window, songs and laughter and soon he fell asleep.

ZOOT & CLOVER

They were just leaving the basement room, Zoot leading Clover in the hallway towards the echo of the arena further ahead, when they were met around the corner by a cloud of trainers and medics swerving a wheeled stretcher.

Twisting in fitful pain on the gurney was a sight familiar to the cast of wrestling: The Starlit Claw. A doctor was trying to keep oxygen going into the wrestler's mask, but the big sad claw was waving back and forth protectively. "No! El Monstruo!" he tossed in delirium.

Zoot and Clover held themselves flat to the wall as all that passed them. Clover took a half step towards the exit, but Zoot caught him, "Don't worry! You're okay!" He grabbed Clover's hand, "You've got the ring," he hissed. "Now come on."

Even so, Clover followed him like a shadow, his flag cape of conquered country spilling off his shoulders. The ceiling beat with stomping.

WHEELER

Wandering everyplace, he watched for disaster. He combed the clouds for fatal silhouettes, checked the cages for opened animal doors, listened to the air for despair, spent the rest of the carnival hours ready to spring to help. By the time the steam calliope poured out its last notes and the carrousel slowed and the mellotron sighed, all the rides closed eyes and the circus sounds pulled their oars back on board for the slow glide to a stop.

A man on stilts was walking everyone towards the gates, out. Wheeler stayed in a dark pool of shadow where only some pale green reflection of water from somewhere fluttered on him.

He wasn't sure what he was waiting for—some last minute accident that he could prevent with his leaping super-powers?

"Hey man, you want to help me?"

Wheeler was surprised but managed to stay connected to the ground. He turned smoothly towards the voice.

"Can you help me move this tank?"

"Certainly," Wheeler replied. He left the dark and green and grabbed a hold of the big aquarium tank.

"We gotta put it in there," the voice at the other end of the aquarium told Wheeler.

"Okay." Wheeler felt the weight land into him and he strained like a cello. This wasn't his calling to move heavy water weights. He wheezed, dragged his feet through the sawdust, finally making it to the lip of the wagon and dropping it on. While he heaved the side of the glass edging, he caught a glimpse of a beautiful face looking back at him. Her hair waved in the torque of swaying water. She was smiling at him. Wheeler jumped away from the aquarium.

The circus man heaved it the rest of the way.

He dropped a canvas over the shape. *La Sirena*, said the painted words.

Wheeler wiped the wet off his hands and straightened his back up out of its willowed bend. That wasn't the work of a superhe-

ro—that was just someone helping to put a mermaid on a caravan.

CLOVER & THE ABOMINABLE SNOWMAN

None of it lasted very long and then it was lost in a dream anyway. Clover began tossed down the arena aisle, stung by hands reaching out, shouted at, bounced up, under the ropes, into the glaring lights of the ring. He raised his arms to the hundreds of boos. An echoing microphone threw words at him he couldn't dodge. He looked for Zoot but couldn't see him.

Then he was cut off from everything as brassy music shook through him. His opponent was arriving. Clover was mesmerized by the flashing bulbs and waving Aztlan flags surrounding him, crowing far up into the ceiling bleachers. He was in a whirlpool.

By the time The Abominable Snowman appeared, it was a relief. He felt no terror or fear of being pulverized. The two of them locked eyes and Clover remembered his dream and almost laughed and when he brought his ring up to his nose, he breathed and he was there, asleep, safe and sound.

GOMEZ

Gomez woke up. Cars were moving around them in the field, spreading out headlights as donkeys and horses pulled wheels against the weeds, black sorrel and sleeping scrub flowers back towards the exit. Mina held Mira curled on her lap. Lamps swung orange and shadows over them.

He flicked the reins starter and the sleeping donkey in front of them moved them too. Everyone was tired. It was a gentle trip from here to home, and bed, and dreams like movies.

WHEELER

This is a part of his legend…He was just walking along an alley in an unknown town in Aztlan, and while he was thinking about his destiny, something was thrown out of a window and it hit him. It caught on his arm. In the lack of electricity, he held it up to what feeble light came through the clouds. Still, he could tell what it was. It was exactly what he needed.

MORNING

Aztlan welcomes the next new day. Over hills, trees, walls, rivers, bridges and buildings, the sun rises, wakens slowly with stirrings. A dripping faucet, birds, a donkey tugging at its lead, shutters, motors, windmills turning, the wind that remembers a million years moving over sea and land and more to come. So say hello to what is happening.

She led him from a darkness to this morning.

Clover felt her touch and the cool water spilled upon his face as he awoke.

"Good morning," she smiled.

Only remembering the wrestling, Clover woke with a start and sat up on the bed.

"It's alright."

He felt her hands on his skin. That was something.

She was sitting on the bed beside him. She said, "I got rid of your uniform. You don't need that anymore."

She closed her eyes as she felt movement within her.

Clover's hand on her opened her eyes again.

"Will you be with me for something I really need from you?" she asked.

Clover nodded. He held the hand of hers close. He loved the soft hold. He would do anything for her.

GOMEZ

6:43 woke him up. He had to get out of bed before the alarm choked the whole family rest. He staggered out of bed to stop the clock. A click and he was on the way to the shower.

He found the little tiled room and ended up in hot water. Even while it poured over him, he thought about water, how it formed, and fell from the sky and then was pushed into the contraptions, giving him what he needed to wake up.

He showered and like he always did, he sent his thoughts in the form of a morning prayer to those who are listening. He hoped for a safe, good day at the factory and the same for his family. Simple…The steam in the little room left out the opened window like a ghost getting lost into the day.

WHEELER

With his long cape of stars, red sleeves rolled up to his elbows and blue tights standing amid the cactus, Wheeler was all bright second-hand colors in the sunlight. He was a picture of a super-hero reading a book about flowers.

He had some time before the papers in his briefcase would take him to his rendezvous. *The Key to Plants and Places of Interest in Aztlan,* had come all this way with him. It seemed a perfect thing for a superhero capable of great powerful leaps through the sky, to be humbled by the simple, small beauty of Abronia Villosa growing in the sand.

Her eyes opened wide, "Mom!" she called. "Where's dad?"

Mina said, "He's at work."

"Oh…" Mira said. She got out of her little bed and jumped into bed with her mother. "I had a dream about him."

Mina made room for her to get close. "Yeah?"

"I can't remember what it was now. When does he get home?"

"Oh, you know…Not for a while…In the evening."

"Maybe I'll remember when I see him."

"Yes," Mina said, "I miss him too." For all the hours he was taken away from them, he was half lost in the dream their life had become.

CLOVER & VIDA

Clover looked into the eyes of every donkey on the lot before he decided on the one he wanted. Vida waited in parasol shade, resting. She had a bottle of cold lemonade. She waved at Clover's choice.

When Clover began to peel money out of his pocket to match the number painted on the fur, the salesman came over.

"That's a good choice. For your lady?"

Clover nodded and paid him and pulled the rope lead towards Vida.

"Here," the salesman added. He tossed a green blanket over the donkey's back. "You have to take care of her. You ever been a father before?" He laughed at Clover's open stare. "Looks like you'll be finding out—maybe today!" He laughed and clapped Clover on the shoulder as a farewell. He smiled at the quiet and gentle way Clover set her up on the donkey, remembered feeling things as they left into the dust, commotion, and timeless sunlight coming down on the marketplace.

WHEREVER IT FALLS

The factory was spinning and they were all well into the routine of it, feeding parts for the velocipedes, when the metal heart of it suddenly stopped. The quiet cut them. They looked around to see if someone had been hurt.

Gomez set the tightly rolled muffler guard down, sprouted it to the cement floor and stared as the boss approached all of them. He whistled and gathered them around.

Holding his hands up, he told everyone, "I'm sure you've all been wondering for a while what was going to happen to the factory now that Aztlan has taken over. I've just been waiting for the American company owner representative to arrive and tell us what's next. He's here now, so I'll let him tell us all." The boss turned and waited for the space in the office doorway to fill.

The light in the office went out and a dim figure grew into the frame, then walked out into the factory's fluorescent light. What they all saw was Wheeler in Clover's thrown-away wrestling uniform, the American empire remains, covered with stripes and stars. He paraded up next to the boss and began to speak to them with a heroic radio voice. "You are the workers of Aztlan now. Your own country, your own today…So it should be up to you to decide your own future." He paused and looked them all over. "I hold here in my hand the ownership deed for this factory. For the moment it belongs to America, but—" he held the paper up in the air, "I am taking this last opportunity to see that, wherever it lands, it will belong to whoever catches it." Wheeler brought his arm down and quickly worked to make airplane folds in the sheet of paper. "Wherever it falls," he said and let it fly.

GOMEZ

The brush rushed and untangled, opened a path for him running, going home early with happy news.

183

September 6, 2002

ROSE PETAL LANTERN

"I will live up to the expectations of the motherland, and will try my best to make every part of the mission success-ful."

Yang Liwei

China's first man in outer space

1.

They chose to meet at the Venuti Cement factory. It's been closed for years, there hasn't been a living soul in there since the last whistle blew. Nobody could walk about in there anyway without leaving a trail in the thick gray dust that coated the place like eternity. It was the perfect secret graveyard.

Ray was having it rough, trying to breathe in there, but he followed directions. Follow the footsteps, he was told. So up and up he went, along the next catwalk. His shoes sunk into two inches of cement powder. He passed another blacked out floor. Something ran away from him. Maybe the place was haunted.

Ray froze beside a conveyer belt that dropped from the heights off to the dark main floor hundreds of feet below.

Whatever it was had melted, but now he heard something else. He looked above him. A steady scratching noise and the metal slats of the floor up there blinked with a pale electric blue light. For a moment he wondered if he was going to meet a robot up there. He had to be ready for any mystery.

Like the very last steps digging into the peak of a mountain, Ray followed the path to the end of the stairway and stopped as he looked at the sight in the dark up there.

Sky sheared down pointed beams of silver from the seized roof. A film projector, clacking an empty reel going round and round made a fan of blue foggy light across the room. It poured into a white square on the wall where it seemed to show a movie of a spirit. There was a real life man in a gray suit waiting for him.

"There you are," the man said to Ray. He shifted in the light and shaded his eyes.

Ray stepped into the thick silt that heaped on everything.

"I'm from Hollywood," the man continued inside the empty movie, "I represent my client who needs—"

Something ran low away from Ray and the man suddenly had his derringer out, pointing an arm outside of the light.

"A seagull…" the man clucked and holstered the gun. The

bird made a purple silhouette in front of a rip in the tin siding as it took off into the air.

Ray brought his hands down from his ears.

So there, in the dismal nowhere of the dead factory, haunted only by seagulls and the two of them, Ray listened to the man from Hollywood.

2.

As with every dangerous case he took, he went to see his girl first. You never know if you'll return. Some things are like that. Besides, he thought she just gave him luck.

He parked the old Ford Gerald in the shadowy salute of a telephone pole. It was a hot day. He left white foot prints from the curb along the sidewalk. It couldn't be helped. His shoes were caked with the ancient cement. So were his clothes. Before he opened the door to the bus station, he brushed off his sleeves and pants and coat. It didn't help much, but he wanted to look good for her, not like a ghost.

The station was pretty dead. It must have been between buses or something. There was a guy sleeping across a few wooden chairs, but that didn't mean he was waiting for a bus necessarily. The ceiling fans were going but the room was hot. His dream girl was reading a magazine. She didn't even notice him til he got there and tapped his finger on the marble.

"Hullo," he smiled.

"Ohh...hello," she replied languidly. She kept a hand inside the closed cover of her magazine.

"What are you reading?"

She told him, *"Hollywood Star."*

"Mmm…You read that every day, don't you?"

She flipped a page.

"Movie stars and candy," he tried to joke with her. "You sure are surrounded by candy, outnumbered," he tried to joke with her. She was though—she sold boxes and sticks and bars of the stuff. "It must be hard to resist."

"It was at first, last year, but not so much anymore. You want something?"

She had read his mind! Well, he guessed, that's why people came to her counter. He was no different than anyone else, but one day he would ask her for something more. "Yes," he said and pointed out something on the wall.

She took enough money from him and gave him the wrap-
pered thing.

Oh, he mumbled the usual somethings before she returned to
smiling and reading about her stars. Leaving her, he thought how
maybe next time he would ask her to see a movie. That would
be great.

He put the candy into his coat pocket with the rest of the
silver paper sweets from her. He had been collecting them. The
pocket was full of them; he could have stopped a bullet with all
that tinfoil.

He saw his reflection in the glass of the station door. He was
lucky she didn't notice the ghostly prints that were still covering
him. Ray left the station brushing at that dust, finding the sunny
telephone pole again where he got into his car.

3.

The Gerald was a piece of work to open. Ray didn't know if it was all the recent rain or what, but he had to pull on the handle with both hands. All the hot air trapped inside blew out in a thick cloud. Getting into it on a hot day was like getting into a teapot. He was prepared to steep in it. He found the key and started the engine. He had a case now and an hour drive ahead of him to go.

Ray tried to drive onto Aqueduct Way but the car had a mind of its own, steering the opposite way. Then he remembered. The odometer didn't have to remind him…Whenever he tried to go too far, like it or not, the Ford would return him to his mother. It was programmed. It was trained like a carrier pigeon.

The steering wheel ran away between his hands taking the familiar roads to her home. He folded his arms and watched it happen. After the shopping center, they went west on Meadowlark and were almost there to Punchbowl Hill. He closed his eyes; it was that kind of a thing.

When the car stopped at last he opened his eyes and there they were, the car parked in front of the gently keeling rack of wisteria.

"Okay," he told himself, "I can't stay long. Just ten minutes, then I have to get going."

"As if…" replied the car speaker, just before it turned itself off.

He frowned at the console, then was out the door.

Flowers were everywhere and he had to brush morning glory out of his eyes.

"Ray!" His mother peeked over the fence, waving a towel at him, "How nice of you to stop by. You're not at school?"

He was mumbling as he stepped around the picket fence to greet her. The house sailed on flowers.

"Oh Ray!" she exclaimed. "Look at you! You're a mess! What is that powder?—flour?—cement?"

"No," he quickly replied. "I was helping out at…the theater.

It's stage makeup. But I have to go soon, I'm—"

She shot him a look, "Well, never mind that. You can't go around looking like that. Come inside, I'll give you something to wear."

"Mom, I'm sort of in a rush. I can't—"

"Nonsense," she cut. "I have something of your father's. I've been meaning to give it to you."

"Uhhh," he groaned, following her into the house.

"Oh Ray, I know it's just the thing for you," she said when they got inside. "I'll bring it to you. You go back there and take those terrible things off." She pointed him to the black paneled screen in the corner, then she hurried away.

Slowly and button by button, leaving more dust on the floor, Ray undressed and tossed his suit over the top of the screen. He waited for his mother, staring at the Chinese herons pictured in gold lacquer. They flew over mountain peaks where people and deer grew. He could almost fall in.

His mother's voice returned, "Your father wore this for the last time in Monte Carlo," spoken with sadness, as she held the tuxedo up before her.

"Ahh…" Ray sighed, "I can't wear a tuxedo where I'm going, Mom."

"Of course you can," she answered. She passed it to his arm hanging over the screen. "You make a good impression with this."

"It's just that it's not exactly a tuxedo place where I'm going." But he took the hanger from her, pulled the suit over, knowing there was no point in arguing it.

There wasn't. "Let me get you your lunch. You forgot to take it with you this morning, Ray."

"Okay." The tuxedo stayed on him, but fit him like water. His father's roundness left shallow pools billowing over him. Still, it was quite a suit, handmade in the Honolulu of long ago. Ray washed around the screen and met his mother in the kitchen.

"Oh Ray!" she delighted, "You look like a picture!" She tipped and tucked at the tux.

"I better go," Ray said. "I have to go."

"Yes, yes, dear. I'm so glad you stopped by. Now…" she gave him a little box, "Here's your lunch."

"Okay, thanks."

They said goodbyes. Ray left with a kiss on his cheek and took a shortcut through the bushes and flowers to get back to his car. He broke the long silver bridges the spiders had made that morning. Their lines stuck across his black cloth.

The Ford Gerald gave him a wolf-whistle as Ray approached scouring out of the colors in his tuxedo. "Nice threads," the automated voice observed and the car door popped open for him.

"What? Since when did you start opening the door for me?"

"Since you started wearing tuxedos," the machine-voice replied.

Ray patted the hood and got into the vehicle. He set his box lunch on the other seat and started the car. He backed out of the driveway, loosing the thin light green tendrils that had since crept onto the chrome.

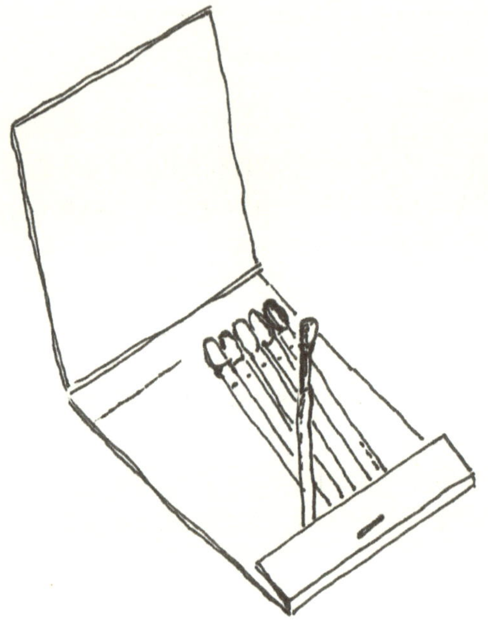

a faulty magician

4.

By the time he got away from the thick sight of the city, into the farms, and the trees backing into them, Ray was getting hungry. He reached for the lunch box, taking his eyes off the road.

A sudden bright flash of light, like sun off new aluminum, blinded him. He had to heel on the brake. Then the Gerald took over, keeping itself from crashing. The car slid along the gravel shoulder and skidded up against the rail and shuddered.

"You okay?" Ray asked, gripping the wheel like an astronaut. "Are we okay?"

"Couldn't be helped," the car trembled. "Right bumper is damaged."

Ray's hands were shaking. He pushed at the door and got outside into the cold air of the trees. The car had dug itself into the soft unpaved ground. The car was bruised and a long scratch cut its smoothness.

Next to the road where the bright shock had flashed, stood a strange, quiet man watching Ray.

"I'm okay," Ray told him. "Something blinded me, I lost control."

Ray was still spinning. He took a deep breath and looked at the man again. He was wearing a black suit too. Sunglasses covered his eyes.

Ray asked him, "Maybe if you give me a hand, we can push my car out of its tracks?"

The silent man took one hand out of his coat pocket and put it on the car out of Ray's line of vision. With not much effort, he pushed it sideways out of the pine needles, dirt swerve and gravel, up onto the tar.

"Thanks," Ray blinked. His reality was still tumbling. "That was a close one…I'm going up there," he pointed at the steepening land. "Do you need a ride?"

Whoever he was moved towards the car. The Gerald automatically opened its passenger door and the figure slid inside.

Ray got back behind the wheel and restarted the car.

"I'm going to the lodge," Ray explained.

The car was deep in firs and fantastic views when the road curved out along the mountain edge.

Ray just drove the winding quietly. It was like sitting next to a shadow.

That's what it was like for more miles, then suddenly that blinding light flashed again, this time right next to Ray and in the shroud of confusion, the strange passenger was clawing at the door with his hard sounding hands.

The car was filled with smoke, choking and coughing and it shut itself down.

The doors clapped open and as the stranger leaped out, Ray fell onto the road. All that burning furnace smell rolled up like a nest of bees into the tall dry branches and needles.

Ray rubbed his eyes and got slowly to his feet. He looked through the opened car but Dr. Jekyll was gone. The ferns swayed where he had retreated, down the bank, towards the sound of the river.

"Hey!" Ray called him. He didn't like the thought of going after him. Anybody apt to blowing up like a faulty magician wasn't a good traveling partner.

He did go over to the crushed leaves to get a look down the hill. The woods smelled like a charcoal drawing. Ray picked up the man's pair of sunglasses. The river shook over stones somewhere down below. A tear of black cloth had raked off in the Oregon grape and thorns.

Just beyond, Ray saw a deer not so far away, watching him. The animal, breathing the cool forest air in and out, was steaming, as if a fire was coming from inside of it. Ray stared hard at the deer as it turned and disappeared. It was wearing black suit pants on its back legs. Or…No…It must be a shadow…

5.

After that, there was no way to talk the scared car into going on up the rest of the mountain. Its tin voice cut back at Ray's begging attempts. The steering wheel went out of Ray's control again and the Gerald puffed back through the sloping, dropping shadows for the city below.

"Now will you let me drive?" Ray finally spoke as they joined traffic on Aqueduct Way. "You can stay parked at home if you want to. I'll see if I can borrow my mother's Oldsmobile."

"Certainly not," retorted the car. "You're going to do what you should have done this morning—you're going to school."

"What?!"

"If you insist on solving crimes, you can do that on your own time—when school is not in session. I shall not be a party to your vagrancy."

Ray groaned. There was nothing he could do but sit there. The Gerald was programmed, the doors were locked. Ray could only watch as they approached the metal fences and institutional brick buildings.

The Gerald swung next to the sidewalk and stopped. "I believe I spied Mr. Jensen behind that juniper."

"I don't want to see him! Whose side are you on? Look, I—"

A dark green swirl of brush shifted with the weight of a one-eyed man cradling a telescope. Mr. Jensen, the truant officer, hinged a long leg out of the shrub and the rest of him followed, unlocking like a carpenter's tool.

Ray was able to unroll the window. He waved. "Everything's okay now, Mr. Jensen, my mom needed my help at home. I better get to class now." He waved again. He could put the car into gear and steer.

"I've got my eye on you," the reedy voice got lost in the Gerald rattle.

Ray scratched his black hair and shook his head. He drove around to the south parking lot, past rows of other cars and pedal cabs. There were some horses in the oak shade. It was late in the day. He circled and found a spot at last.

Getting out of the car, he groaned at the dream scenario unfolding. He stood by the car another moment, then shut the door soundly.

"Ray, is that you?"

He sighed and turned, knowing already who he would see approaching him. Ray held out his hand stiffly in a mock salute to his rival…Ever since they were ten, when their games would match wits on maple lane arenas, bicycles and backyards, they had been rivals. Ray spoke mechanically, "Yes, hello Britannica… and Peggy."

Britannica Brown and Peggy Eubanks strode lightly across the gravel towards Ray.

"I detected your absence from the schoolgrounds much earlier," Britannica spoke in his clipped accent. "Could this tuxedo be the explanation? Were you being fitted for some convocation?" Peggy smiled and cupped a laugh beside her companion.

"No, I—well, yes in a way…" Ray lowered his voice. "I'm on a case actually."

"Oh really!" Britannica brayed. "For whom? The Maharajah?" Peggy grabbed his tweed suit coat to keep herself from falling over laughing. "You can't be serious?" The two of them leaned on each other. She held to his ascot like a puppet. "And you solve crime…wearing a mildewed tuxedo…driving that *jalopy*?"

Behind him, Ray heard the Gerald steam. The angry door popped open and struck him against the back of his legs. "Get in," the squawk box gritted, "We've got a long way to get far away from here."

6.

A pretty girl dressed like a black and white photograph was standing beside the doors of the lodge, holding a sign that said his name: Ray Chan. She wore a long black coat with white stockings. She had the look of waiting.

Ray was light in the air, 5,000 feet above sea level, his eyes taking in the wide blue and the skin of the mountain. He stopped next to her and told her, "That's me," pointing at the words.

Her smile was a little worn, "What took you so long? I'm the third girl to wait for you today." Her eyes slid over him at an angle while she turned back to the door, "Nice tux though. Follow me."

"All the time I've lived down there in the city, I've never been up here before. It's amazing! This is like another planet."

"Yeah," she said. She hurried him down a hall and opened a door. "He's in here, I think." She stood next to the door.

"You've been waiting all day beside doors?" Ray noted. "Well, thanks."

The room held a desk, with a woman sitting on a chair behind that, and a painting of a mountain view that could have been a window.

"Mr. Chan?"

"Yes, I'm here. I apologize for my lateness. I had some car trouble."

"I'm not sure how much you've been told about your assignment."

"Actually, very little..."

"Well," she continued, "your name comes highly recommended in our world of film."

"Not just movies," Ray corrected, "Chans are in books too."

"You may be aware," she went on, "or not, there's a film crew up here making a Hollywood feature. Simply put, the star of the picture, Sylvan Moore, has been receiving threats. We'd like you to keep an eye on him and make sure he's safe during the shoot.

And…" her voice went up, "If possible… Discover who's threatening Mr. Moore."

Ray listened to her. He was following her, but he had found something strange in his pocket. When he took his hand out, it was dripping something black. "Ahh!" he exclaimed in surprise.

"What's the matter?" She stared at him with underwater eyes.

He realized what the black wax was in his hand, "Sunglasses!" It was those glasses he picked up and put in his pocket. They had turned into a soft wax that ran candles over his fingers. "They melted."

"Here," she said, passing him a box of paper tissues.

The wax came off his hand easily and he threw the dough in the little tin pail on the floor. He smiled at her. "Anyway! Yes, when do I start?"

Her answer was like pulling a green apple off a tree. "They're up at Artist Point right now. You can drive to the end of the road and take the gondola the rest of the way there."

"Well great. Thank you. I'll be on my way." Ray stood up and left her sitting in her chair as quiet a part of the room as the painting on the wall.

The girl with the sign was gone, not in the hall and nowhere to be seen in the lodge or guarding the doors to outside. Ray guessed she had done her job.

The air at this altitude was a rare color and heavenly to breathe. He felt like wrapping himself up in a blanket of it.

Ray got into the Gerald and followed wooden signs to the gondola. The road steeped up a switchback to another wide lot planted with a couple black limousines and trucks and vans. "This must be the place," he muttered.

Giant Golgotha gears fed trolley wires to an even higher place on the mountain where all the actors and movie makers were stamping out some new dream.

"I'm leaving you here for a while," Ray told his car. He tried to get out the door but couldn't. It was locked.

"For how long?" the Gerald's voice rasped.

"I don't know, a while. I have to talk to a movie star up there. You'll be fine here. Now would you let me out?"

The latch in the door unbolted with a slow scrape.

"Thanks," Ray huffed and he left the car. He tried to be nice to the Gerald, keep it clean and serviced, but cars ruled their people and they knew it. They always had to remind you.

"Wow!" Ray had to say, a tiny voice of human wonder, as he stood at the gondola landing and looked over the rising alpine.

Far up, a twinkling silver gondola was descending. The heavy steel cable overhead pulled, twitched and sung out whale sirens.

While he waited, Ray stared.

The gondola gave a pleasant whistle as it neared. Ray couldn't help waving even though he realized it was all automated and empty on board. There were meadow flowers skirted around it, the landings with earth had rubbed them on. And Ray laughed when he saw the name *Heidi* painted in curled, stylized letters on the door.

"Beautiful day, isn't it, Heidi?" he said, but she was quiet, with door opened. Maybe she couldn't talk like his car could. Maybe she was just a simple creation that mechanically did its job all day. He boarded.

She whistled something two times and then another and Ray, staring from her window inside saw Gerald reply with blinking headlights. Ray waved. He'd never seen Gerald do that before.

Heidi lurched and they were going up. Ray stood there peacefully beside the glass, going up like a prayer.

The angle of the mountain went by rock slices furled with green and dry, crushed landslides. When the window view finally came up over the ledge, a hidden new world appeared.

A wide flat grassy step floated up against the edge of white snow. There were pale yellow tents and dots of people surrounded by their stalks of cranes and camera equipment—all that strange vision needed for showing illusions in the dark.

The gondola bumped, touching down, and the door slid aside. "Thanks, Heidi," Ray said. What a strange day, he thought, leading him all the way to this place in the sky. Walking towards the phantom sight, he wondered if that cement dust he had started this adventure in was quarried from this very mountain. He thought how it all made sense that he would be led back to the source now.

"Boy!" he unbuttoned his collar. It was hot being on top of a mountain in a tuxedo. Ray didn't want to get in the way of the picture so he stood against a crop of lupine. He tried to blend in. His father had been a part of this world for years but that was long ago. His adventures were film history and the late, late show, and who knew how he was remembered today? He was in the play of time.

"You Mr. Chan?" a turtle-faced little old man waved his clipboard. His eyes were crisp with excitement.

Ray nodded, "Yes."

"Aw, I been waiting for you to get here, Mr. Chan!" the old man practically boiled over. "I was friends with your pop! You're the spitting image, you are!"

"Thank you…"

"Here, let me take you over! They're setting up the last shot. You can watch with me."

Ray followed the bent-over slow walk and they stopped beside the boom mic arcing out overhead to where Sylvan Moore stood bathed in reflected light, knee deep in the snow.

"This is it," the old man whispered, near to Ray's ear, "They'll start filming now."

Sylvan Moore cupped his hands to his mouth and yelled down at the snow, "Are you in there?! Can you hear me?!" Then he let his face crumple into a new mood, "Well, I'm tired of searching. If you want me, I'll be at the lodge!"

With infinite cool detachment, Sylvan Moore tore himself free from the snow and walked out of the camera's eye.

"That's it!" called the director, and like a clock falling apart they all started separating from the last scene.

Sylvan Moore told someone, "I really am going to the lodge," as he moved in Ray's direction.

"That's him, Mr. Chan. You'll have to catch up to him," the old man insisted, giving Ray a light push, calling after him, "I'll be seeing you, Mr. Chan!"

Ray waved to the old timer and hurried after the movie star. He jumped over an electric cord pulling itself through the grass.

"Excuse me, Mr. Moore," Ray leaned.

Hands thrust deep in pockets, Sylvan Moore glanced over his slooped shoulder, still walking for the gondola.

"Mr. Moore, my name is Ray Chan. I was sent up here to—"

"Hah!" Sylvan Moore flared like a trumpet, "That tuxedo must be fifty years old!"

"Well yes, probably, it belonged to my father."

"Last worn in some Algerian adventure or in a luxury train compartment, surrounded by suspects?"

Ray nodded, "Perhaps. Anything is possible."

"And now you've come here, wearing this infamous relic, to save me from the clutches of a murderous criminal?" Sylvan Moore threw a cape of stage laughter over that.

"My services were requested," Ray stated. "If you don't—"

"Nonsense!" Sylvan Moore slapped him on the back. "I couldn't be more delighted to see you. I expect you to begin immediately by escorting me safely to the lodge." He said it with that famous crooked mouth full of white teeth, the smile that broke just short of a sneer.

The gondola opened its door. Sylvan Moore waved his arm, "You first, Chan. You never know—the floor could be wired for electrocution."

Ray tried to keep his humor. When he got on the gondola his life didn't end. He could turn peacefully and allow Sylvan Moore on.

The Hollywood king seemed to be enjoying the situation, "Don't forget to watch the parapets. There could be some assassin disguised as a goat, pointing a blowgun."

"Perhaps, Mr. Moore, you could tell me the nature of your

threats."

"Hah! You know I'm just giving you a hard time, Chan. I don't take this very seriously. How can I take anything seriously? This whole life of mine is nothing but a dream! Merrily, merrily…It's the studio that needs me to be watched like a million dollar egg." He stopped to strike a match and light a cigarette.

The gondola began to move. It took to the air and moved with its peculiar swaying metal motion.

"The nature of my threats, Chan? You know, the usual letters made out of newspaper words…A dead chicken hanging on my door…Someone just doesn't like me, Chan. Nothing unusual in that I don't suppose." He paused while a shadow went over him, opening up the next spill of words, "I'm not scared, Chan. I've seen this world from both sides of the screen. Everything is doomed to short life. Nothing lasts forever. That's how it is, right, Chan? It's the sad way people are, so I just feed them some dream to keep them calm for a while."

The gondola gave her whinny, they were back.

"Why the sour face, Chan? You can shadow me, it's all right, we'll have fun, you'll see." He gave a laugh and opened the door for him. "Come on."

Ray's tuxedo shined as he stepped into the sun again. There was a black limousine waiting beside the Gerald.

As soon as Sylvan Moore emerged from the gondola, something bomb-sized and black shot from the open window of the limousine. Ray jolted with fear for the star's safety, but Sylvan Moore let a shout of affection boom, "Haynes!"

A penguin scrambled across the rough ground. Like magnets the two of them were pulled to each other.

Ray observed their reunion from a patch of snow and trampled berry.

Suddenly Sylvan Moore was a man in love with life. He carried the penguin like a bouquet of cold flowers, hugged to his chest.

"This is Haynes, Chan." He kissed the penguin and set the animal in the snow so he could watch adoringly. The bird climbed and slid and rolled and came back to a waiting embrace. "Haynes has been waiting for me to do a film in the snow. So here we are. I even got snow put in my new contract. I look out for Haynes. Next film we're doing is *Call of the Wild II.*"

"Hello Haynes," Ray pet the sleek head of the penguin. "I never guessed you had a penguin, I didn't know people had them as pets."

"Sure, that's a whole story in itself, how I got Haynes. We're developing that as a script. A real heart warmer…How about you, Chan? Any animals in your life?"

"My mother has a parrot. It's been in the family for a long, long time."

"Say, would you look at that car," Sylvan Moore suddenly pointed over Ray's shoulder. "It looks like love to me," he laughed.

Ray stared at the sight of Gerald and Heidi. Sylvan Moore was right, it looked exactly like love. "That's my…car," Ray groaned.

"Hah!" With an embrace of penguin, Sylvan Moore laughed and got into his limousine. "I've got a couple hours before the next shot, Chan. I'm going to the lodge. You need a ride?" he grinned.

"Uhh no, Mr. Moore, I better see what my car is up to."

"Fine. You know where I'll be. Unless of course something unexpected happens to me," he added as the long car pulled away across the crackling gravel. Hopefully it wasn't the last sighting of Sylvan Moore.

With sand filled limbs, Ray let the limousine go, as he walked heavily towards his Gerald.

This wasn't going to be easy, he had a feeling. The Gerald's lights were aglow and Heidi was there, flowers and a musical hum.

"Umm…We have to go…" Ray tried, "And ummm…" he pointed up the rocky slope, "That film crew needs the gondola to get back down here."

The car answered him with one mechanical word, "No."

"Oh, come on, we'll be back later. I promise."

"I'm not leaving her."

"Look, I have to guard Sylvan Moore, I don't have time for this," and Ray opened the car door.

Before he could get inside, the Gerald began to sink.

"What?!" Ray took a step backwards.

All four wheels let out their air at once and the Gerald flattened against the ground.

Then the air above twanged loudly as the gondola let go of the wires and splashed down next to the car. Heidi and Gerald weren't leaving their bed of meadow.

"So…I'm supposed to walk?" Ray guessed.

7.

By starlight, Sylvan Moore relaxed in a bubbling hot tub. On the cedar deck beside him, Haynes floated in a wooden tub filled with ice water and cubes. A record player within arm's reach swung its needle across another melody.

"Life is but a dream, eh, Haynes?" Sylvan Moore crooned his song.

He reached over to play the record again when a voice called his name in the darkness.

"Who's there?" Sylvan Moore bellowed back. He put his hand on the derringer he had hidden under a white towel.

"It's me…Ray Chan."

"Hah! Oh, I see," Sylvan Moore yelled into the night. "You're out there protecting me?"

"Well…"

Sylvan Moore laughed again. "Here," he said, "Come below the balcony and I'll drop the keys to you."

"Okay."

Sylvan Moore sloshed in the water and leaned over the wooden edge. In the gloom he could hear rocks sliding, footsteps, branches cracking. "You alright, Chan?"

"I'm okay."

"Can you catch these keys?"

"Yes, I see you. I'm underneath."

"1, 2, 3," he let go and in a second heard them land with a clink. "You caught them?"

"Yes."

"Good. Well, come on up here, Chan. You've been gone for ages."

"I know."

Sylvan Moore sunk back into the hot water and sighed.

Haynes looked half asleep, floating in that stew of ice in a circle. The steam from the hot tub drifted over ghostly against the swale of black night. Haynes opened both eyes as footsteps clocked onto the wooden porch.

"Chan!" Sylvan Moore exclaimed.

Ray was quite a sight, his tuxedo was torn and stained all over by the rocks, riverbed skree and soil and leaves of the mountain.

"Ohhhh…" Ray collapsed into a chair.

"What happened, Chan?!"

Ray sounded like a pulp magazine from 1937 as he formed the words and dropped them. "You're never going to believe this." He breathed deeply and exhaled like an old balloon.

"What happened to you? You've been gone for hours." Sylvan Moore leaned on his elbow, "Five hours?"

"Okay. I left my car—that's another story—then I fell underground. I saw something…I don't know. It took me a lot of trouble to get out again. All I know is I have to get back there and take a look, make sure I wasn't just seeing a dream in my head."

"Chan, it's the middle of the night," Sylvan Moore told him, "It looks like you fell down the mountain. Or through it! You need some rest, Chan."

Ray was still in the dark and the shadows under the eaves, he didn't let his gaze go up with the disappearing steam into the starry poured Milky Way. Then he let his face fall into his hands. "Ow!" he cried. His numb right hand was all wrong, hard, it had hurt him.

Sylvan Moore squinted through the steam. "What's that you're holding, Chan?"

For a moment Ray didn't think he could speak. His hand wasn't his hand—it was a hoof. He stuffed the shape deep into his pocket.

"Chan! What's the matter?" A splash and wave as Sylvan Moore came closer.

But what kind of dream could that have been? Ray could move fingers inside his pocket again, his hand had returned to him. He felt the cloth and paperclip things in his pocket. He took the hand out carefully to stare at it and make sure it was his.

"Chan?"

"Oh…I surprised myself…It's nothing."

"Listen Chan, you sure you didn't get sapped or poisoned? Maybe you got what was meant for me? Sure, that must be what happened." Sylvan Moore grabbed a towel and wrapped it around himself, getting out of hot water.

"You know, Chan, you surprise me. You're not like what I expected. No wise sayings like your father, not much to say at all. In fact, you're a quiet sort. I understand though, you're deciphering." Sylvan Moore was wearing a robe now and Haynes had got out of ice. "Let's go indoors. We'll talk it over." He slid open a glass door. "Well, I'll talk. You can listen and filter through all the silt for the gold." The Sylvan Moore smile. The movie star paused as if on camera, lit like his whole life was that, moments posed and moving. "Maybe you need a shower, Chan? I've plenty of clothes in that steamer trunk. Help yourself. After all, if someone is going to drag you down a mountain thinking they've got me, then I better have you dress the part. It's the least I can do for my shadow."

Sylvan Moore paused before following Haynes into the next room. "Go ahead, Chan. There's a new tuxedo in that trunk with your name on it."

Ray stared at the star's steamer trunk. The thing had wandered the world with Sylvan Moore. Ray stepped closer to it so he could read the stickers all over its skin, the places it had been. He tried to imagine Japan. China. India. Egypt. Ethiopia. London. Paris. Lhasa and Peru. Cities and lands near and far, and here, he was brought here too. Ray wondered about Sylvan Moore, treated like a royal angel here on Earth, thinking that surely he was sent to me as much as I was to him.

Even though that might be, Ray felt close to letting go and starting out that door once more for who knows what force had taken away his hours. He looked at his hand. It wasn't changed. It was back to normal.

Sylvan Moore was singing a popular jazz ballad in the other room.

With slow might-as-well motion, Ray opened the well-traveled box full of famous clothes. Another tuxedo practically fell out on him. "Okay," he said. This is what he was fated to wear.

He drew it out and took the black cloth to the bathroom to change into. First though he needed a lot of water to wash over him. He could be a whole new person. Then what? Sleep? What if he woke up and forgot what was out there?

He paused. What should I do? What should it be? Comfort, rest, or the discovery of a mystery waiting for him in the middle of the night?

8.

Ray laughed. Of course he landed out under the stars again, freezing, still wearing the old torn up fragments missing from a fifty year old tuxedo. It must have been the father in that suit making Ray go out on the mountain like this, he laughed again.

When he left Sylvan Moore's room by dropping off the balcony onto the dark rocks and tree shadow rows, he climbed the minutes until now.

This spot where it was so quiet was where Ray remembered reappearing. Not more than a few hundred yards away, the snow line formed, making the white mountain you could see from hundreds of miles away. At this hour though, who would be out here? What mattered when sleep was everywhere else? Was there really dark mystery here?

From the ragged tuxedo pocket, Ray brought a spool of white string. This dreamy memory was a favorite belonging of his father. When done with a crime, the old man used to fly his kite up on Punchbowl Hill. Ray handled the spool, found the tucked-in end and got low to the ground. He made a tight knot to a scrub pine, attaching it to him, then he let it reel.

Ray paused on a table sized flat rock. He tested his voice. It seemed to stop, not far in the black in front of him. A bat would have known exactly how far...Ray sighed. He thought of his hand, those melting glasses, and that man who might have been a deer. It had all the appearances of being a mystery, but his father would surely have something to say about deceiving appearances. Yes, he should look underneath.

Ray spread his hands back behind him flat along the stone. He breathed in the night sky. It was worth taking a rest to stare at the night. Why didn't people write more books about looking at the stars? "I guess they do..." he mumbled. Astronomy, astrology, science fiction, there was a whole lot written taking off from this...Sitting before something vast in the dark.

Ray told himself he returned to this spot to hope some clue

or memory would be revealed, but he also hoped whatever happened before would happen again and, "This time I'm awake for it..."

Maybe he was awake, for another second or so, as the rock revolved and the world seemed to whirl and he spun underground again.

9.

The sound of pebbles and chips of bark hitting window glass woke up Sylvan Moore. After minutes of thinking it was in his dream, he rolled over and stared for the noise. "Haynes?"

Another stone pecked the glass.

Someone was throwing them at the window. Sylvan Moore had seen this before. Sometimes people sent him notes in balloons, or carrier pigeons. Best thing to do was get up and make it go away.

He peered into the blue gloom. He could see someone out there waving arms at him. "Is that—? Haynes! I think that's Chan!" He laughed, "The amazing, disappearing Chan!" He went to the balcony sliding door and let himself out into the cold. "Is that you, Chan?" he called down.

"Yes…" came a sigh with no more words attached.

"Why don't you try the door again, I'll let you in." It was cold out in that mountain space. Sylvan Moore hurried to put a robe on. "Can you believe it, Haynes?"

Sylvan Moore tossed a blanket over the female form curled on the bed. "You better change back," he said, "Chan will be here shortly." He walked over to the wall and made orange light come out of a lamp. "I'm interested to see what Chan found out." He looked through a drawer and found a cigarette and lit it with one untrembling hand. The smoke came out of his famous smile. He whiled the time humming one of his jazz songs until the knock on the door. Opening it changed his smile. "Chan?!" he gasped.

"Mr. Moore…" Ray crackled in tatters. "A most interesting riddle has presented itself to me out there, but I would feel safer if you accompanied me." He pointed back at the black.

"Chan!" Sylvan Moore declared, "What have you been doing out there? You okay? Come in, sit down. Let me get dressed and I'll follow you."

Sylvan Moore collected some clothes off the end of his bed. The penguin brought its languid face out of the blankets to look, then went back underneath. "It's alright Haynes, I'll be back. I'm just going to see how much Chan here knows." Catching his song again, Sylvan Moore disappeared into the bathroom to change.

10.

There was enough pale glow from the dawn on the way for Ray and Sylvan Moore to see the rough path across the stones.

"I haven't been on this mountain long, longer than you Chan, but long enough to begin to understand and experience some of the mystery here. It isn't only this place though…Maybe it's the air here that makes it seem more clear…What people have done to the world has upset the balance. It's so tipped now, heavily, that, well you can expect some changing…Transforming."

"Excuse me, Mr. Moore," Ray stopped, "This is the spot." A fine skeleton line tied to a root led under a flat trapdoor rock. "This last time I went underground I took the precaution of leaving a clue." He gave the taught line a little tug. "I have to go back in there, but I need you here in case something happens to me down there. I may need help returning."

Sylvan Moore stared at the string disappearing into the crumble. "What's down there anyway?"

"Something I need to see again." Ray set his hands on the flat stone and pressed his palms along it. "Somewhere there's a way it opens…"

"Chan," Sylvan Moore spoke urgently, "Can't you see? What are you doing wasting your time underground? The answers are out here, all around you, I'm telling you."

But Ray had hit some switch and the stone turned, revealing a tunnel growing in. Loose rocks skittered down into the dark. The kite string scribbled along. Ray paused and told the movie star, "One mystery at a time, Mr. Moore. I'm sure everything is connected. Whatever I find out down there will lead me to answers up here."

"Alright, Chan," Sylvan Moore sighed. "But you know, I can't wait out here for five hours while you crawl around searching for who knows what."

"I understand." Ray was already half gone. "I just needed to show you where I'm going. In case I'm gone for a terribly long time, you can bring help and dig me out."

Sylvan Moore threw his hands in the air, "Okay, Chan! There you go. Good luck."

Before Ray left, he asked, "You'll be alright without a body-guard?"

"I've stayed safe this long without you around," he smiled.

Then Ray went into the tunnel and picked up the kite string at his feet to lead him through the shroud. He stumbled as he went along, putting another tear in the arm of his tuxedo. The string was his lifeline though. He wasn't worried about finding what was up ahead.

The dark began to be softly dawned with early morning blue glow. The string was leading him to it. In another twenty feet he could see the rough cut tunnel he was in and he didn't need to stoop and let his fingers run through the line. He was coming to the source of the light.

The tunnel ended in a sort of chamber, a room cut into stone and held with old wooden ribs. In the middle of the rocky floor was the strange sight that had brought him back.

It was a boat. Who knows how the lifeboat got here, inside of a mountain. Letters along the gray wooden slatting spelled *U.S.S Lincoln*. It had heavy yellow canvas covering it.

Around the boat were four thick columns of ice, each holding a tipping lantern, the cause of the cold blue light. The light must have frozen in them a long time ago.

Ray approached carefully. This was the closest he had been. He didn't know what the *U.S.S Lincoln* had been, but the lifeboat looked years old, like it must belong to the early steamship age.

The iron nails holding its seams together left rusted tears all along it.

With careful slowness, Ray took hold of the canvas covering the bow. He had to know if there was anything hidden under-neath. Maybe there were some boxes of old crackers, or rolled documents lifted from a sinking ship? Maybe a skeleton crew? The thick material crackled, and splintering crystals of ice showered off as it uncovered.

Ray lost his breath when he saw what was revealed. He gasped for the air the shock had taken away.

There was a man laying in the cradle of the keel. There were some gray tubes running from tanks up to his face. A glass globe holding ticking, delicately balanced wheels and spinning gears seemed to be the heart keeping this man fed and alive. Or was he alive? Eyelids closed, the face had a wax statue look.

Ray watched the heavy fur coat covering the man's chest. He couldn't detect the rise and fall of breathing, but that didn't mean it wasn't happening. The man, with his thick polar clothes, looked like an arctic explorer from the dawn of the twentieth century. What wasn't possible? Ray wondered.

And now, he also thought, what should I do?

Anyway…Who was this man and should he be disturbed? What if Ray put the tarp back over and left this ice experiment in this hollow earth to float on in the *U.S.S Lincoln* lifeboat until the dream ended or til it all caved in? Then again, Ray decided, I could wake him up for a little while, ask him some questions, maybe get some answers to things, and then put him back to sleep again.

So Ray reached into the boat and put his hand on the mask covering the man's mouth and nose. He broke the seal lifting it off.

There lay the man's revealed waxy features. He had a thin moustache like a movie star, like Sylvan Moore. He looked familiar that way. He really didn't look much like a real explorer at all, but then who really knew until—

The man coughed as he drew in breath. His eyes sprung open. "What time is it?" he gasped. "What—?" then he seemed to catch himself, calming himself to breathing and remembering. A smile grew across his face. "I've been discovered," he grinned. "Who are you?"

"My name is Ray Chan. Who are you? What are you doing down here?"

It was only his first minute of air in this new world, "I'm still waking up," he said. He rubbed his hands on his face. "Uh, what's…Oh, I remember. I had to put this on my skin to preserve me. It worked, I hope," he smiled. "I don't look bad for a time traveler, do I?" He sat up so he could see over the hull. His hand stuck out towards Ray, "The name's Sid Canova."

Ray held the freezing ghost-clasp for a second. "Sid Canova," he repeated and thought.

"Yeah! You know me?"

"I've heard your name somewhere…"

"Doesn't surprise me. There was probably quite a stir in the papers when I went missing. I'm sure the world must have mourned." Sid's eyes glowed almost merrily at the thought. "Another brilliant talent taken away too soon."

"Sid Canova," Ray let the name go again. It may have been spelled out in lights above the passing streets of somewhere long ago, but Ray just couldn't place it. American history is paged with names that come and go.

"Well world, Sid Canova is back!" the long buried voice rejoiced.

The smile and regal flow of the mystery man again reminded Ray of Sylvan Moore. He thought he should tell the star what was going on underground. "I have a friend up above. Perhaps he could help out with your return to the limelight. He's a star himself. He's the lead actor in a movie they're making here on the mountain."

"Yes!" Sid beamed. "This would make for an amazing newsreel story. Yes, by all means, tell your friend I'm here. Tell him to prepare for my reappearance."

Ray said, "Okay," and so left the sky blue glow that Sid floated in like some man in a bathtub. The rocky tunnel became the usual stagger he had made several times now. He held to the string until he arrived in the moonlight beneath the opened stone.

"Mr. Moore!" Ray called. He shifted on the scattered slope of broken rocks. "Mr. Moore!" Then he let go of the kite string and used both hands to climb himself out into the surface air.

Well, he thought, Sylvan Moore must have gone back to bed. Maybe hours had passed again, but it didn't seem so. The sun would be coming up soon. Ray hadn't been gone that long…It didn't seem long anyway.

Half out of the underworld, he looked around the climbing view above the tree line and saw no waiting silhouette of Sylvan Moore. Still though, there was someone watching Ray. He felt it and hearing a faint sound, turned to see what it was.

Not far from where he had last seen Sylvan Moore, a raven now perched on a jagged chin of rock.

Ray nodded to the bird. Ray felt compelled to inform those twinkling eyes, "I made a remarkable discovery. I'll be out soon." Ray was satisfied to see the raven take notice of his words, as if it had been Sylvan Moore after all.

"Alright then, that's all." Ray went back into the murk, pulled along by string. Even after it snapped and trailed off into black, he wasn't worried, he knew where he was going in the unseen.

The glow of blue grew and soon he was in Sid's cavern.

While Ray was gone, Sid had been working.

There were two pulleys hung over the boat connecting it with thick rope.

Sid hailed him, "Come aboard, it's time we got going."

Ray stood next to the lifeboat, "Got going?"

"Sure. Let me explain, Mr. Chan. I had this all planned out long ago. Here…" he leaned out and took hold of Ray's hand and steadied him getting into the boat. "See, I know the only thing that ensures the fame of an artist such as myself, is time. If you can last out the years, keep your work alive, they'll finally catch on to what you're doing and presto! You're on the sunny side of the street."

Ray settled himself on the creak across from Sid Canova. So he's an artist, ran through Ray's mind, still not knowing him though. It wasn't that surprising though—Ray's apartment had some postcards on the wall, the bookshelf had some paperbacks and records and a transistor radio for the baseball games—he didn't know many artists. His hours were filled with criminal reason and he dreamed in a mirror of the day.

"I've been missing for long enough," Sid said with a smile while he reached for the ropes connected to the pulley. He set his other hand on a lever hidden behind the starboard. "Hold on tight, Mr. Chan. The city is awaiting."

Ray barely had a moment to start a question when the lever caused the floor to give out. The boat rocked violently, they were suspended by the pulley, swaying. Below them rushed the sound of water, close to the keel.

All Ray could do was hold on to the boards of the lifeboat as they plummeted in the splashing, dark swerving river underneath the mountain.

Sid Canova howled in front of Ray.

The boat creaked and seemed to snap its seams as the rush threw it back and forth. It was black but Ray could feel the pull of gravity taking them steeply down. Like the switchback road that brought him up here, the river hooked and dropped and shook back and forth at any second, either direction. The only thing he could do was hold on to the boat.

11.

Sunlight dappled leaves green beside the banks of moving water. Trees drifted past, hillside brush, berries and big log piles cracked up against rocks that wouldn't move until the new thaw flood. Ray was awake. The river and gentle life around him made music in his head and lulled him into sleep again.

When he woke up the next time, the river was soft. He lifted his head and saw the wide path of water gliding them through farms.

"What do you say?" Sid Canova asked. Huckleberry Finn, he was pleasantly, lazily rowing the lifeboat. Standing off like November was the snowy mountain above the blue fir hills. They had come a long way asleep.

Ray yawned and stretched his tuxedo arms. He looked through the ripped seams. There went the country. "Merrily, merrily," Ray replied. A song stuck in his head. That's what Sylvan Moore would say. He looked again at the mountain that left them miles ago. A white cap topped into the blue sky.

"You sure were tired, pal. You missed all the rapids. It's all smooth sailing to the city now." The way Sid let the oars sip in the water and out showed he was in no great hurry to get there. He was happy to let the river pour them there.

Ray gave a last yawn. "I've had a tiring time on the mountain. Finding you was the end of a lot of running around."

Sid Canova laughed, "Well, I don't feel like sleeping ever again! I've been stuck in a dream long enough." He gave the silver flow a tug with the oars.

"What do you plan on doing in the city?" Ray asked him.

"Hah!" Water dripped diamonds off the oars, spreading circles. "I just want to see all their faces when they see me again!"

"They're going to think you were lost in Antarctica," Ray observed.

"Oh don't worry about that. This was all planned to perfection."

Ray watched the shift of the clouds above the hedges and a sudden burst of black birds. "How did you set it up? Your trip through time, I mean. Why in this lifeboat? Why on top of a mountain?"

Sid laughed, "How, why, why? Well, I'll tell you, Mr. Chan. I haven't quite seen the sights of this time I've arrived in, but I come from an age that was surrounded with everyday magic. Flying machines, moving picture shows, steam engines and talking machines. It wasn't impossible to dream of something and find a way to make it happen. With plenty of wizards to choose from, I followed the leads. I found a fellow on Myrtle Street who could drop me to sleep for fifty years and I figured that would be long enough for my fame as an artist to catch on." He threw a laugh overboard. "Now it's up to this, our drift into town, where we'll find out if my sleep was worth it."

"Yes," Ray agreed. The river seemed to be picking up speed.

12.

The water told of town. Deep, gray colored and run through with broken limbs, masonry, metal bends and things fallen in, the tense surface reflected bridge shadows and telephone poles. The plash of spilling pipes added city runoff. The bow lopped into an oil slick rainbow that curled around and joined their wake. The turning mountain stream had nearly found the ocean. Ray was surprised by a salmon kicking its tail through into the air.

Silt and gravel and rust scraped under the keel as Sid tucked the oars in and landed them. The beach he chose was haunted overhead by low branches and leaves. Ghosts of colored plastic bags were pinned in them. Fishing line tangled up and down around orange forgotten car parts.

Ray hopped out to tie the bowline around the thickest trunk.

Sid still wore that smile and as he stood in the boat for the last time, he shed the heavy polar outer clothes he had been wearing. He was finally warm.

Even in this shady place, his stage uniform caught every dot of sunshine and shot it back off the golden scales that covered him. He left his old skins flayed over the wooden seat and leaped overboard like a Chinese restaurant dragon, into the inch of sink.

13.

They decided to part ways in the shadow of a tree, where a bus stop sign grew. Sid Canova was going to continue on foot, hoping to start a parade, on his way to his talent agency downtown. Ray would grab the next bus to Punchbowl Hill. The two of them were a sight you couldn't help but stare at—the man in electricity gold, and his companion in tuxedo remains.

"If you lose this phone number," Ray was saying, "All you need to do is find a telephone book. That's the big book of names they have in telephone booths. Just look up my name. If I'm not at home, I'll be—"

"Relax, Ray. Everything will be swell. Next time you see me, I'll have the key to the city."

The bus was approaching behind all the slowing traffic.

"Here comes your ride, pal. It's a funny looking thing too."

Not to Ray, it was an ordinary white and blue bus. "Well, you know what to do if you run into a jam."

"Sure, sure, don't worry about me though. You'll see." He slapped Ray on the shoulder while the bus rubbed up against the curb and a door hissed open.

"Alright," Ray waved and stepped on. He reached in his pocket for the fare. "Ohhh," he said, trying other pockets. He may have lost his money in the caves. There were enough holes and tears on him.

"Let me guess…" the driver rasped, "You forgot your money in your other tuxedo."

"No—it's just—"

"Nevermind, this ride's on the Public Transport Association. Maybe you can buy us a new bus in return."

There was a museum of laughter that fanned out down the aisle.

Ray mumbled a thank you and quickly found a seat. It was a ten minute ride up the slope to Punchbowl. He'd be glad to get out onto the street lined with graceful, sturdy old trees. This time he sure looked forward to seeing his mother. He hoped she wouldn't be appalled at his father's tuxedo. Probably…Well, maybe she had another tuxedo. That would really be best. Sid Canova had his starlight suit and a tuxedo was what a Chan was supposed to wear. He thought of his father and maybe some of what he thought was imaginary, or spun up in movies. Still, everywhere he went was just moving where others had been. People came and went while he looked out the traveling window. Then it was his time to go.

The hilltop had a quiet street. The bus, cushioned on maple shadows was carried away and Ray began the walk to his mother's house.

Little birds hopped alongside him in the wicker-looking shrubs that guarded someone's fence. A sprinkler blurred the yard in front of a house. Ray began to whistle. He wondered what would become of Sid Canova. If worse came to worse, Ray had connections at the police station, in case Sid landed there. That glowing suit might be asking for trouble. Ray broke his whistle to smile.

"Hey!"

Ray turned around.

A police cruiser had silently idled up next to him. "Is that you Chan?" the voice turned into surprise.

"Yes. Hello, Earl." Ray stopped and nodded. "How are you?"

"Oh, I'm good. What happened to you? I thought I was going to have to run you in."

"Me? No, please excuse my appearance. I've been…It's a long story."

Earl looked concerned. "You okay? You need a ride somewhere? I can loan you some clams if you need it."

"Don't worry, Earl. I'm fine. I'm on a case right now. I'm just going to my mother's to change and maybe get some lunch too."

"Okay, Ray. Well, I better go. You give Mrs. Chan my regards, will you?"

"Sure Earl."

"I'll be seeing you." The cruiser slid away and Ray continued.

He thought about his car, how much easier all this would be if it hadn't left him. Who knew what was going on with Gerald and Heidi? Love, he hummed.

By the time he arrived at his parent's house, he had wondered about three other things. There was a lot that needed sewing up on the mountain. As soon as he could, he would go back.

His mother didn't seem to be home. The doorbell rang and rang unanswered.

So he bent down to the parrot statue that stood between the potted flowers. He picked up the clay bird and retrieved the key underneath. Setting the parrot back on its cool blue outline on the porch, Ray returned to the locked door and let himself inside.

"Hello?" he called.

The telephone was ringing.

14.

Sid Canova couldn't make much sense of the new world. For the future, it sure felt backward. Where were the things predicted, the silver and glowing wonders everywhere? After a while, he started to imagine he was still asleep in the mountain, this was just a dream. So he took it as such.

His wandering brought him to Myrtle Street. "Hah!" he laughed out loud. This sign post looked battered and old but he adored the letters. "Let's find that wizard," he said. "If he's still alive…" The wizard had some explaining to do.

A dog ran up to Sid. He pet its crazy face and it ran away. The cars parked along the street were heavy, blockish-looking things. He wondered again, what am I doing in this strange land? Then he remembered who he was; he could stop in just about any house and look at their music collection and there he would be. And here he was now, returned in the prime of his life. The sound would be heard across magazines and newspapers.

Of course, Myrtle Street was different. He laughed at some of the things he saw.

The house he recalled was different too. There was a bent young hawthorn tree in the yard. The old one must have died…A shame…Cropped yellow grass…Little pale flags in the eaves… He stopped walking to stare.

A boy he hadn't noticed came around the dry cedar tree. The boy stared hard back at him.

A motorcycle went by. A car followed.

Sid lifted his golden sleeve. "Hello." He felt like a moon man.

The boy took a few steps towards him. The lawn cracked underneath him. He was holding a stuffed toy lion.

Sid didn't remember the wizard having a family. A lot could happen in fifty years though…This might be his great grandson. Who knew?

"I'm looking for someone who lived here before," Sid tried.

"Are you a superhero?" the boy replied. He wasn't afraid of the gold suit and he came up closer.

"Uhhh…"

"I know all about superheroes," the boy said. "I can read."

Sid had to admit, there was a familiar look to the boy. He had the wizard's eyes and features. Oh, all the time Sid had spent looking over the crystal ball at that wizard! Yes, the boy had to be from him.

"Do you know the wizard who lived or used to live here?"

The boy held the lion with one dropped hand. "I live here with my mom and dad. My mom is doing something. My dad is at work. Can you fly?"

"Sure," Sid said. "I like it up there." He took a look at the blue sky without any clouds.

"I can do a magic trick."

"Oh yeah?"

The boy took a little plastic black box from his pocket. He slid it open to show a gray nickel inside of it. "See this quarter? I can make it disappear."

"Oh yeah?"

"Watch…" He closed it, his fingers thumbed over the edges. When he opened the box again, the coin wasn't in the drawer.

"Hotcha!" Sid acclaimed.

"I can do other magics," the boy said. "I'm going to be a magician."

"I can tell." It didn't surprise Sid that the wizard would have a magician waiting in the wings. "Can you tell me what your father does? Is he a magician too?"

"He gets to take money from people. He works at the 7-11 store."

"The 7-11 store? What's that?"

"It's over there. We walk there every day to bring him his lunch."

"Over there?"

The boy nodded. "Are you going to fly now?"

"Nope. I'll walk. I don't mind. Thanks for your help. That was a great magic trick too. Keep it up, you'll be a great magician."

"Maybe I'll be a wizard instead."

"Okay, kid," Sid laughed. He took off for the store the boy told him about. He couldn't believe the future still had 7-11s. When he was a kid, he remembered going there on allowance day for candy and comics.

He left Myrtle Street. So far he didn't see any futuristic things about him. The future must have taken a few steps back. Economic depression, or a war, or…He didn't know. He walked past the dun colored houses and their lawns.

The magician boy was right. At the corner, Sid saw the plastic 7-11 sign stuck overhead. Bulky cars went by loudly. People looked bored and made of clay. Sid almost tried not to take in too much of this time—he was here as an astronaut, not a part of it—but he clung to the hope of the reward.

He was happy to stop and pet a cat that appeared on the sidewalk. He wrapped his hands around it and really rubbed the fur. He laughed at the lazy cat's half-closed eyes. The cat rolled over. "You're alright, friend," Sid said, "You take care," and he had to leave the cat lying there watching him in a coil.

The 7-11 lot was poured old tar. A big yellow car doped on it. He couldn't believe it, where were these people?

Inside the pushed door was another surprise. There were rows of things he remembered with greedy child eyes. Candy, packets and trinkets and an ice chest full of ice creams. The glass wall in back was filled with soda bottles and cans.

The man behind the counter had already made eye contact and was watching Sid.

"Hiya," Sid said.

"Yeah?"

Sid went to the counter. "I have a funny question for you. You're the father of the boy I met over on Myrtle Street?"

The man shifted and changed. "Yeah?" he sounded like loading a gun.

Sid smiled and dropped his hands onto the glass counter.

"It's only that I'm looking for someone who used to live in your house. I'm hoping I can track him down. He helped me out years ago. He was a wizard."

"What?"

"This was way back, but he lived in your house. Do you know about a wizard who used to live there?"

There was a button underneath the counter that connected to the police. Whenever anything like this, or worse happened, the push would send for a cruiser. The man in the gold suit would have to go with them.

15.

"Hello, this is Ray Chan." The telephone was like a seashell held to his ear. He heard the dull flood of air from somewhere else. He was about to hang up when he heard the voice.

"It's about time you got there. If you want to see your mother alive again, come to the bus station. Wait on the bench next to the shoeshine stand. You'll get your orders."

"What?! Who is this?" He clicked the phone, but Ray could only hear the buzzing dial tone. The villain had already dropped out.

Ray left his half eaten sandwich and ran for the door.

16.

His shoes on the pavement slowed him down. Ray stepped right out of the frame of his childhood bicycle and wheeled that red three-speed in the doorway of the bus station.

The clatter of others echoed up the marble pillars and tiled floors. It was hard to search the crowd suspiciously when he didn't know what he was looking for.

He steered through a class of students on a field trip. Some laughed behind their hands at the sight of him and his tiny bicycle. The spokes clicked from all the rainbow plastic straws stuck in when he was eleven.

The shoeshine stand was well over by the lockers, on the other side of the station. First he knew he needed to stop and see his girl for luck.

He passed some girls unwrapping candy from there and then he was there.

She had the *Star Reporter* movie newspaper held up before her eyes. There was a picture of Sylvan Moore grinning at him. She put the paper down when Ray's bicycle creaked against the counter.

"Hello, Darla," he said.

This time she noticed his tuxedo. "You look like you fell out of a coffin."

Wasn't she supposed to smile when she saw him? Couldn't she see who he was? He sometimes wondered. "I have some bad news."

Her eyes came back his way with no shine.

He sighed and tried something else less pained. "Is that Sylvan Moore you're reading about?"

"Yes," she clutched the paper to her breast. "He's gorgeous," she gushed.

"I've been up on the mountain with him. He's a friend of mine."

She stared at him in suspension. When her eyes had become

large as blue buttons, she asked, "Is that true?"

"Yes, of course. In fact, he's waiting for me to return."

She moved forward. "Will you take me?"

"Well, I…I have to take care of something first."

"Your bad news?"

"Yes, I have to see that through first."

"Then could you take me to Sylvan Moore?"

"Sure, if everything works out."

She smiled past him dreamily. "Sylvan Moore…" Those two words seemed to bloom from her. "Go do your thing," she said, coming back to earth. "I'm going to close this place so we can go. Don't leave the station without me!"

"I probably won't be going back to the mountain right away. I—" he stopped. She was gone already.

That smile of hers was really something though. He could almost forget all the world woes.

No, he couldn't. He had something on his mind that turned him away and around toward the other wall.

A goat pulled a wagon in front of him…A man with a wooden trunk on his shoulder…A woman selling roses made from painted newspaper.

Ray sat down on the empty bench. He was close to the shoeshine stand. It was just to his right. A man with a broken leg was having his cast shined. That's odd, Ray thought…He read the message written in marker on the cast. It said, For a good time, tap my leg. Ray quickly looked away.

It could be a long wait, so to bide the while Ray got back up and took out a coin for the tea machine.

He dropped the silver in and a paper cup fell into its place. The machine hummed a high pitch waiting for the selection. Once done, it poured out a steaming four seconds worth of green tea. Ray took the paper cup back to the bench where his red bicycle leaned on its kickstand. He sat down, wrapped his hands around the tea, and waited.

It wasn't long. The crippled shoeshiner lamed over to him,

"You got a phone call, sir." He pointed at the wooden booth where the phone hung from its cord.

"Thanks," Ray left the bench and led his bicycle over there. He took a deep breath before he stepped into the deep shadow of the booth. He put the cold metal to his ear. "Hello?"

It was that strange voice again. "You're in luck, fellah. The old lady's been returned to her house. She's fine. It was all a mistake. That's all." The phone went dead.

Ray caught his forehead and set the receiver back. For a while he sat there frozen inside the booth in the echoed stereo of the bus station. He wasn't listening to the chimes, the footsteps, loudspeaker, a radio, a dog, the conversations…All that melted into a blend…He had fallen inside of himself in relief.

"Hey! Hey!"

Ray looked out the phone booth doorway, out the dark into the flickering scene of the bus station. Darla was standing there.

"Can we go now?" She reached in and grabbed him, "Let's go see Sylvan Moore, okay?"

Ray put his hand over hers. "I need a minute, Darla. I have to make a call to make sure everything is okay at home."

She rolled her eyes and stamped away.

He put a coin in the phone and dialed numbers.

"Chan residence," a pleasant voice answered, someone he didn't know.

"This is Ray Chan. I'm calling to see if my mother is safe and sound."

"Oh yes," the woman replied. "She's resting now. I'm caring for her. She'll be fine."

"Who are you?"

"I'm a nurse from the Screen Memory Guild. I'm caring for her. She got lost but she's not been harmed, Mr. Chan. She's very tired. I'll mind her until your adventure is over."

"My adventure?"

"She told me about you."

"Oh…Okay. Thanks, I'll try to call her later."

"Yes. I'll tell her you called, Mr. Chan. Good luck."

Hmmm…He hung up and left the dark.

Darla spun over to him, "Now are you satisfied?"

"Yes, I suppose so."

"Good. Let me get us a car."

"A car?"

"Sure. To get to the mountain, of course. You weren't planning on riding me up on that bicycle, were you?"

"No, I…Well where can I put this in the meantime?"

She groaned, "Here, we'll put it behind the candy counter. That'll do." She unlocked the door to the little stall and he steered the wheels in with her newspapers and chair.

"It's no problem closing up the shop for a while?" he asked her.

"Of course not." She locked the padlock again. "To tell you the truth, confidentially, the candy counter is just a front. I'm sure you won't tell," she shot him a look.

"A front?" he whispered.

"Sure. The mob. You must have heard of these things before, haven't you?"

"Yes…" Ray nodded solemnly. "It happens."

"That's right," she pinched his arm. "I'll be right back. Let me get the car. Meet you out in front of the station." She was gone out a door behind the counter.

Ray turned around and was surprised to see a familiar figure on the bench, shining not so bright as the sun anymore. It was Sid Canova, bent like an old brass maple leaf, with his arms around his knees. He stared past his feet at something burned into the ground and gone forever.

"Sid!"

Somehow he lifted his head to turn an eye.

Ray hurried over. "Sid, what's going on?" Ray couldn't believe Sid the star wasn't somewhere aloft in the air.

"Oh…Hello, pal." His suit looked like the dark chandelier in a torpedoed steamship. He looked like he had drifted for miles, then up out of the water into the cold heights and buried in an avalanche for another hundred years. "I got an official request to leave. That's why I'm here." Sid straightened up some more as Ray sat down on the bench next to him. "I've been all over this town and nothing's the same. Places I thought I knew…"

"Well sure, Sid. It's been years since you were here."

"Years…" Sid repeated. "Years in the wrong direction! I understand it now. Things are strange not because I woke up in the future, but because I woke up in the past."

"What? What do you mean?"

"I haven't even been born yet! Not for another ten years. That contraption in the mountain sent me back in time, not ahead."

"What are you talking about?"

"The wizard I was looking for—He's just a kid in this time. He cast this sorcery on me much later in his life. His idea of a trick joke, I guess. Some laugh. Anyway, here I am and I don't exist."

Ray shook his head in sympathy.

"Yeah, it's crazy alright. So…I don't really know what to do now. I was planning on taking this stuff," he rustled the paper bag holding tubes and oxygen tanks, "back up to the mountain and going under again. Maybe that's all I can do. But…Is that what I should do? What if I stay here? What will happen when the other me is born? And *will* the other me even *be born*? Will I be me? It sounds nutso, I know. But if I'm not me, then who am I?" He groaned. "See, it gets crazier the more you think about it."

A black sedan pulled up outside the bus station windows and blared its horn.

"Why don't you come with me, Sid?" Ray asked, standing up. "That car's going to the mountain. We can try to figure this out together."

"Yeah…I guess so…Sure." Sid Canova, future star, or never-was-at-all, got up, fetched his paper bag, and followed Ray to the rumbling car.

17.

The car was powered by chatter of Sylvan Moore.

Darla hadn't stopped talking about him in the hour since they'd left town. Ray was silent in the front seat, Sid was withdrawn and leaning with the turns in the back seat. At last, thankfully for her passengers, she pulled the sedan off the road onto an unpaved drive, into a gravel parking lot surrounding a tin-sided building. She stopped the car engine and got out.

Ray got out too and was waiting for her when she came back from the car's trunk carrying a heavy looking suitcase. "Can I help you with that?"

"No," she told him quickly. "You don't want to get involved with this. I'm just making a drop-off, then we can get going again. Pretend you never saw this happening," she told him over her shoulder just before she entered the building.

Ray shook his head. He kicked a stone and watched it bounce away into the ferns. He could hear the distant river…A jay made off through the boughs of firs, then the sound of the car window being rolled down.

"Who is she anyway?" Sid asked him.

"I'm beginning to wonder," Ray replied after consideration. "I'm trying to fit all these pieces together." I don't know if I can, he thought. He stared at a keyhole that opened to beyond the wall of trees, showing the white and gray steepness of the mountain. "I hope we find out when we're back up there." He scratched an itch on his hand and got back into the sedan.

18.

Another half hour passed on the switchback road, the trees thinning out, the rocks coming through and Darla's never-ending radio of Sylvan Moore stories.

Ray and Sid were both out the door before the car was quiet.

The lodge was a welcome sight. Up here in the altitude, the cool air breathed right through you. Fog played on all the many rills of the tiled roof of the lodge, swirling off and haunting the corners.

Sid breathed in deep. "Ahh, it's nice to be back."

Darla got out. "Is he in there?" She tucked her hair around her ear. "Or is he filming somewhere?"

"I don't know. We'll find out," said Ray.

She joined him on the path to the lodge door.

"I guess I'll come with you too," Sid Canova took up behind them. "Just to see what happens."

"Sylvan Moore sure knows how to pick a romantic movie setting," Darla glowed. "This is even better than *Cross Country Havoc*. I wonder what his next movie will be?"

"It's a sequel," Ray said. He waved at the familiar girl at the door. "Is Sylvan Moore around today?" he asked her.

"He's out there," she pointed beyond the lot, up the flank of meadow and rock. "He's waiting for you."

"Thank you," Ray said and he led his group around the building. He knew that other side well—it was where he had gone underground and found Sid Canova. He supposed Sylvan Moore would be waiting at that stone where the tunnel began. "It's not far," he told them.

"I hope we don't get lost in that fog," Sid observed. The stuff was thick as sheep herded down the hill.

"I just hope we can find Sylvan Moore," Darla worried. "We've come all this way to see him."

They walked silently while the fog writhed towards them, across the stones and clover. Ray could feel it sigh around his feet like an animal. It grew deeper as they climbed steeper. Soon they waded in thick white cloud. They slowed to keep from stumbling, taking each step carefully. Finally Ray called out, "Sylvan Moore! Are you out there?"

Darla grabbed his coat. Sid had disappeared somewhere behind them. They stood still and listened.

They heard a rock trickle down the slope to their right. The fog made them stand in a nothing of white.

"Where is he?" Darla whispered. Close as she was, ghostly, she seemed to fade and reappear, at the whim of the air.

"Sylvan Moore! It's me, Ray Chan! Are you out there?!"

Sylvan Moore's voice snapped like the crack of a bone, "Hello, Chan." He was there in front of them in a space free of fog. He was leaning on that same rock where Ray had left him. "Where have you been to? I've been worried about you."

"It's sure good to see you," Ray smiled. It really was too. He had missed him. And it wasn't anything like star-struck movie dizziness, there was something grand about seeing him again. They were connected.

Darla's stark next words took him by surprise.

"You're over, Sylvan Moore." She had drawn out a derringer pistol and was pointing it at her idol. The fog had slipped in to curl over the barrel and over her slender, exposed wrist. She pulled the trigger and nothing exploded. She was quick to try again. Then again…But nothing happened.

"Everything's okay," came Sid Canova's voice as he slid from the billows. "I took the bullets out of that thing."

The fog made a ghost out of Darla for a moment.

"How?" Ray asked him.

"When we stopped back on the road. You were outside the car. I figured you needed a Watson to expect the obvious."

Darla threw the dead gun down.

Nobody knew what to do. The wind blew the fog around them.

Sylvan Moore was the one to speak. "So you tried to kill me."

He grinned. "It's alright. You're not the first one. I'm not trying to make enemies. I'm alive to what happens. It all figures itself out." He turned to Ray, "Well, Chan…What do you make of this?"

"Oh…I didn't think this would happen. Honestly, I had no idea. This is how it goes, I suppose."

Sylvan Moore laughed. "So why be worried? We're all still here. Hey there!" he called to Sid, who was half closed inside the clouds. "Mister! Come here, I want to thank you."

The fog made everything go.

There were four seconds before a shape was formed. Sid wasn't there. A deer was in his place. He was a photograph until he moved, alongside the fog, then gone into it, lost on the mountain.

10:27 PM October 3, 2003

COPPER KETTLE

The Water Operation

Starfish

The Sinister Backdrop

Wherever World

20 Dollars

Start With the Ending

Chapter One:

A BARGAIN FOR FRANCES

The wind came through the broken blinds into the basement and woke him up.

"How long have I been out?" he asked his daughter.

"Only a couple of minutes, maybe," she said. "I've got the carotid pressed. He's still alive. You can save him when you're ready."

George smiled, "Okay," and took over the life of gangster 'Charlie' Benodonci quickly and skillfully. His tired voice continued, drawn like charcoal, "One of these days I may not return from that black sleep. You'll be looking at me but I'll be gone. But don't worry," he looked at her with awakened eyes. "That will be your chance to escape this racket." He sewed the life back into the gunned down hood. "It's drawn into the contract. In the end, we'll both be free."

All the blood that covered Charlie could have killed him, but he found the crime doctor just in time. His wound was healed and the doctor was suddenly falling asleep beside him.

Frances caught her father before he fell over the table. She led him back onto the stretcher. He needed some rest now.

She left them, doctor and patient, closed the door on that place and went into the other room.

She was facing a counter, a cash register, and a mob of children waiting for her. "Uhh, who's next?"

"I'm next!" piped up Crybaby Johnson. He had his gang of fourth graders all crowded around him. Their eyes barely made it over the counter but they were all looking at her. "I want a pound of Whoppers."

"Of course," Francis smiled while she spun around. She noticed some blood on her hand as she unscrewed the jar. She wiped her hand on her black apron, poured a paper bag full of malted chocolate and returned. "Two ninety five," she said.

"Is that a pound?" Crybaby squinted at her.

The boy next to him rattled at her, "Yeah, is it, dummy?"

"Weigh it," the little voice ordered.

"Yeah, dummy. Weigh it."

What could she do? She put up with them. She set the paper bag onto the silver scale and everyone stared up at the red moving arrow. It stopped on one pound exactly.

A moment of silence passed, then Crybaby said, "Not bad."

"She's cheating!" shrieked his partner. "She's a big dummy!"

Crybaby Johnson gave her a long look. "No…I don't think so."

"I've been doing this a long time," she said. "Here you go then, one pound. That's $2.95." The bag plopped down onto the glass.

"Pay her, Louie," the boy leader snapped his fingers softly at some other nine year old as he grabbed his candy. "Let's scram."

She watched them leave. The shrill little crowd of bird voices flying away, all except for Louie. He was left at the counter, standing on his tip-toes counting through a pile of silver and copper coins. He tipped his glasses and tried again. "Sixty three, sixty four…seventy four…" he mumbled. All the money was a math problem for him.

"That's okay," she told him with a wave. "You can go with them."

The relief shined out of him. "Thanks, lady!" and he pulled his hands away and ran. The bell over the door rang as he left.

With the store quiet again, she raked the coins into the cash drawer and yawned. She was about to go check on the operating room when the door rang back open.

Wind and some flicks of falling snow blew in a tall thin man, wearing a black coat, staggering like a mechanical wind-up toy.

"I need the doc," he gasped.

"I can see that." She slid around the counter and caught him before he collapsed into a tower of chocolate boxes. "I'll help you."

"Never saw it coming…They had Tommy guns," he coughed.

She wiped the blood off his mouth, "Take it easy," she urged. "Follow me to the back of the store. The doctor's in there." She clawed open the paneled door and yelled, "Wake up! Bullet wounds!"

Her father gave a jerk falling up off the flat stretcher, "Nobody's bulletproof," he muttered to life. "Lay him down on my table, I'll get my tools."

He had a bad habit of falling asleep at any moment. Even if his life was broken up by dreaming spells, this place was his calling; when he was awake, he saved lives. As he prepared his patient, he recognized the scars from one of his previous jobs next to the fresh wounds.

His daughter had already placed the mask over their patient, feeding him gas.

A bare light bulb stuck in the wall above the door was flashing. "Oh!" Frances cried, "Someone needs me out there. Will you be okay?"

"Sure, sure Frances," he grinned, "I could do this in my sleep."

"Well don't! If you start fading out, give me a shout before you go," she said as she left.

The shop was silent and looked empty, until a girl with green eyes jumped up above the counter level. "Can I have twenty cents of taffy, please?" she hopped.

"Yes, of course." Frances scooped an arm into a jar. "Here you are."

"Thank you," said the girl, adding, "Ummm, this is for the doctor, from Tiny Snopes." She put a gray, soft looking statue on the counter. It looked like a guitar wearing a dress.

"Wow! Another one…Will you tell him thanks?"

"Mm-hmm," the little girl answered. With five cents of taffy chewing away, she sunk, out of sight until she got to the other side of the floor and opened the front door. "Bye."

"Bye bye."

Frances thought about locking the door, putting up a Closed sign, but what would their customers do? The doctor was in business saving the lives of the underground, the element who would die in the street if bullets weren't taken out. They needed their store.

She put the cold flesh-like statue on the wall shelf, in the row full of more guitars wearing dresses. There were slight variations on the theme. Or was he just getting better?

A year ago, the doctor had sewn new hands on Tiny Snopes. Every month or so, another sculpture would arrive. Maybe he was getting better.

Frances opened the door to the next room.

She was glad to see her father's back, standing there at the table while she followed the tiled floor to the sink. "We got another present from Tiny," she told him. She smiled, turned around to face him, "Another thanks to you."

Quiet…Except for the slow drop of blood onto the floor… Her father was asleep standing up, with a saw cut stuck in the arm of his patient.

In the next second Frances clicked out across the distance to wake him, shout him out of it and reverse the cold death taking over.

"I'm sorry," he muttered for the hundredth time, "I'm sorry," again. He quickly put his knowledge into saving what he might have lost to sleep. The hovering specter fled as he cut, sewed and fed new blood into that dying form. From that moment to the next, he worked the miracle. Frances passed the tools to him, followed his directions, until another gangster's life was going again.

She reached and touched his shoulder. "You okay?"

"Sure." He had a smile after all. "I'm tired though."

"Okay, dad. Take a rest now."

By the time she settled him on another cot, he was already gone. No, there was nothing she could do about it. He came and he went. She dimmed the light in the room. It was alright. There were already two patients resting, plus her father. While they all slept, she crept to the door and went back to the store.

It was quiet in there but nothing was wrong. She found her

seat behind the counter. She picked up a book that hadn't been read for an hour. There was a page marked where she left off. There was always time for poetry when time allowed.

The door belled open with a crash.

"Tiny!" she yelped. The book fell from her.

Snow falling off him, he tottered through the candy displays like a small, slow motion mummy. "Can you hide me?" he asked her. "For a while?"

"Yes. Of course..." Frances pointed at the wide cardboard display of a chocolate colored cow. "You can hide behind that. There's room back there and nobody can see you."

He was already gone.

"Thanks for the new statue," she whispered.

The quiet was slow before she lifted her book again. The page remembered her.

With a sighing, the door behind her opened and her father stepped out. He put a hand on her shoulder, "Frances…We're a little low on ammonia. Could you go to the store and get some more?"

"Of course," she said. Her book caught that place where she left it. "Are you okay if I go?"

He laughed. "Go ahead. Don't worry about me. I've given myself an injection. I'll be here and I won't fade."

"Really?"

"Don't worry."

Outside wasn't a place she went very often. Out there was where gangsters got shot. Death roamed where she let herself out and it was snowing.

The black sky showed between all the tall grown buildings with the wind scattering white. She looked for the Moon but there was none. The street was so cold she felt difficulty going in that dimension. She hurried as fast as she could go.

Across the street, in the distance, Food Castle was a burning sight of haloed neon, pale blue in the night. She cut across a dark parking lot, over the curb and street to the next block. She directed herself towards the light of it. She and every moth in the neighborhood flew to the same bright place.

She walked by parked cars turning into white sloped and sleeping silhouettes. It could have been a peaceful walk until she got closer to the corner, where she saw a dog thrown down on the sidewalk and a man holding its paw.

She sped up. She was sure it was someone she knew…He was.

"Can you get us to the doc?" the big sad face of Don Benny begged her. "They shot him…This crazy dog took the bullets meant for me," he choked.

"Here…" she reached and took the dog's pulse, her hand touching fur and snow. "We have to get him back to the store."

"I can carry him, lady. I'd walk ten miles for this dog."

"Alright, Mr. Benny. We have to hurry though."

He staggered after her across the parking lot. The three of them made a monster movie image, wading away.

"You've gotta save him," Don puffed clouds in the cold air. The dog was draped in his arms. Its breath made ghosts, it was still alive.

"We're almost there," she told him. They crossed the street. The light was a blur in the curtained, candy store window. As she hurried ahead to unlock the door, she noticed fresh footprints running from the wall.

"What?" she said aloud as she read the badly spelled graffiti left behind—*DUME*. It took her about five seconds, then "Ohh…" she said as she realized, sounding it out like a school grader and solving it. It didn't spell "DOOM," it was "DUMMY."

"Lady…" Don Benny wheezed up to her, straining and resting the dog over his leg.

"Yes!" She quickly found the handle and they went inside.

"We're here," Don Benny told his dog. "Everything's going to be alright."

Frances led them to the back door. She brushed snow off of herself and pushed the door open.

Ahead of them the doctor was okay, sharpening a blade with

a whetstone.

"Bullet case," Frances announced to her father. "Here, you can lay him here, Mr. Benny." She straightened the fresh sheet on the table.

Don Benny's hands and gold coat buttons were wet with blood. He stared like an owl.

"A dog…" The doctor approached and looked at the wounds. "What's his name?" he asked while he went to work.

"Agnew," Don Benny rasped.

"Agnew…Agnew?" the doctor looked up for a moment until the next.

"Can you save him, doc? Can you fix animals?"

"Of course. We're all animals, Mr. Benny. I remember one time we had a racehorse in here. Sniper got him. I put him back on the track though. You'll see, Agnew will be good once I get these bullets out of him. All he needs is a lot of blood."

"That's what I'm here for!" Don Benny suddenly rolled up his sleeve. "Take all you want." He held out his arm. "What's mine is his." He thumped his heart.

"Okay. You want to sit him down, Frances? And get an I.V set up." There was a plinking rattle as a bullet dropped into the tray. "There's one," he said.

Frances guided Don Benny onto the cot beside the operating table. "Lay down here, Mr. Benny," her voice poured while she prepared the needle and the tube to connect him to his dog.

"There isn't anything I wouldn't do for Agnew."

"I know, Mr. Benny. Now relax…" she tied off the vein, "This will only hurt a second, just take it easy. The doctor will take care of you both."

Don Benny let out a yelp when it bit and the blood flowed out of him.

Another bullet clinked into the pan.

"Oh!" Frances turned to look at the door. The light bulb above it was flashing.

"Go ahead," her father answered. "This is fine. I've got company and man's best friend."

"Alright. I'll be back soon as I can."

"Go sell some candy."

"Okay." She smiled back at him before she left the room.

Opening the door she had to push on someone leaning against the other side. Registering the police uniform before her, she tried to hide the operating room from sight as she slid into the store.

The officer was absorbed in something else though.

"Can I help you?" she asked him.

"This thing." He hefted one of the sculptures in his hand. "Where'd you get all these things?"

Cautiously she said, "I'm not sure…Maybe from—"

"This is pure opium," he interrupted.

She stood blocking the operating room door, with her body pressed against it and the frame.

"So this is what's going on around here." He was getting louder. "We've been watching this place." He carried the sculpture to the space in front of the counter and plopped it down. "All this candy in here is nothing but a front," he pointed at the chocolate boxes and penny bins, "Opium is what it's all about, isn't it? Opium!"

Frances didn't say anything, someone else's voice did. "It ain't opium."

"What?" the policeman spun to see who was in the corner.

"It's Connie Francis." Tiny Snopes stepped out of the darkness. "Stick your hands up, copper." He sneered, "*Opium…*" He chuckled. He was holding a little gun pointed at the policeman. Tiny steered the conversation into the middle of the room. "You got a chair for the lawman?" he asked Frances.

"What are you going to do?" she asked.

"Let's just get this lawman com-for-table." Tiny Snopes let it drawl.

She pulled a stool across the wooden boards. "I don't want anyone getting hurt."

"Noone's gonna get hurt, precious," the little man sneered.

"Not if everything goes alright. So sit down, flat-foot."

"What do you mean Connie Francis?" the policeman finally spoke. "Is that something new? Slang?"

Tiny Snopes growled.

The policeman bristled, "Listen, outlaw—"

"What do you know about opium?" Tiny waved his gun at him.

"We know this place is crawling with opium. There's more officers outside. They're waiting for the signal from me."

"These are just statues I made." Tiny confessed, unfazed, "Art for an angel, Connie Francis."

"You made this, huh?" The policeman's hand began to squeeze. The gray form mushed and spilled out between his fingers.

"Hey!" Tiny Snopes shrieked. "That's it! No mercy for you! Nobody hurts Connie!"

Frances wanted to step in and stop whatever was building into happening, but just then the operating room door flung open.

"He's alive!" Don Benny lurched into the store. He trailed a loop of tubing taped to his arm vein. "He's alive!" When he saw the policeman though, he turned instantly malevolent, hissing, "Copper..." as he reached into his coat.

"He's mine!" Tiny Snopes shot. "I've got a plan for him. Oh yeah..." he grinned wickedly. "Why don't you give me a hand, Benny?"

Frances was worried about this. "Listen fellows, I think we should stop this."

Tiny Snopes hissed at Don Benny, "Bring me the rest of those statues."

"With pleasure," Don Benny grinned. He filled his arms with Connie Francis idols.

The policeman stood there frozen, his numb face watching his fate unfold.

Don Benny and Tiny Snopes worked efficiently, tucking the statues in all over the silent policeman.

Then Tiny Snopes took a roll of wire out of his coat pocket.

He spun the thin copper coil back and forth, round and round the blue uniform, connecting the charges. "Opium!" he spat laughter.

Don Benny wheezed with delight. "Yeah, opium!"

"What are you going to do to him?" Frances asked at last. "That's plastic explosive, isn't it?"

"Flatfoot here is going to take a little walk," Tiny Snopes leered. "He's gonna go out there and call off the raid, see. He's gonna tell all his pals he was mistaken and—" he jerked the end of his wire tied to the policeman like a leash, "And if he makes any stupid mistakes…It's curtains."

Don Benny laughed like a dry sprinkler. "Fourth of July!"

"Get walking!" Tiny Snopes snapped the wire and began to let out slack.

"This won't work, Tiny," the officer warned. He took a couple steps toward the door, pulling wire along, pausing.

"Walk!"

Onto the leak of light coming from under the operating room door, Frances faded from the store, swung through the wall and locked the latch behind her.

The operating room was an underwater green. There was that dog Agnew sprawled across the table, striped white with bandages, sleeping off the effects.

"Dad?" she called. She looked around. She followed the smoke signal cloud coming from the corner, behind a Chinese folding screen.

She peered around and caught her breath in surprise.

Atop a cushion, her father rested with a long black pipe laid across his folded legs. He smiled at her and lost some smoke.

"Opium?" she sighed, realized.

"Yes…" George whispered slowly. "Opium…The mob keeps me supplied…I'm addicted…I belong to them…But I made a bargain with them." He took another tug of smoke and drifted into a nod.

"Wait! We have to get out of here! This place is surrounded

by police."

He was smiling. He was asleep and didn't mind at all. Then he awoke for a breath and his words walked out. "This is your chance, Frances. I always told you it would happen like this. I made a bargain with them…They own me, but when I'm gone you're set free…My life for your life." His hand moved, "Use the passage…" He motioned the pipe at the bookcase. "I've got my escape. Now go while you can." George's eyes closed him down. He was gone.

Frances heard a crash behind her and she spun around. It was the dog, Agnew. Either he had rolled off or pushed himself off of the table. The will to survive staggered him in his mummy cloth, his bleary eyes searching for a way out.

"This way, boy," she called. "This way!" She ran to the bookcase full of medical tomes. Pushing the shelf to the side revealed a creaking passage opening beyond.

Chapter Two:

SAM AND THE FIREFLY

The crash startled the fragile man into trembling spider-like motion, up off the daybed and across the creaking floor to the door. George hadn't been sleeping, at least he didn't think so, but maybe his mind had been playing tricks on him. He pushed the door open into the small room that served as kitchen and everything else in the apartment.

Not surprisingly, Sam had broken their new wooden radio. Crushed splinters of it, gray tin foil and mechanics, heaped smoking on the scarred floor. Out of it croaked a last crazy word or two more. It was still plugged in by a thick black wire. Then the heap crackled a spark and died.

"Sam," he rasped, "Maybe you shouldn't listen to the radio for a while…"

For a moment his gigantic roommate really became the super-villain of those B movies he starred in. That was the face Sam made when his submarine ran aground, or whenever the Empire suffered a temporary loss.

"Relax Sam… That's my advice to you, as your doctor."

Sam's big hand went into the radio rubble. Giving a huff, he caught the Firefly between his thumb and forefinger. He held it up to his gaze like a jeweler with a diamond.

A tiny voice appealed from it, "This is a possession of the United States of America. Any resultant breaking of applicable laws is considered a felony and punishable by law."

Sam made it dust when he shut his fingers together.

Sam growled, "Why can't they just play music?"

"You know, I told you. That's not the way they do things in this country, Sam. On radio you have to have commercials and news. I told you, just turn it off when that happens. The music always comes on afterwards."

The words hissed out of Sam like pistons of a steam engine,

"The Empire will not be defeated."

"I know…I know…" the doctor held up his hands placating, then with a smile he tapped the wristwatch on his right arm. He pressed the button, starting music from of a little warbling speaker. It hummed like a cricket on his arm.

"Cornelius Barter," Sam nodded. The effect was immediate and soporific. Sam dropped back dreamily into a straw-backed Van Gogh chair.

Chapter Three:

GREEN 17

The late afternoon windows were raining. The radio song had calmed Sam and he reflected back the weather's celery color. This was a good time for George to take a walk.

He quietly put on his overcoat, scarf and the gray fedora that rode just above his eyebrows. He left the watch in front of Sam, still spinning Cornelius Barter jazz. He had a clear premonition of the watch's fate—it would be smashed flat when he got back. So what? Time and radios weren't built to last.

He went out the kitchen door. The rain pattered on the dark wooden stairway. The wounded stairs tipped and showed wet, chipped yellow paint. They crawled down one floor to the alley. Clothes hung like band-aids from the laundry ropes strung above. The air rolled smooth and cold and smelled like the ocean. George held the rail and went down into Chinatown.

All the usual creaks…He was used to this place. It had been a half year since the explosion leveled his lab and candy store and here he stayed. Everything had been blown away that day. It was okay. He didn't need to go back to the ruins and pick up pieces. There was nothing to remember. He didn't need the mob anymore either. Sam was keeping him supplied. He could lay low forever. It was best if he seemed dead.

In his black coat and slouch he moved in the rain like a nobody. He walked on the sidewalk along bricks and window shine. A tree strained tall out of the cement. Other green, smaller leaves were finding their way out of the pavement too. He remembered why—it was spring. The unfreezing rain was another reminder. Then, for a sad moment before he turned into the corner bodega, he thought of his daughter.

Fortunately, the music and Mexican movie posters overpowered him. George nodded at the man reading a newspaper at the cash register. He drifted by the Spanish words on produce lining the shelves and stopped instinctively when he reached the green labeled can of cactus juice. "Why this?" he mumbled, his thoughts analyzed, "What a thing to be craving." As a doctor, he observed this phenomenon—the body signaling a specific deficiency. Perhaps, he concluded, a diagnosis was in order? So he turned the can in his hand to read the ingredients, "Water, Agave, Saguaro Puree from Concentrate, Cane Sugar, High Fructose Corn Syrup, Citric Acid, Beta Carotene, Green 17."

He speculated. He knew the effects of all active ingredients except Green 17. What could it be? Why would his brain order it? And what could it do?

Anyway, he carried it to the counter and set it down next to the newspaper reader.

George had time enough there to stare into the front page as if it was a tabloid mirror. *Dos Pedros* were in the bold headlines. The words went on below with a photo. He was leaning to look at it when the paper snapped down.

"Fifty cents."

George managed to find the coins in his change purse.

There was an old fashioned bell and clang of machinery and George was gone with the can.

Outside it was starting to really rain. He tucked the can under his coat and bent into getting wet.

"Hold it, doc."

The shrill voice sapped George in the back of the head and he turned around.

"Yeah…It's me…" The little face of Tiny Snopes sneered at him. "I finally caught up with you." In a quick motion, he had a pistol in the air. He snarled, "I hate talking to you!" then he pulled the trigger.

The blow hit George over the heart. A stream of green looking blood poured out the puncture in his jacket. He gasped for air to breathe.

"Martian!!" Tiny Snopes squealed at the sight. "I knew it!" The tiny man recoiled so fast he bumped against a stack of garbage cans. They crashed all around him and knocked him down. When he got up, he was running away.

Chapter Four:

THE NIGHT BALLOONS

"George is my friend," Sam took a hand off the steering wheel and pointed at his grim passenger on the car seat next to him.

The guard nodded, "Yes sir, Mr. Samsara," and returned to the kiosk to open the studio gate. He had to walk past the rumbling, long engine under the silver hood of Sam's car. The pistons churned and pounded the ground for fifteen feet in front of where Sam Samsara drove the colossal bullet shaped car.

When the striped yellow gate rose over the airstreamed grill, Sam took his foot off the brake plate and the automobile roared forward. They were already there when he hit the brake again, fit in a runway parking spot between a row of potted palm trees. Sam turned the ignition key over and one by one the valves shut down with the growl and sparking cough of a dragon. The silence in the air afterwards was deafening.

George had never been to the film studio before. He only left the apartment for short walks. Today though, Sam had requested his services as his personal doctor—he was doing a stunt that had the possibility of going very wrong and he wanted George along just in case. From the swinging grip of his left hand George carried a black leather bag.

"This used to be a horse track," Sam grunted. "Even has an old radio tower…That comes in handy."

A big stable in front of them had been converted into a film stage. A studio jeep pulling a torpedo on a trailer drove in the wide rolling doors. "There it is," Sam told him. "That's where we film."

Even before they got there, George could smell the horses' ghosts. After he turned his head, he saw the abandoned field inside the dead track. It was overgrown with mountains of blackberry vines. It was a briar patch like Uncle Remus or the Brothers Grimm. In the middle, some white balloons were tied to piles of garbage.

"Those balloons are in today's shoot."

George said, "Mmm." They walked by a parked truck. The back of it was filled with standing sheets of plate glass that reflected them walking past. George got a good look at the two of them—Sam wore the uniform of the Imperial Japanese Navy—George was dressed like the Invisible Man. What a sight, what a horror, George thought. Then they were met at the open door.

"Sam! Sam, good morning!"

"Wervers…" Sam told George. "He's the director."

The nervous fellow gimped up to them. He carried a copper tea kettle. "You got your lines memorized?"

Sam tapped his temple. "Photographic."

"Oh yeah!" Wervers laughed, "That's right, Sam. Well come on in, we need you now."

George took a step into another world. The light inside was brighter than sunshine. A crew was dismantling the last scene. They were ripping out the nails of a jungle. There was a big water tank filled with fog and a ship on the miniature waves. George followed Sam to the edge where ferns were propped and a couple folding chairs waited.

While Sam perched himself carefully into his creaking chair, a cup of green tea was quickly poured from the copper kettle. The china cup fit in his hand like a hummingbird nest. Sam inhaled the steam and liquid then held the empty cup out for more.

"I got a neighbor lady who thinks you're great!" the old man gibbered while he applied makeup to Sam's face. "Course she's nuts about all the bad guys, but she likes your pictures most of all. I told her I know Sam, I work with Mr. Samsara, he's not like that at all. But she just gives me one of those looks, you know. One of these days I'd like to get your autographed photo. I'd sure love to see her face when I drop that on her!"

George was watching the last of the jungle fade away. It was being carted away and replaced by gray walls, painted windows that showed a harbor view, battered furniture and a single red rose in a slender vase. The last thing one of the stagehands brought in was a big cardboard contraption. It was a box in shape, with silver aerials crowning rows of phony levers and dials. Then the floodlights went back on and George had to shade his eyes from the bright yellow.

"Okay, Sam. This is it." Wervers left his side and went to the camera.

Sam stood up and took big steps onto the set. He sat at the table. He let the last preparations go on while he laid hands on the prop machine and waited for the director to yell, "Action!"

A sour voice came through a close-up on the desktop speaker, "Are the radishes in the garden?"

Sam leaned toward the transmitter and turned a knob, "Yes, Master. They are ready for harvesting."

A chuckling laugh replied, "Then carry out your orders."

Sam nodded and snapped a switch. He stood up and looked out the window, the sight of the harbor, the sleeping city fading out at the sound of seagulls.

The next chair George was sitting in was under a cloud of gulls, staring over heaps of garbage, car and kitchen parts that framed the scene of rubble at the junk yard. This film was rushing along like a train through a dream.

The camera leaned towards Sam as he took out a bomb from a red wheelbarrow and tied it underneath a white bobbing balloon. He moved from balloon to balloon, arming them with bombs, letting them quietly drift airborne.

After that scene, Sam came over to George and explained. "That was for Chapter 4, The Night Balloons." He jabbed at the weak afternoon sun, "This is supposed to be nighttime. They put a dark filtered lens on the camera."

"I see," George nodded. "So you're sending out weather balloons to blow up clouds? Making storms? Interesting idea."

"No. The balloons are heading for the city. Over there…" Sam pointed across the harbor at the tall buildings along the shore.

George stared at the toy-like scene.

"Well done, Sam!" Wervers clapped his hands together, "That was great. Talk about cliffhangers! The kids will be lined up around the block for the next installment."

They stood there and watched the film crew. It took five people to push the camera on tracks through the thorns to the next location.

In the distance, across the water, the silhouette of skyscrapers dotted with orange explosions and black smoke.

The sound rolled towards them like thunder.

"Holy—!" Wervers staggered.

The crew hurried to push the camera back up the hill.

A smile winched down the corners of Sam's mouth.

George fell backwards into his folding chair and blacked out.

Chapter Five:

IF YOU DON'T MIND

Frances woke up without moving. Crows were squawking outside her window behind the blue flowered curtains, but her eyes wandered down her bare leg thrown out of the covers. She noticed the long thin red scrape and began to wonder. She slowly wriggled her toes. The nails were dark with dirt underneath. Her feet were stained green yellow and stuck with leaves of grass.

The crows all at once flapped in a clatter. A wing bumped the glass as they left cawing away.

Her arm was heavy to move, to bend to her face so she could look at her curved fingers. They too were scratched and soiled, as if she'd been running on all fours in the middle of the night. She sighed, tried to breath in the new day without too much pain in her ribs. "Ohhh…" she moaned, as she noticed the state of her room. "Not again."

The door was bucked off its hinges. A force stronger than the metal latch had snapped it free. Everything in her bedroom had been friction bent by that whirlwind. What remained of yesterday's purple blouse was a rip of cloth looped around her left wrist. She shook it off. It was the moon at fault—it was the full white face of it howling from space that had done this to her again… Another werewolf night…

A little cry left her. It was like the first breath of being returned to life. She pushed herself to move off her bed, with that same slide out of darkness she knew from time and again. Where had she been? What had happened? She slipped a bathrobe on.

Her memory painted fierce images. Was she on someone's lawn? Was it the park? She tried to fight the fog to figure out where she had been…Lots of trees…Not much ground cover—it had been gnawed away to the dirt…She padded across it. When she got to a tall chain link fence, she easily climbed over it to the other side…That was all for memories.

A gray violet morning light flooded the hallway behind the splintered door. It was quiet. Frances stepped around the door and onto the panels of daylight falling in from the kitchen windows. She looked down the hall. The front door was closed. It was quiet but she couldn't help feeling like she was being rolled along tighter in a spider's web.

The kitchen clock tick-tocked above the stove. Spring leaves swayed on the branches beyond the window. The screen was open, she could hear a mourning dove breezing on a wire across the street.

Something scratched the linoleum floor under the table. Frances shot a look at it and suddenly she saw the claws curl up, the panting big teeth, the glinting eyes and dark fur.

She was so relieved by the friendly sight she cried out his name, "Agnew!"

The dog whined and scratched and licked at her hand.

"Oh, Agnew. Good old Agnew." The gangster's dog had been with her ever since their escape from the candy shop. He had kept her safe from police and crime all this time. She patted him gratefully. "I'll get you some breakfast, Agnew. I could use some tea, I don't know about you." She opened the cupboard door and jumped at the face looking back.

It was herself reflecting from the shiny, warped tin surface of a can on the shelf. For a second though, she had seen a fanged beast. "I'm a little scared still," she tried to laugh, explaining to him, "Last night was another full moon."

She took down the can, placed it on the counter and opened it for him. Agnew remained under the table, the same place he would crawl whenever there was thunder, or fireworks on the 4th of July. She tipped half the food onto a blue and white china plate and set it down gently by the chrome leg of a chair. "There you go."

Some music would be nice, she thought. That might go a long way towards making her feel better. First some water in the pan to get the tea going.

After the pan was filled and put on the gas burner, Frances reached and switched on the wooden radio. It took a moment to warm and turn gold.

Instead of music though, the station chattered with news of the attack downtown. The radio panicked and shrieked with voices that had seen it happen. It was war! It had to be, they said. In one quick spin like a safecracker, she wheeled the radio dial out of there and it hit on the sound she had been looking for. Cornelius Barter played "It Never Entered My Mind." The trumpet poured it out sad like some dented flower.

When the song was over, Frances was staring into the iris of a boiling silver pan of water. The announcer rattled to the microphone. "And Cornelius Barter will be playing tonight at the Lucky Note. That's set for an eight o'clock show. As far as I know, that's still going to happen. Cornelius Barter in town tonight… So…Let's…Uh, let's play another cut…If you don't mind."

Chapter Six:

THAT SAME MORNING

That same morning, Wervers strode back and forth at the studio with hands deep in his pockets. The rest of the crew watched him go on his wind-up way, hoping he would stop before too long and say something else or point cameras anyway. They were all in a dull shock, but at least he was moving.

Finally, he did stop. Next to a boom, he turned to face them all. He touched his chin and said, "On the other hand…It's not like anyone *ssaaawww* us release those balloons, right? I mean, who could have known where they came from?"

"That's right," a woman in a pilot costume agreed. Some other murmurs echoed around the stage.

Wervers continued, "And it shouldn't stop us from making our movie, right? We can't let this disaster—this horrible disaster—defeat us." He put his foot up on a chair to think. He weighed the copper tea kettle rounded on his open hand. He tried to Hamlet out the words for them. They were watching him, they needed some poetry…They were waiting for that tragedy and meaning.

From the end of the room, a door clapped open and the light threw someone in. "We're off the hook!" The door banged shut. The secretary ran across the wooden floor towards the filmmakers. "It's on the radio! The Nazis did it!"

"What?" Wervers stared at her. "Nazis?"

"Talk about luck." She laughed nervously.

"What do you mean, Nazis?"

"They're saying Nazis attacked us. They said this is just the start, that more is on the way." She shook the thick pile of paper script at him. It seemed to take the timed burn of a fuse for her news to pop. She grinned, "That means we can keep making the movie!"

That was the message Wervers had been waiting for. He was overjoyed. He leaped over to her and hugged her tightly and suddenly the pages of the movie fell away from her grip and splashed all over the floor. He swung her around and let her back down. Everyone felt the same way. What was a grim room before, reacted with shouts and laughs and hurrays.

"Well!" Wervers rejoiced, "Let's set up that next shot down at the bay. Let's go, let's go!" Equipment had to be loaded onto trucks, all the actors, all the props. Wervers caught Sam's arm as he bowled past. "Wait a second, Sam. You can come with me in my car."

Sam nodded. He snapped his fingers at the swaying doctor caught in his shadow. "Hey George, follow me."

Out in the lot, Wervers had a blue Packard sedan. It looked like an automobile version of himself—rusted on the edges, and faded to silver by years of weather—but it started up eagerly once they all got in. The old man pulled at the wheel and turned them around the hurrying crowd, down the road between stage buildings and the track. "Sam, what do you make of what happened?" he asked. "I can't figure out why those were real bombs…We're lucky we weren't all blown sky high."

With a shrug that could have bent a trestle, Sam grunted, "Don't know."

"Well…I think we better keep an eye on things. It's up to me to get this movie made and I don't want Nazis or whoever sabotaging us like that again." He waved at the gate man and they drove out of the studio onto the two-lane road.

After a pause, drifting on the edge of the wildflower shoulder, Wervers continued, "Do you suppose it's possible that Nazis might have got on our set and switched the dummy bombs with real ones? I'd hate to think it was an inside job."

Sam kept quiet.

"If they really are using our movie for their war, forget it. I couldn't be a part of that."

The Packard bucked over some potholes, slowed, turned to follow a small side road that made a run for the ocean. "We'll shoot down there." They shook across a rail line, into the iron colored flats that bordered the sea. Now the harbor was revealed and the city shimmered across the waves. "Those balloons floated this way yesterday," Wervers traced a crooked finger across the windshield slant. "Phewww!"

They hit another rut and George in the backseat thumped against the window. He slumped like a human cargo.

"Is your friend okay back there?" Wervers asked Sam.

"He's fine," Sam said. "He's tired."

"He's a doctor, right?" Wervers' eyes filled the rear view mirror. "Maybe he sat on one of his hypodermic needles?"

Sam glared at his director. Was the old man playing a game with him? What did he know?

"One time, on a film we did up in the canyon, we shot a cougar with one of those tranquilizers." Wervers was warming up to the story but he stopped his thought and his car at the sight of a soldier waving a gun at them. "Woah!"

Sam's fists clenched. George bumped against the front seat.

The soldier came over to Wervers who unrolled the window.

"What's your business here?"

"Hello there, soldier. Name's Wervers. I'm directing a movie. The rest of the crew is on the way. You need to see the permit? Papers?"

The soldier stared past Wervers and his face beamed like a lamp. "Hey! You're Sam Samsara, the wrestler. I've seen you in those serials too!"

Sam nodded at the man.

"You fellahs making your serial here today?"

"That's right," Wervers told him. "Soon as we get set up."

"Aww, I can't believe my luck! I thought I got stuck with boring guard duty and now look! Hey, can I watch you guys film?"

"Yes, of course. Maybe I can even put you in it somewhere."

"In a picture with Sam Samsara?" the soldier rubbed his eyes. "This is like a dream!" He slapped the car, "You go right ahead, Mr. Wervers. I'll do whatever I can to help out."

"Thank you, soldier. We'll park up there on the bank. The rest of the crew should be coming along shortly."

"Hot dog!"

Wervers saluted and restarted the car. They pulled ahead over gravel and dry ryegrass.

Chapter Seven:

THE 4 AGNEWS

She still had connections. Don Benny paid her to walk his dogs every day. She made a living that way. Later in the morning, she took his three greyhounds for a walk to the park. The straining end of the leash kept them from running away. Her dog Agnew tried to keep pace with them, but Don Benny's dogs were all retired racers. "Agnews!" she called, getting louder, "Agnews! Agnews! Stop!" Frances was still sore from the full moon effects.

Finally, all three of them halted instantly. The greyhounds turned their puppet-like heads to stare big black watery eyes at her.

"What's got into you Agnews?"

Her old Agnew panted to her side rustily.

"The park's not going anywhere..." She took a breath. "Just take it easy."

They started again and before long they were running again. Frances held the shrouds of the dog sail. The park appeared like a green island beyond the meridian.

Once they passed over the cement curb onto the cobblestones into the leafy shade of it, the three Agnews caught her by surprise with a quick rip that took the leash out of her hand. They bolted gone across the lawn. She couldn't hope to match their speed in her long skirt and this daylight. A hundred yards away she saw a rhododendron lash as they whipped into its cover.

"Ohhh Agnew..." she sat down on a bench. Agnew lay in the slatted shade underneath, panting. Agnew was a gift from Don Benny—when he found out Frances was still alive, and heard about her heroic rescue of Agnew from the candy store blaze, he gave her the dog. That was kind of him, but more than he could bear; he soon bought three more dogs to replace his old friend.

She rubbed her sore calves. "They're probably after a rabbit. I'm not going running after them right away." She slipped off her shoes and socks. The grass felt good and she remembered last night. Fast pieces of it flew at her like jagged glass—someplace she had been before—fragments of a dream—parts of a whole she couldn't piece together…Why did it always have to disappear when she woke?

She stood up and splashed into the cut grass. "Come on, Agnew. I guess we better go now."

There was a man running a kite with his daughter. They got it going into the air in blue swoops back and forth. Frances looked away at her shoes in her hand. It still hurt to think about her father…Don Benny got out of that burning room but not him… Don Benny told her all he left behind in there was fire and smoke.

"Agnews!" she called. The sky replied with the roaring pass of a Flying Wing on patrol. She held her ears and fumed at the sight of the plane, If they weren't always looking for war, maybe they wouldn't find one. She squinted her eyes at its silver knife shape, glinting with sun. It was quickly gone, leaving a charcoal trail in the cloudless sky. "Agnews!" she repeated.

The Agnews weren't in the undergrowth. The brush and flowers turned back into field on the other side. "Agnew, can you track them?" Frances asked her companion. She pointed her finger beyond. "Where'd they go, boy?"

Agnew crept gingerly through the last of the shrubs. He was camouflaged by a cover of burs, torn leaves and brambles. He'd been through a lot in the past year—seven years time for a dog— and the baleful look he gave Frances told her that in spades. She scratched him, "I know…"

A gust of wind came rushing across the new field like an ocean wave and with it came a faint cry of, "Help!"

"What's that?" In a moment, she heard the yell again.

Even Agnew creaked to his four feet.

More breeze poured off the crown of maple trees towards them, along with the loosened gauze of milkweed pollen that made her sneeze. It was a long minute running over the field to the tall stand of trees. "Look!" Frances yelled back to Agnew.

The Agnews were bunched at a trunk, staring up into the leaves at the thing they had treed. The leash was wrapped around them so tightly it trapped them together, making the Agnews resemble one dog with three heads. They snapped and wheezed at whatever was up there in the leaves.

"Help!" the voice piped down. "Get it away from me, Frances. Please!"

She thought she knew that wretched voice, but he was well hidden in the leaves.

"What it that thing!? Did you bring it from Mars?"

"Is that you, Tiny?"

"Yes it's me! Listen, Frances. I'm sorry I took a shot at your dad. We got a code, you know. Nobody deserts!"

"My father? What are you talking about?"

The three Agnews were joined by her old Agnew who huffed his paws up against the trunk and snapped at the little foot positioned on a limb.

"Aiieee!" Tiny shrieked. "Call your monsters back!"

She almost told him they were only dogs, but she paused instead. "First tell me what you know."

"Okay, okay, I'll talk! What choice do I have? I'll give with it." He sighed, "There was no sign of your father in the crater. Still, I had to know if he was still alive. A guy like that knows too much…It took me a long time to find him, but I did. I'm sorry to say this, Frances. It's the business we're in. He turned the cops on to us when he found a new supply. The doc traded us for a connection straight from the source then he thought he'd drop out of sight. Savvy?"

"No."

"I finally found him and I plugged him. But I didn't plan on him being from outer space…A Martian stool pigeon."

She wanted to say something about that, but she didn't dare. What was her father's plan?

"Not til I saw that green blood spilled out of him did I know. I put the pieces together." Tiny's shift in the tree caused the leaves to rustle and branches clack. The dogs strained below. "When I saw that green blood, I panicked. I didn't know what I was up against. Now I do. I know you Martians have got rockets and monsters and advanced technology and robot armies. Look, can't we make a truce? Can we forget it all? Can you get back in your rocket and go back to Mars? I don't want to start an interplanetary war."

Frances listened without saying a word.

His voice floated another sigh down from the tree, "I don't know if I killed him or not. I doubt it. I didn't stick around long enough to find out. There…That's it…If you want to shoot me with a ray-gun and feed me to your monsters, go ahead. But I promise—if you let me go, I promise you—he's off the hit list. From now on we don't know him."

Frances paused again while she thought over the possibility. Her father bleeding green? That couldn't be…Then he must be okay, somewhere in the city. The dogs whined again. She crept closer and took the leash. "Alright, Tiny. It's a deal. I'll take the monsters back. Give me a minute or two to get away, then you can come down."

"Thanks, Frances…"

She untangled and tugged the Agnews, "Let's go," and they followed along in the deep swerving weeds, retracing the path they had sawed getting there.

Chapter Eight:

UNDER A BLACK UMBRELLA

George watched the world from under a black umbrella. Its broken spokes stuck out and the wind blew the ripped waterproof cloth like petals. It was raining but Wervers was determined to keep the film rolling, setting up the next shot as soon as one was done.

George had trouble with the frantic pace. After a while, he looked away from them, over the edge of the dock to see weeds and kelp floating in the deep green water. A patch of small fish ebbed among the piers. Rain drilled holes on the surface.

Sam was trying to fit, sitting in a low rowboat tied to the dock getting wet. The camera was close to him, framing him against the vast pour of the sea. It was a cheat shot, to make him look like he had rowed a mile from shore.

"Action!" Wervers cried.

Carefully, Sam stood up. He was holding a torpedo across his arms. He slowly turned with it and pointed the silver prop towards a target. He pressed a button near his hand.

All that was supposed to happen…

Then Sam lost his balance as the propeller end of the torpedo whirled alive. It bucked from him like a swordfish trying to escape capture. The sharp blades bit Sam and he dropped the torpedo overboard as he clamped his hand over his wound.

"Cut!" Wervers choked.

In the doomed quiet that followed, rain popped on the dock around the film crew. They all watched the torpedo leaving its traveling wake of bubbles out to sea. Sam stood in the middle of the small rowboat while a trickle of blood cut down his white Imperial uniform.

"Ohhhh boooyyy…" drawled Wervers. Everyone else realized where the torpedo was going too…The collective sigh sounded like summer thunder five miles away.

The lightship was a sitting duck at the mouth of the harbor. For over twenty years the *Harry S. Keeler* had been anchored there, blinking its light in the dark and sounding a foghorn when there was nothing to see.

Wervers cleared his throat. "I don't suppose there's any way to bring it back?"

Nobody could answer.

"Or press self-destruct?"

The torpedo was out of sight into the gentle waves. The *Harry S. Keeler* was celebrating its last moments of floatation.

"I guess we better get it on film anyway…" Wervers decided. "We can sell it to the newsreels if we're lucky."

After twenty seconds of falling rain, there was an explosion. It threw a spray of water high above the flames of the burst-open vessel. It didn't have time for a last whistle, or a S.O.S. It rolled over and sank quickly, leaving a swarm of burning wreckage and an ugly cloud of black, lurking smoke in the background.

In the foreground, Sam got out of the rowboat unsteadily. He was comical as a clown stepping over the side of a bathtub, except for the blood that ran off his elbow. "George," he said. "I lost a finger."

Chapter Nine:

IN ITS MOON NET

Night fell on the city early. With the lightship out of the way the harbor let a blanket of thick fog pile in. It came steadily over the waves, up stone shored beaches, rolled into the leaning red armed madrona hills, then crawled down and followed the roads leading to town. Cars stopped on the street. Their amber lamps were no use. Something with a life of its own had invaded.

So it was a ghostly walk that Frances took to get to the Lucky Note. The fog was thick enough she could lift her feet off the ground and float for a moment. The air was thick enough to swim in. She could wave her arms like a windmill and make snow-angel shapes follow in her wake. Everything was captured in its moon net. Shapes loomed and gloomed and vanished, paging in and out of the white. She heard a trolley that wasn't there. It could have been a mile away, only the sound carried to her. Other sounds, all kinds of sounds, echoed and wandered, became memories that caught and couldn't get out. The whole haunted town had been absorbed and embalmed by a hungry creature sent from the Sargasso, the Sea of Lost Ships.

Whatever dangers of whirlpools, shark dead-ends, or broken rocks that might have stopped others, Frances made it through to the fragile melody of a trumpet. It came from an orange window, a pumpkin eye cut glowing in the dark. A Cornelius Barter ballad reeled out like a blind flower seller, feeling from curb to corner. He was in there spinning and she was pulled to the door of the Lucky Note.

She had not been gone for more than ten seconds when loose chips of brick shook on the road. A cobblestone rat fled behind a garbage can and soon a noise transformed into the sight of Sam Samsara's monsooning car. It submarined to a halt in the alley. Slain fog streaked and beaded off its silver aerodynamic hull. When it shut down there was a groan of engine death, silence,

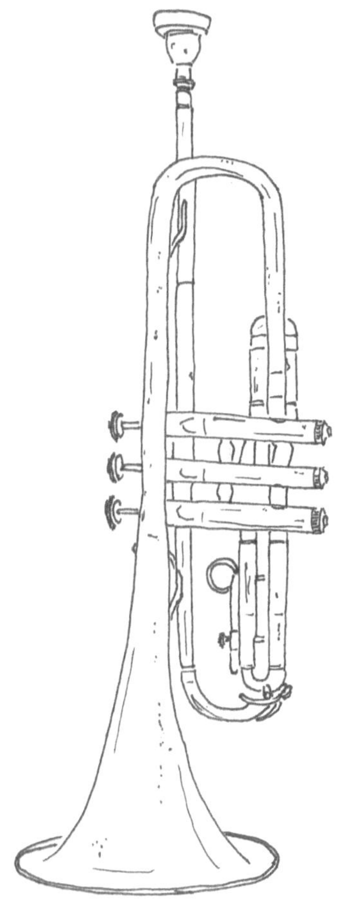

a blind flower seller

then a deep breath later, the sound from the Lucky Note turned up again. Cornelius Barter was singing, "Oh you crazy moon, you broke my heart."

Sam left the car, carried by the swirls of roiling cloud. George watched him go, propelled and buoyed gently to the club. The door opened, a blast of jazz, then closed and George was left alone.

The open cab bristled with the atmosphere. Fog sparked on his face like some watery form of electricity. George was finally coming out of a long day's dream and he needed a minute to gather himself. He lifted an arm, poked the radio button, focused on the little green glow of the dial.

"—broadcasting to all the ships at sea and our armed forces everywhere. Folks, before I sign off on our Dos Pedros program this evening, may I remind you of this: The used fats that you're saving up, while it's swell that you are saving them, but remember they won't do anybody a speck of good as long as you keep them in your icebox. Please turn them in. As soon as you have a can that's full. Not in a glass container please. Any tin can will do. You'll be paid in cash and receive two red points for each pound of used fats that you turn in. Thank you. And goodnight!" An orchestra swelled up into the mariachi theme song. George turned the radio off. The first clear thought he had all day bloomed in his head. A picture of a can with Green 17. He had to go out and get some.

Chapter 10:

THE MARTIAN CONSPIRACY

Where the wind takes things can be a mystery. There are invisible pockets sewn in the sky, clouds disguise dragons, or, on this foggy night, a white balloon with a bomb beneath…It had escaped the fate of the other explosions when it hit an updraft and soared above the ocean a thousand feet. The wind kept it there frozen in place until nightfall. As the air cooled, with help from the dark swivel of the planet, the ocean fog and the clouds, it quietly rejoined the panic where radio waves bounced desperate signals into the ether, a hundred terror stories per hour.

Tiny's Garage was open late. Amid the hammering, a frantic radio kept the little man company. The big swinging door was open on the night and let out a bright yellow-white Titanic light. The oily cement room was filled with a shiny assembly line of red Shriner cars. Tiny was halfway along the row of them, banging a crumpled fender with a wooden hammer.

In a way, what happened was a lucky break for Tiny—that terrible bombing of the city coincided with the Memorial Day parade. The puffs of burning buildings caused the Shriners to blow their practiced figure-8 thrills. It wasn't only the Shriners going out of control—the whole city went haywire and needed repair. Tiny should have counted his blessings for this sudden appearance of twenty damaged miniature cars. They carried a hundred dollars apiece. What a windfall.

But Tiny was living in fear. He had the radio going full blast so he could be sure to hear the latest news while he battered and bashed at the cars. Since seeing the doc's green blood and then his daughter with her strange hunting creatures, Tiny was waiting for the end of America as we know it. Any second it was going to happen—Tiny had seen the Martian Conspiracy!

Finally, when he couldn't take it anymore, he set his hammer on beveled chrome and hurried over to the telephone that held down a stack of paperwork. He dialed the spindle and drummed his fingers impatiently.

"This is Arlo Wilbur speaking. You're on the air."

"Listen, Arlo. You got it all wrong!"

"Is that so?"

"Yeahhh," Tiny sneered. He cocked his head towards the radio blaring among the cars. He heard his own voice broadcasting a five second delay. "Listen, Arlo. You got it all wrong!" He liked the sound of it.

"Sir—Sir, you'll have to turn down your radio," Arlo said in the receiver.

"Yeahhh," Tiny's hiss squealed out of the speaker.

"Okay, okay," Tiny barked at the telephone and he left it for a moment.

"Sir—Sir, you'll have to turn down your radio."

"I know! I know!" Tiny screeched as he slapped at the wooden face of the Philco, turned and raced back to the telephone. "There!" he growled and panted, "Now listen up, Arlo. I know who's behind these bombs and it ain't who you think."

"Really sir?"

"Yeahhh."

"Even though the Nazis have publicly taken credit for—"

"Enough of the Nazis already!"

"Sir, this isn't the time or place for hysterics. We need to—"

"Listen, Arlo. We're up against an enemy that ain't even human!" Tiny raged, "I've seen them! They're from Mars!"

Suddenly the telephone got cold; it was like holding a curl of ice to his ear.

"It's Martians that are doing it," he muttered. "Did you hear me, Arlo? Martians…" he repeated. "We have to figure out how to stop them."

Arlo Wilbur was gone. The phone had lost him overboard.

"Hey!" Tiny jiggled the cradle. The dial tone hummed in his ear. "Agghh!" He threw the phone down on the sliding papers and ran back to the radio. Arlo Wilbur was lecturing sternly, "—

got to maintain our faculties and reason in what will surely be a very trying time for our great nation. We must continue nobly and settle for nothing less than victory. I hope this next caller—"

Tiny snapped at the switch. He grabbed his wooden hammer and swung it in his clenched fist high above the radio. Only a blur of motion in the doorway stopped him from striking down.

Glowing in the swirling gloam of fog stood a ghost holding a candle. Actually, it was George, holding a fifty cent flame, with a can of cactus juice in his coat pocket, but when Tiny beheld that vision he dropped the hammer. It hit him on the head and clattered to the floor.

"Oohoww!" Tiny shrieked. He rubbed the sore knot on his forehead. When he took his hands from his face, the doc had blown.

Chapter 11:

WOLF O'CLOCK

Her change was occurring a lot faster than she could control. At first she thought she could shave her wrists and hands and that would hide it for a while more, but by the time she got to the bathroom at the back of the Lucky Note, the full moon was taking its fearsome effects. Frances just had time to slam the door and scream into her muffling paw.

Cornelius Barter bopped his buzzing soundtrack to the transformation as she grabbed the wall and howled. Powerful arms swung around and gripped the porcelain sink. It was so easy to tear it out of the tiles and pile it at the door.

Water broke across the room in jet sprays, flicking diamonds on the fur grown all over her. There wasn't much left of Frances in the creature she became. Some white stocking. Her eyes were closed when she was done; she seemed to purr with the sound from the other room. Yellow eyes snapped open.

The door was being shoved. The music was pushing in loud around scrabbling hands and nightclub yells. The bathroom was a mess of debris and waterfalls.

Frances bounded to the window, going out in a leap, luffing the curtains, gone. Mid-air she writhed against the full moon spotlight pinning her like a moth on its backdrop, before the fog spirited her down.

She was falling at a world that already had another life going, that didn't know anything about her arriving.

A white half candle flickered on the dashboard in front of George. He had carefully tabbed open the can of cactus juice and was drawing it towards his mouth, really looking forward to it, when something like a loosened turning dam turbine slammed into the long engine cowling. The crushing kerash knocked George down onto the floorboards.

Frances popped up beside the car spectrally, an outraged phantom that shook the fog. She snarled and snapped in a circle. The only thing directly near was a telephone pole that she hit with enough force from her claws to slice into it like butter.

George cowered down near the foot pedals. He held his breath in and didn't move again until he was absolutely sure that the falling rocket—or was it raining lions?—must have calmed. Only then did he pull his crumpled legs and arms out from him, uncurling himself like a night flower, to push up onto the seat. The can of cactus juice clacked empty to his feet. The contents were all over him again. He smiled wide enough for three photographs…It was the second time Green 17 had spilled on him and saved his life.

Chapter 12:

George pushed through the crowded Lucky Note. It resembled a subway terminal at rush hour some holiday night, people standing in the rumble and haze. The Cornelius Barter Quintet was done and standing around a pillar talking with Sam Samsara—the grin spread on his face looked like a carved and painted mask. Smoke from cigarettes made a fog. Everyone was talking and Symphony Sid boomed platters from big speakers. The air was a lot like outside, George realized, on his maze way over to Sam. He supposed there was fog was in here too, poured in through the door and windows.

Sam was handing Cornelius an ornate oblong wooden box. Japanese characters skirled around its five sides. George hated to interrupt him to tell him about the car, but it turned out he wouldn't have to.

"Excuse me," Sam added quickly, "Can you please accept this award from our government." The hinged wooden box, opened to show a gold sun medal with red and white ribbon attached.

Cornelius put his hand on his head, "Wow…" he said.

All at once, the music stopped and a microphone asked, "Will the owner of the silver land yacht get it out of the alley. Or else it will be towed… By a couple of elephants if that's what it takes…" The music cut back in.

Sam bowed, flustered, passed the musician the gift and eased away. George followed in the path Sam broke to the exit.

The announcer had the misfortune to stop the music a last time, "If you got a greyhound bus for a car, I've got news for you—it's breaking the law to park in an alley." That was all he managed before Sam reached a straight arm over the blue counter and chopped him. The monitor jolted just enough to start running the jazz again. Like a movie, everything continued as before.

George took a passing look at the man sinking with the microphone slowly below the counter. He sighed. There wasn't much a doctor could do.

The door shoved aside to let Sam out into a midnight of fog.

George caught up with Sam, stopped at the crunched hull of his car.

"Hmmm…" Sam grunted. He ran his fingers over the crushed metal topography. He regarded the skin of it as keenly as a detective, then, reaching under the damaged, bolted panel, he pushed the crumpled shape of it smooth. He cleared his throat in a satisfied manner and said, "Okay, George. Let's go."

The moon net had trapped more sounds since they were inside the club. Now, amid the echoes of roaming souls with radios and wind sounding slightly out of tune, George felt a howl creep up his spine. He wished he could have believed it was only the steam whistle on a lost train, but he knew there was something else out there.

Sam got the monster engine started and George was glad that roar was all he could hear. He folded his hands on his green splattered suit. At least that was funny, he thought.

"That…" Sam pointed at the Lucky Note, "was great!" Then he sent the wheels spinning. Each cobblestone drummed faster underneath as they picked up speed. "Cornelius Barter!" Sam yelled into the slipstream. "Hey, George!" he yanked the wheel hard to get them onto the road.

Good thing the road's empty, George reflected. Sometimes their way wasn't so lucky and something would get pulverized. George would try to think of it as the law of nature, survival of the fittest. Right now the law of the road favored them; they were the biggest thing; a battleship on cement.

"Hey, George! Start the record player!"

Below the space where the radio was constantly replaced, George pressed a button. The mahogany panel slipped downwards, cupping a turntable with a record already circling.

"Yeah!" Sam bellowed.

The needle dropped into the scratched groove.

An old Side-B song from years before materialized, when Cornelius Barter and his quartet recorded in a basement near the ocean…Beautiful and sad, drums brushing, a muted trumpet, a bass bowed and a celeste…They drove the night around the car.

A few minutes later the fog was gone. The giant car broke out of its wall to emerge magically, flying on wet moonlit sand. The beach ran for miles.

The jukebox dropped down another jazz record ring. Sam mashed his shoe into the pedal and red sparks shot into the clear, salt air.

For this feeling, shooting on a perfect arrow of high speed with angel music pulling them beyond, for finding heaven while you're still alive, that's why they were going. Everyday-people were long asleep by now, while Sam and George were burning up like a meteor.

Green dials on the dashboard, fiery glows from the stacks cut in the cowl ahead, the car could have roared on and turned around to go back and forth until dawn…Or until the gasoline ran out…In any case, it didn't matter because there were little shipwrecked fires to avoid.

Sam grunted, "What the—?!" The car swerved a bonfire and the left wheel hit smack into fireworks. Another near miss and they were sliding sideways for a second, then Sam had them going okay—a couple seconds of relief—except they didn't see the snapped ribs of the washed ashore *Harry S. Keeler.*

It seemed like they ran into a big white billboard.

George was lying on his side. He could hear the slowly beating heart of the surf. Wake up, he made himself move. He dragged himself out of the flipped over car. He dug his fingers deeply into the sand to pull himself further away, fearing at any moment it might explode…Until slow motion turned into him being able to stand and stumble.

"George!"

Vision shuffled like playing cards and settled on a single picture in three shades of dreamy color—blue and black and white.

George heard a name being called. After it repeated a while he realized it was his name.

"Ahh…" he replied.

"George!" Sam waded into view.

"Look…"

The car looked like a rocket smashed on another planet. It was skidded into a mound of pushed sand.

The merry-go-round slowed. George stopped walking. There were burning remains all around them.

Sam Samsara stood there wide as a drive-in movie screen on the beach, his gray suit reflecting all the little bonfires. He moved and they moved like fireflies against the black sky.

"You okay, George?"

"Sure. Sure, Frances," he grinned, "I could do this in my sleep."

Before Sam could respond, another voice called, "Hey! Can you give me a hand?!"

George and Sam looked around themselves.

"Down here, fellahs!"

There was a man's face looking up at them. Bits of broken glass twinkled. "I'd sure like to get a hand out of this sand, Mr. Samsara."

Sam bent down. "Oh, it's you…" He recognized the soldier from the morning's shoot.

"Yeah…I was out on the lightship when it blew. Guess I washed up here. Lucky thing the gulls didn't see me buried like this, huh?" he laughed a wheeze.

Sam brushed the sand from around him and dug his hands in to find shoulders. The head rolled against his shoveling hands. Sam let out a scream.

The head screamed too. Staring straight up into the stars, "Where's the rest of me?!" it yowled.

Sam shot a terrified look at George.

George sat down. "Shhh." He laid a hand on the head. "I'm a doctor."

The head's eyes rolled at George. "Yeah? So—so—tell me

then…How bad is it?"

George scooped the soldier's head gently between his hands and lifted.

Chapter 13:

SOME DREAM CONTRAPTION

George made room in his doctor's kit bag for the soldier's head.

"Don't close it all the way!" he pleaded, so George left the bag open.

"Everything will be fine," George reassured him. Sam was the quiet one, green with moonlight, staggering along like an oak tree on a moving treadmill.

George led them away from the shore towards a soft glow settled in over the saw grass and sandy hill. "Everything will be fine," George repeated.

By some fortune they found a violet path and tracked up that sand. At the top of the rise, they were looking down on other fires, not dots of wreckage, but campfires and candle lanterns. The lights were strung around a big shrouding tent and the gloomy dinosaur shapes of amusement rides.

"It's a circus." George tipped the doctor bag so the soldier could see it.

"Hey!" the soldier brightened. "I saw these guys setting up this morning before I left for work." He chirped, "We're not far from my house. 412 Maple."

Sam had his eye on the animals tied in the tent shadows. "I bet those elephants could pull the car back to the road."

They followed the path down. Sand slid in front of them in sugary gasps.

Soon the soldier asked, "Do you suppose you could drop me off at home? I'm not sure yet what I'm going to tell my wife…But I think I should be there."

George nodded down at him, "We'll get you there. Let's talk to these circus people first."

They went towards the nearest burning campfire, trampling the last of the beach grass as the ground leveled into shadow.

Weird scraps of burning paper took to the air, whirled and jerked into nothingness.

Someone saw them arriving and stood up.

George waved his arm that wasn't holding the soldier steadily. "Hello!" he called and stopped.

Sam stopped walking right next to him. "We had a crash on the beach," he graveled. "Could you spare a couple elephants?"

After a dead dropped silence, "Hah!" was drilled back at them.

George looked at Sam.

"Sammmmsara!" someone at the fireside yelled.

George and Sam froze in criminal poses.

"Where have you been?" Wervers yelled, "Join us over here! Wait til you hear what happened."

While he spoke, George and Sam got closer. They were a little amazed to find Wervers where they were.

Wervers made a raspberry sound, "Our movie's over. The studio brass showed up and shut it down. They didn't like the dailies we shot. The balloon bombs and the sinking lightship were a little too *realistic* for them." Wervers laughed.

George and Sam walked into the floodlight with the moths.

Wervers smiled an ivory set of teeth, "So they took us off the film, boys. It wasn't going the right way. But guess what? They gave me the choice of two movies to accept instead... *The Crybaby Gang Meets The Gong*, or *Frankenstein's Hand*."

George and Sam were caught in the amber circle of firelight.

"It's probably no surprise to you though," Wervers continued, "No way am I going to work with that Crybaby Johnson, or his rotten gang ever again." He made a sour face. "I had no choice but to take the monster movie." He paused dramatically, "Of course, I thought of you first. You'd be perfect for the monster, Mr. Samsara."

Sam shrugged. Movies were all the same to him. He'd been every other shade of villain. He didn't mind being Frankenstein too.

"That's great!" Wervers explained, "That's the reason I came here, to get help. That's Fled Magyar over there. He's going to do the special effects. He makes puppets and he can do the make-up." He laughed, "Believe it or not, I'm looking forward to doing this. It's got a great beginning." Wervers kept the story going, kept them hypnotized reading from the script, building and building the movie into some dream contraption, reminding them that tomorrow was the start of *Frankenstein's Hand*, and before they knew it, the sky was rolling over to dawn, tomorrow was today.

Chapter 14:

THE UNFILMED BEGINNING

Wind brushes across the field in a ripple effect pouring up to the road. Next to the worn-out gray tar a fence post with a silver, dented mailbox. The red flag is up. A car engine can be heard approaching, wheels stop and the driver reaches out to grab the mailbox door. The latch snaps open and a sudden huge green hand springs, reaching out of the dark:

FRANKENSTEIN'S HAND

Chapter 15:

THE RAINY MOVIE

Frances stared at her reflection on the ice wall. Behind the thick frozen window, a couple salmon moved like rocking chairs in the current. Smaller fish hurried past, upstream or downstream, she didn't know. This was a good place for her to end up, she thought, after everything she had done. Some moonlight was getting on the ice and even though the electric effect of it may only be enough to run a train set, it was powerful enough to keep her a werewolf.

She remembered everything…Tying real explosives onto the white balloons…Arming and setting a timer on a torpedo… Howling in the fog last night…She covered ground on all fours and made it to the top of Jupiter Hill, where the Mayan-looking windmills powered the city.

The newspapers and radios were already chattering about how it happened—using cover of the fog, a skilled team of Nazi saboteurs had struck! Even far underground she could feel the rumble.

Would they ever know it was her? Far above Frances, the doomed windmills tilted against each other, broken shells of them were scattered around. She had torn down power lines and used them to rope all the sails together and bring the whole fleet of windmills crashing into each other. No wonder her arms were sore. After that and the fall, she could barely move at all.

So this is why her father kept her inside all those years of full moon nights…It wasn't so much a dangerous world…It was a dangerous *her.* She relived watching her destruction sparking against the black sky, swoop like fireworks, then the explosion and the ground gave way. She fell into an old mine or well. Far below, she was in a room-sized cavern. It would be black if not for the flickering moonlight coming from the ice.

She leaned a wolf's arm against the frozen projection. The ice traveling down her arm took its time, freezing her and transform-

ing her into a statue. She took on the whole city and she couldn't
be stopped, only by herself. Maybe it was best for her to stay
entombed…She was too tired to fight anyway. In front of her,
the ice steamed with her breath. Her breathing slowed from one
minute to the next. There wasn't much to do but lean on the blue
window and watch the rainy movie of the swimming fish.

Chapter16:

421 MAPLE

In the doctor's black bag, the soldier's head had gone off, quiet and marble gray. The morning sun was painting Monets over the canvas big top tent.

"Do you remember where he said he lived?" George asked Sam in a sigh.

"Yes. 421 Maple." Sam touched his forehead, "Remember? Photographic memory."

George clasped the doctor's kit shut. "We better take him home."

Sam thought about it for a moment, then he agreed.

Wervers got the circus to loan them some transportation so they could hurry back, get their car and drive to the studio.

After a last cup of green tea, they were freed into a jitney cart pulled by a zebra, trotting out of the circus into the other world.

The sky was mad with Flying Wings burning contrails. For a while the thick green canopy of cedars and maples hid the swarm from view and George was glad. A crazy war was starting and there was no way to stop it. He thought about the doctors in the cities that would be bombed. They won't get any sleep. Their distant streets will be filled with terror.

Sam interrupted him, "I never drove one of these!" His face was gleeful. He held the ringing bell reins like an antique, staring at the zebra's amazing stripes, the look of a star struck moon man crowning him. There was no shouting motor or crushing speed velocity; the clapping hooves on the road were all they needed to hup along.

"There's Maple," George pointed at the green street sign pressed in a lilac tree. The zebra responded to Sam and they turned the corner. Sedans were parked under the awning of leaves. Yards with mowed lawns led to big houses. The sound of the jitney arriving on the quiet street brought faces to windows to see a zebra rattling bells. Little did they know how it hid a wonder as apocalyptic as some folklore portent; the two men were arriving with a severed head.

George looked nervously back into the bag. "What are we going to say? He never told us what we were supposed to tell his wife."

Sam shrugged.

They shook to the next block. A dog barked along a slatted fence.

"421," Sam said. There on their right was the house. They clip-clopped to the grassy edge of the curb and Sam pulled the reins to a stop.

The zebra reached out for a mouthful of dandelions.

Sam looked at George. "Let's go."

"Okay…" George got out and stood next to the short white fence. Rose petals patterned across the yard on the other side, scattered by the windblown night before. George read the name on the little swinging gate, "Parrot Residence." It was painted on a flat piece of driftwood. George hefted the zipped bag in his hand. "Okay," he sighed.

Sam pushed the gate open and led the way up the stone path. His shadow threw down a cloud.

"What should we say?" George hissed, hurrying behind him.

"We'll find out what happens."

Sam's big hand tightened into a rumpled fist and he knocked on the door.

A woman with a baby in her arms opened the door. She stood there surprised. "You're—!" she stammered. She looked into her yard for cameras. She noticed the strange zebra contraption eating her flower bed. "Is this one of those sweepstakes?"

Sam shook his head regretfully, "No."

"Sam Samsara!" she laughed and stepped aside. "You can come in, I'm just making tea. Can you stay?"

"Yes please." The giant had to duck under the eaves a bit. George followed quietly, carrying that bag with her husband…

What was left of him. "George is my friend," Sam told her.

"Hi," she smiled, "Edith," and she took them by the photographs in the hallway to the kitchen. The baby stared over her shoulder at them. A teapot was steaming. "I wish Archie was here! He'll never believe Sam Samsara was here! We used to see you every Monday when you were a sumo wrestler. Of course everyone did. Now we see you in the movies and magazines. What a world, huh?" she laughed. "Please take a seat." A table was prepared with a candle and half a bowl of oatmeal.

Sam sat down and rested his hand on the windowsill and asked, "Can I turn on the radio?"

"Yes, of course, Mr. Samsara."

He did so, deftly spinning the dial to his station and landing on it.

George was relieved when it was Cornelius Barter. It would have been a nightmare if Sam smashed her radio right away. Hopefully the music would last a while.

Edith opened a cupboard over the sink and took down three cups.

George startled Sam as he plopped the black bag onto the tabletop.

"Excuse me," Sam remembered, "We have news about your husband."

"Archie?"

"Is he in the army?"

"Yes…Oh no! Did something happen to him?" She hugged the baby tight enough to make his arms windmill. "What happened?" Then she whirled around so she wouldn't see them tell, busied herself pouring hot water into three cups.

George glanced at Sam, wishing he had a script, something really heroic he could say, like in the movies.

"Ms. Parrot—"

"Edith," she urged Sam.

"Your husband had to guard the circus last night, that's why he didn't show up yet. He wanted you to know he'd be late."

"Oh—" she let a laugh go. "What a relief. I thought—" She turned to hide her face again.

George gasped as he saw the kit bag inch forwards. He clapped his hands on it. The baby was watching over Edith's shoulder. George opened the bag some and said, "Shhhh…" into it.

Sam whispered in a croak, "Is he alive again?"

"He must have been sleeping, I guess."

Edith carried two cups over for them, holding her baby pressed to her. She was still a little rattled.

"He—" Sam tried, starting a new story for her.

The soldier spoke up, "It's okay. You can tell her."

"What's that?" she asked George with growing alarm.

The hidden voice called to her, "I'm in here, darling."

"Uhh…" George stood up with the bag held closed against him.

"Is that my husband's voice?" she pointed.

"No!" George yelped.

Then Edith's confusion abruptly managed another nervous laugh, "This is one of those sweepstakes, isn't it? Is there a telephone in there?" She reached for the bag.

George grappled Sam's arm. Cornelius Barter was fading out. "Oh no…" He reached and tried to turn off the radio, quickly, before it got crunched. To his horror, the head rolled out of the bag with a plop.

Edith screamed.

The song ended. George knocked the radio off the windowsill into the oatmeal.

Edith screamed again. The baby was crying.

The soldier stared up at the woman and child. "Who are you?"

She bit her hand in terror. "What is that?!" Her screeching son crabbed in her arms.

"She's not my wife," the soldier's eyes rolled gruesomely at Sam and George.

As the radio clucked the news bulletin in a grim monotone, Sam flinched and flashed a block fist onto it, crushing it all into pulp and oatmeal.

George jumped, the head teetered, Edith screamed again.

"Sam, I think we better leave."

"Yeahh," the big man stood, "Sorry for this, Ms. Parrot. We found him on the beach like this. He asked to be brought here."

"Actually," George tried to soothe her, "I think we got the wrong address."

"Thanks for the tea though," Sam bowed to the woman, "I apologize for your radio. I'll have a new one delivered."

She was holding her baby and staring in shock at the table— the shattered bowl and radio, the candle knocked down, rolled against a cup of spilled green tea with a man's head planted in the middle.

Sam batted the head into George's bag and they left the kitchen in a sprint, down the hall, and they bashed out the door.

"That went well, didn't it?" George panted, but Sam was approaching the crowd of boys ganged around the jitney. He cracked his knuckles and they turned around.

"Samsara…" It was Crybaby Johnson. "What are you doing riding this rig? You doing a circus picture?"

"No."

"It looks like you'll be in our next movie."

Sam pushed through them.

"We started production today, in a haunted house," Crybaby Johnson continued.

In two strides Sam got back up into the creaking jitney. George sat next to him.

"We'll be seeing you, Sam," Crybaby Johnson tried to make words sound rough as sand dollars.

Sam clicked and flicked the reins across the zebra's back.

"Want me to count the stripes and make sure they didn't take any?" George asked.

The Crybaby Gang stood in the garden watching them go, grown no taller than the lilies and the half eaten weeds.

"You brought me to the wrong house!" the soldier gasped inside the open bag.

"I don't understand," Sam murmured. "I thought I had photographic memory. I'm very sorry."

"That's alright, Mr. Samsara. Heck, after *that* scene my wife will be a breeze."

"412 Maple," George looked ahead. "That sounds right to me."

"Yeah," the soldier agreed. "412 Maple is where I live. Hold me up, let me see."

George obeyed. "Just don't fall out again."

"Hey—a zebra!"

"There's 412," Sam said. "That's the place, correct?"

"Home sweet home."

"Alright, let's do this right this time," Sam said as he pulled the zebra to a stop. He bounded out.

A spray of little birds flew out of the overhanging mimosa tree.

George got down and patted the zebra for luck. *Saturn Circus* was stamped on the white of a stripe.

"Don't worry fellahs, my wife isn't loony."

"I hope you're right," George replied. He kept the bag open to dapple in the light of the front yard, to the porch and the screen door that Sam opened.

After a rap on the wooden frame, they all waited listening. Sam rapped again and one last time. "She's not home," he decided.

"Look," the soldier piped. "I don't want to be any more trouble to you. There's a key over the door. Just let me inside and you can go."

George looked at Sam.

Sam shook his head. "No, we cannot risk another misfortune. We will all return later."

"Aw! You can put me on the mantle. I'll be fine there, Mr. Samsara. Honest."

"No!" Sam burred villainously and he looked like he was on the verge of snapping, Imperial flag unfurling in the background.

It would have been the perfect start to a movie.

305

Chapter 17:

REVENGE OF THE SHRINERS

The old men stood outside the drawn down garage door. They all wore the same peculiar uniform of wine red fezzes, blue suits, festooned with ribbons and ranks and heraldry. The Shriners had been there for fifteen minutes in the blue shade of Tiny's Garage. They knew he was in there—the mad sounds of hammering, the whoosh of an arc welder, Connie Francis' ululation echoing—Tiny was in there alright, like an oyster shut up tight with the industry sounds of creating its pearl.

"What's he doing to our cars?"

Four or five of the vanguard addressed each other before the shrill cacophony.

The elder with the most lean into his cane picked the weight of his arm from the mottled door. "Rennie!" he bleated.

The less silvered Rennie stepped forward eagerly with sun blasting gold on his black rimmed glasses.

"Rennie, I want you on stake-out in that phone booth over there."

The whole daffodil contingent turned to stare at the phone booth. It looked like it had tumbled onto the street corner off the top of one of the warehouses. The booth was a sorry sight—bent frame, cracked and shattered glass panes, the phone hanging to a twisting cord.

But Rennie saluted smartly.

"You can keep yourself busy with this phone list." The elder Shriner took a parchment from his coat pocket. "These are people you can hit up for contributions," he explained. "You know the routine. And..." he added, digging into another pocket, "Use this quarter for the calls." He dangled a coin that was sewn through with a loop of thread so it could be pulled out of the machine after each call. They all chuckled, making the dry rasp of forest leaves.

"Let's get back to the 249." He referred to the lodge by its familiar codename. While Rennie took up residence in the phone booth, the rest of the Shriners ambled, hobbled and steered chairs past the garage to the alley in between Tiny's and Shelton's Packaging.

Their parked squadron of miniature red motorcycles waited in rows. Some of them had sidecars for the less nimble. It took them a while to prepare helmets, goggles, get seated and start motors. They had done this for hundreds of parades, but time made them slower and slower.

Chapter 18:

THE WATER OPERATION

Sam Samsara was in a rowboat again. The oars were stowed and he leaned over. The small boat tipped dangerously as he stared past the glassy surface swerve. The high tide floated him over the sight of his car, sunk shoulders in the sand below. A flight of sticklebacks flecked across the shining silver submarined hull. It seemed a peaceful part of the sea. There were weeds and anemones already waving to it. It would belong to them in a few more tides.

With slow unreeling, Sam let an anchor line descend through the green. He had to scull an oar to catch the car's bumper on the second try. He pulled. It was tight. He let the line unloop around the oarlock to keep it caught while he rowed back to shore.

The boat hushed up onto the sand. Sam stepped out trailing the lasso. It cut a taut trail back to the ocean.

George had already drifted from the scene at the beach. He didn't feel like watching elephants pull a waterlogged car, he was busy wondering. It occurred to George that he hadn't slept for a long time…Had he? He felt warm in the glow of the climbing sun of another new day. Then he darkened with the breaking thought—what if he was sleeping right now? What if this was a dream? How would he know? This world seemed as real as a dream. These worries carried him away from Sam and the elephants and the water operation.

He left soft footprints in the sand like the Invisible Man fading from view across a thin white layer of London snow. By the time he passed around the rocky bend of the cove, he was a mile away. The city showed itself across the bay. Gray barrage balloons made buttons in the sky over the buildings. The war had started. He wandered on to the next beach holding the soldier's head in the bag. He stopped when he remembered and looked inside.

"You okay?" George asked.

"Sure."

George said casually, "What are you thinking about?"

The soldier didn't worry over words, "I'm thinking about what will happen when I'm back. Look what's left of me…How am I supposed to be when I get home? Mister, my mind is thinking a hundred miles an hour."

"I know," George said. His eyes were on the distance too. "Do you mind if we take a walk to that pier way over there?"

"No…Go ahead."

That was all they said for a while along the high tide chalk mark. Like a strange two-headed machine, steam powered by hundreds of thoughts, George followed the washed up flotsam, ribbon bits of weed, beautiful stones shining wetly in sand, shells, bird prints and odd remnants of man-made things.

Each time George looked up from his feet, the dock materialized closer and clearer as if it was building itself. It had the look of something that was built very swiftly. It leaned crooked angles, there were boards missing, light shone through its planks like a rickety piano keyboard.

"There's someone out there at the very end," the soldier said. His head was half out of the doctor's kit bag so he could see.

George nodded. He switched the bag to the other hand.

"Woahh!"

"Sorry. My hand's getting sore," George said. He was curious to see what the silhouette on that cartoon dock was doing. He wasn't expecting to know who it was, but he did.

It was Cornelius Barter playing his trumpet to the sea.

"Look at that," the soldier stared.

George was. Cornelius Barter was actually playing directly into the ocean. The bell of his trumpet dipped underwater. George didn't want to be a disturbance, so he stopped near the rocky shoreline.

The water was hopping around the horn. At first George thought the bubbles and chop were from the sound of trumpet air. But he soon realized there were hundreds of thrashing fish gathered around Cornelius. It reminded him of a summer a long time ago when he was out in the woods and he heard the ecstatic water slapping of those carps in the lagoon. The fish had gone lovestruck or something. Maybe Barter was playing in a particular key that caused such a reaction in that species of fish? George thought it was certainly a possibility and yawned. He looked for somewhere to lie down for just a minute; all this excitement and wonder made him tired.

Beyond the fish, the ballad reached into darker and deeper water…Into veils offshore where the cold current welled, a Japanese submarine drifted in riveted silence. Sailors crowded around the receiving monitors while a reel to reel live recording was made for Imperial Broadcasting Services. It would be pressed next week into long playing records labeled, *The Cornelius Barter Water Opera.*

Chapter 19:

STARFISH

George stared at a black and white photograph of Frances. He stirred in real terror, not knowing yet if this was a bad dream starting. Her picture was on a green can and the words above it said, *Have You Seen Me?*

George grabbed the can from Sam Samsara. He turned the can around trying to find something out. Cactus Juice. There was no news about Frances, but he tipped the can to read the fine print on the side. Water, Agave, Saguaro Puree from Concentrate, Sugar, High Fructose Corn Syrup, Citric Acid, Beta Carotene, Green 18. "Green 18?" George gulped.

"That's from their factory," Sam told him.

George lifted himself off the park bench.

There it was, filling air with deep throbbing of living machines and furnaces. Smokestacks roiled out green colored smoke.

"You got this can over there?"

"They gave it to me," Sam shrugged. "I'm a movie star. You should give some to the soldier. Maybe it will grow the rest of his body."

"Not funny, Mr. Samsara!" the head chimed.

George turned in the direction of the ocean. "Did you see—?" Cornelius Barter wasn't out there anymore. "What time is it?"

"Relax, George," Sam laughed. "The car's out of the water, those elephants were swell. Take a look." Sam took a couple steps back and motioned. The silver car, crumpled as sheets of abalone metal, was parked up on the grass off the road. Like a steamship boiler it hissed, like a sunken ship dragged ashore, it was covered with barnacles and weeping leafy camouflage.

"It still works…" George's floating words were as hollow as heron bones.

"Come along. Wervers wants us to meet him on Jupiter Hill."

"No, I can't. I have to find out about this can. This picture on it is my daughter." George held it out to Sam and the giant began to laugh.

"Your *daughter?*"

George looked at the can again, turning it quickly in his hand. *Have You Seen Me?* asked the bold letters above the picture of a shepherd dog.

"Your daughter," Sam repeated as if he had to remember that punchline later for the camera crew. He slapped George on the back with a weighty hand. "Let's go."

A hallucination, George decided—I saw the wolfish dog and I thought of her; it's all a trick of the subconscious mind…After all, he had been asleep, it was nothing more than the last melting imprint of a dream…Absently he put the can into his bag.

"Yiiii!!" the soldier yelped.

"Oh—sorry." George fumbled the cool green can from the face.

"Careful there, doctor. Don't ever forget I'm in here."

George put the can into his coat pocket, thinking who knows, it might stop another bullet. And what about, "Green 18?" he muttered, barely audible. What was Green 18? Was it an improved Green 17? Would he be able to run some experiments? Or was it up to fate for him to find out the difference?

Sam was halfway to his car when he turned to check on George who shrouded slowly after him. "My daughter," Sam husked.

Closer to the car, George could see light stripes of rust banding it like a tiger. The rattling engine wheezed out charcoaled smoke from cut holes and torn tin edges—it had a hard time in the sea.

Sam crawled into the big harpooned shark. There was a splashing sound. While George caught up, Sam bailed out handfuls of water.

When George opened the door on his side a small waterfall poured out onto his shoes.

"I still have not got all the ocean out," Sam apologized.

"I can see that," George answered. He put his bag down and

sat in the aquarium car. He stared at the starfish on the dashboard. They probably think it's low tide and all they have to do is
wait for the ocean to return.

313

Chapter 20:

THE SINISTER BACKDROP

When the road reached the top of Jupiter Hill, they were slowed by a hive of studio trucks and sedans, black and white police cars, military vehicles and finally Sam's car was brought to a stop by a yellow tape strung across the tar.

Sam grumbled and turned the rusted, protesting steering wheel towards a glade under a tree.

"What's going on up here?" George said. "This assembly can't be for *Frankenstein's Hand*, can it?"

"I don't think so," Sam answered. He killed the motor and a last spasm rippled from the engine, down the frame, and coughed out the exhaust. "Oh no…" Sam suddenly groaned. "It's that guy."

A tall white cowboy hat rode above a thicket of actors and crew. Bronson Griffith strode towards the silver car with a big smile prepared on his face. "You old son of a gun!" he lowed. "Sam Samsara!"

George closed his hands protectively over the bag and followed Sam's lead getting out of the car.

"You on this picture too?" the cowboy boomed. He dropped a fist through the air and caught Sam for a handshake.

George sogged along the long ocean scarred hood of the car. He stopped when he saw one of the rivets moving across the metal. When he realized it was a gray shelled hermit crab, he moved on around to Sam's side.

"It sure is something…" Bronson Griffith shook his head, cleaving a hand in the windmills direction. "Wait til you see, it'll take your breath away." He squinted his eyes seriously and confessed, "But I'll tell you what. I'll never forget what they did to us this day, Sam. And I'm here to tell the people, I'm coming back swinging." Then, as he pushed back the brim of his cowboy hat, a loud sneeze came from the bag George was holding.

"Whu—?" Bronson Griffith leaned to look in the gap of the bag, expecting to see a small dog, his features going from mild curiosity to a frightened mask he'd never shown on the silver screen. He squeaked, "Whu—?" again.

"Holy cow!" the soldier's head chattered back at him, "It's Bronson Griffith!"

George quickly snapped the bag and with a juggle of words hurried to explain, "That's a prop—a puppet! Funny, isn't it?" he grinned haphazardly.

Sam gave the cowboy a thud on the shoulder with his oar-sized hand. "Yes, we must be going. The set is that way?"

But the cowboy actor was still waxed and attached to that spot like a statue imitation.

"Excuse me, we will find it," Sam nodded, leading his companions away, slipping into the crowd carrying light stands, ladders and rolls of wire. Jupiter Hill had gone from hilltop home to windmills to a spilled out anthill. Sam and George were caught in the flow and carried on the crushed lawn past hedges to an amazing sight. Every windmill was strung together with thick white ropes going over every angle and blade up and down, lacing it like spider web.

The soldier in the bag sneezed again, but nobody noticed. Sam and George approached the swarming remains.

After another sneeze, the soldier head said, "You know, I think I'm getting a cold."

"This is the biggest budget I've ever seen," Sam confided, "It looks like an Alfred Spinster movie."

George was just amazed by the expert knots and surgical skill involved in tying the windmills. He almost felt like laughing.

"Sam Samsara."

It was Alfred Spinster.

"I should have known you'd be paying your respects up here," the director remarked into a quick rattle. "Yes, it's a terrible shame this thing had to happen. Still, here we are. So tell me Sam, you think you could make an appearance in my film while you're here?"

"Sure," Sam said. "I'm…"

"I'm glad you said that. In fact, I was hoping you would. I'm very happy with the result. Okay Sam, I've got a part for you. I want you to picture a little town beside the sea. You can see movement when the dawn hits. People start getting ready for work. They're out the door and either they catch a gondola or they walk. That's where you come in, Sam. That's where the camera finds you." Alfred Spinster stopped to take a stare through a kaleidoscope camera lens. "No, no, no!" he cried, "I'm not in focus!" While there was a scramble of crew, Sam felt a tap on his shoulder.

"Sam Samsara." Wervers was there. "I'm glad to see you. We're—"

"Hah!" Alfred Spinster spluttered. "I seem to have forgotten your name. Oh wait—I remember now. Wervers, right?

"Yes," Wervers nodded. "Good to see you again."

"I suppose you're cashing in on a picture up here too? Probably using some of my sets when I'm not looking? That's alright, I don't mind. It's all in the nature of the beast."

"Actually," Wervers broke in, "I've been waiting for Sam so we can get started."

"There you are, taking my actors too. I wonder what kind of slip-shod production you're up to this time. Monsters on the loose? Ghouls? Let me see, let me guess. This whole tapestry of wound-up windmills is only the backdrop to a more sinister, paranoid reality. The world is plunged into war and the only one who can stop it is this heroic Sam Samsara." Imperiously, Alfred Spinster leaned back on his heels to coast in the wind of his words.

Wervers cracked a smile. "I suppose you guessed it."

Chapter 21:

WHEREVER WORLD

Very slowly, with brushes, Fled Magyar applied the green make-up of Frankenstein's monster. Classical records played on the wooden player, one after another as time passed by.

George turned another page of an Edgar Allan Poe book. The bag sat on the plastic chair beside him. The soldier seemed to be sleeping away the long waiting.

"There we are," Fled said at last.

Sam was allowed to lumber out of his chair. His feet were already worn into thick soled boots that made him even taller. He took big, chopping steps away from the chair, one by one. What a monster he was, as he walked from Fled to the door.

"Let's go, George," he growled.

George followed, holding the book up to his face like a rare flower, or the window to an underwater or wherever world.

Sam opened the tin trailer door. Rays of sunset made him squint his green lidded eyes.

"Hey, don't forget your bag," Fled called.

"Oh!" George gasped.

Fled Magyar held the bag and it was open and he was looking inside and smiling. "This is good work," he told George. "You make this?"

"No," George answered with resigned slow motion, taking the bag back. "To be honest, I found it on the beach. I don't even know how it stays alive. It defies my medical knowledge. What can I say?"

"Hmmm," Fled replied. "Not unheard of though. You should come by the circus later tonight." He stared at the green under his fingernails. "I've been keeping something under wraps at the sideshow. It's a body…Without a head."

George stood there like paper mache.

"I assure you, it's completely alive and only waiting for a

chance like this to come along."

"Oh…I don't know," George said. "I'm sort of looking out for him."

"Yeah, he's my guardian angel," the soldier brayed and sneezed. "Listen doc, you bet I would like having a body again! You fellahs have no idea. This is torture."

George said, "Well then…Sam…Would you mind if I—"

"No," Sam burst. "I need you here. This is a dangerous place. There's a war on, I could get hurt again. I need to have my doctor nearby."

This speech coming from a green Frankenstein made George smile and almost laugh. "Okay, Sam. Okay."

"But what about me?" said the soldier's head. "I need that body."

"I may be able to do the procedure," Fled offered. "In fact, I'm sure I could."

The soldier's head looked hopefully at George.

"Well, I don't mind," George finally laughed. "Although…I'll, ahh…It'll be strange not to be carrying that bag all around, protecting it like a mother hen."

"You *did* forget me a minute ago," the head reminded George.

"I know. That was a mistake. I was reading a book." He directed his eyes at Fled, "It's a fairly simple operation to attach the nerves, veins, muscle structure and various ganglia."

"Ugh," the head said. "I don't want to know."

"You'll be okay," Fled promised. "I've been doing this kind of work for years."

"It would be a sort of relief," George sighed looking down into the bag, "Truthfully—no offence intended—I think I'm getting tired out emotionally and physically, making sure you're cared for all the time."

"You know," the soldier said, "I'm so grateful that you and Sam Samsara showed up when you did. You saved my life, I'm really thankful for that. But I need to get back to my wife and I don't want to go back there the way I am. It's crazy! What'll she do, put me in a birdcage? If I can be attached to a body again, what could be better? Please doc, give me a chance."

"Sure, of course." George allowed Fled to take the bag from him, though it wasn't entirely easy, it still felt like something stolen off a laundry line.

"Don't worry, friend," Fled said. "A new life isn't far away."

Chapter 22:

20 DOLLARS

"Yes, hello, is this Mrs. Parrot?"

"Yes! What—who's this??!"

"Please madame. My name is Rennie and I'm calling you on behalf of your local Shriners Union."

She sighed a tangled breath back through the receiver.

"Mrs. Parrot, a little while ago you pledged to support our organization with the generous amount of twenty dollars. Now, if you'd like—OH MY GOD!!" he suddenly shrieked and fell against the shaking glass walls of the phone booth, a quarter pulled out like a silver fish on a string.

Chapter 23:

START WITH THE ENDING

Birds painted orange as goldfish had been released into the blue sky. The flock sparked overhead and Wervers said sardonically, "That's what you can do with a big budget…I wonder what Spinster is trying to make up here?" From his copper kettle, he poured a cup of green tea for Sam. "Sam, I thought what we could do is start with the ending, while we already have the windmills and a mob gathered. Now what I want you to do is—"

But it was too late, the end had already started. Sam was on the move. All Wervers could do was run the camera as his Frankenstein heard the music playing down from the wrecked top of a windmill and walked big, slow and apocalyptically.

"That's Cornelius Barter," George whispered.

But Wervers gave him a steely look to be quiet and watch the movie.

Frankenstein moved across a yard full of dandelions and then he pushed his way past the spectators and film crew and entered Alfred Spinster's picture. Screaming people ran from Sam in fear, but Cornelius Barter went on with the soundtrack. It was all a movie to him. Frankenstein just got to the tied up windmill when the first shot was fired.

George bolted from Wervers.

Wervers swung the camera around as he heard a metallic fluttering clattering up behind him. Only years of experience held him from screaming out in surprise, or losing focus.

All that tin from Shriner cars had been welded and torn and turned into a wobbling biplane with ten propellers slicing.

More shots were fired by the military and police.

None of it made any difference to Frankenstein. He had climbed ten feet off the ground, pulling on the white roped ladder. He had clouds and heaven above while ricochets and bullets burst around him.

Tiny Snopes bled and tried to steer, but the aircraft was going down in pain, pouring charcoal and flame. It seared over the trees and slope beyond Jupiter Hill and disappeared from view.

Another fire had started, the windmill was hit by a burning wing. Cornelius Barter played on, as smoke billowed out gray and smothered the sight of them.

A cloud window opened and George saw the apparition. He yelled, "Sam!" and ran towards Frankenstein.

The wounded monster moved with stop animation.

"Sam, are you okay?!"

There were still gunshots; they were in a dangerous war zone. Everything Sam had warned George about was happening now.

"We have to get out of here!" George yelled. When he caught up with him, George felt the blood on his hands. "Are you okay? You're bleeding."

"Let's go…"

"Of course, Sam, I'll patch you up at the car." George let the weight of Frankenstein lean on him as they hurried across the World War 1 atmosphere, somehow clawing to where their car was waiting.

The leaking water made the ground into mud around it. They slid and crushed little flowers they couldn't see as George got Sam to the driver's side. They didn't even see the letters DUME spraypainted on the side.

"Okay?" George said to the crumpled Frankenstein behind the wheel. "This is the time to test Green 18." He unspooled white bandage and poured on the can of cactus juice.

Sam found the key to start the car.

Wrapped in green soaked bandages, Frankenstein was half mummy when George was done and the car began to roll out of shadows in a wide arc onto the road. The car was more ocean than ever, all the seams were water, a starfish rotated on the speedometer.

"Look out!" George shouted. He grabbed the steering wheel instinctively to avoid the white balloon bomb drifting towards them through the vapors. The silver car slid and kicked up wind that breezed the balloon bomb away. "That was close..." George said just before a big orange explosion occurred behind them. The whole peak of Jupiter Hill was like a volcano.

The car shot along the steep hill, hundreds of feet above the drop to waves.

"Maybe we don't need to go quite so fast," George suggested just as Tiny's hellish, burning red airplane cometed over the hill at them.

George saw Frankenstein lurch the wheel—that was the last the doctor saw of him. George was thrown free and out. He almost soared, half bird. If only his arms could have stretched into that wind and flown him miles. No such luck. He was an unconscious sleeper traveling by air.

George hit the soft ground and fell in. He dropped into a tunneled world with ice melting everywhere. Passing shadows of fish crossed where he landed collapsed into shallow water...He was a foot from a frozen werewolf.

Sam had escaped his destroyed car too. At the last moment, when that silver thing had skidded off the plummet towards the sea below, Sam was thrown clear, and left stranded in air, with his arm hooked around a root. Madronnas sighed above him, raving leaves.

Straight up, twenty feet beyond on the road, there was an explosion as more of Tiny's airplane burned cars. Sam dug his boots into the cliff side, dislodging rocks and dirt into the climbing fog from the sea. He winced. Some blood trickled down his green painted hand. He had to hold on for the fog...He knew once the fog got to him everything would be alright...But the fog had to hurry.

As he waited, some rocks fell away from his shifting feet. It was close. Ghostly fog birds felt across the ridge and soared on overhead, leading the way for the rest of the shroud. It was coming to save him. Sam could hear the familiar sounds it carried, reaching to dream him out of there.

Clouds swarmed. A surge of them formed stairs just below his feet. All he had to do was walk up them into the floating world… Just let go and belong to the air.

March-August 2005

Other Books by the Author

Ohio Trio (Bottom Dog Press 2001)

Bowl of Water (Bottom Dog Press 2003)

Another Life (Bird Dog Publishing 2007)

Home Recordings (Bird Dog Publishing 2009)

The Mermaid Translation (Bird Dog Publishing 2010)

The Selected Correspondence of Kenneth Patchen
    edited by Allen Frost (Bottom Dog Press 2012)

The Wonderful Stupid Man (Bird Dog Publishing 2012)

Saint Lemonade (Good Deed Rain 2014)

Playground (Good Deed Rain 2014)

Roosevelt (Good Deed Rain 2015)

www.ingramcontent.com/pod-product-compliance
Lightning Source LLC
Chambersburg PA
CBHW050522110726

47899CB00005B/1550